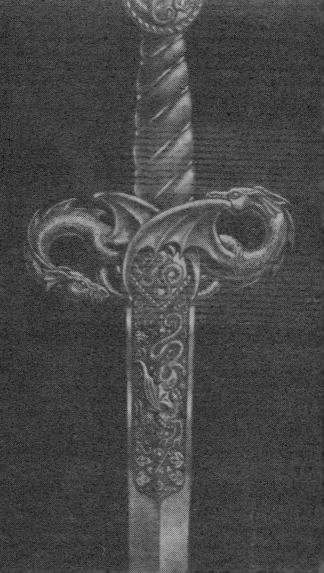

In a flash understanding came. The gods were coming to take charge.

The cloud, no longer serving any purpose of concealment, was being allowed to dissipate, and it vanished quickly. The handful of beings who had ridden it were walking now, already entering the parade ground at its far side, and approaching quickly. The sea of humans occupying the open space parted at the dieties' approach. Four gods and one goddess, each as tall as Draffut, came striding forward without pause, and Mark got the impression that they would have stepped on people without noticing had any remained in their way.

Humanity had hope of being saved, by the beings who had made the Swords, from powers that were too much for it to manage.

THE
THIRD BOOK
OF
SWORDS

THE THIRD BOOK OF SWORDS

FRED SABERHAGEN

A TOM DOHERTY ASSOCIATES BOOK

THE THIRD BOOK OF SWORDS

Copyright © 1984 by Fred Saberhagen

First trade printing: August 1984
First mass market printing: August 1984

A TOR Book

Published by Tom Doherty Associates, Inc.
49 West 24 Street
New York, N.Y. 10010

Cover art by Howard Chaykin/Victoria Poyser

ISBN: 0-812-55333-0
CAN. ED.: 0-812-55334-9

Printed in the United States of America

0 9 8 7 6 5 4

CHAPTER 1

Up at the unpeopled borderland of cloudy heaven, where unending wind drove eternal snow between and over high gray rocks, the gods and goddesses were gathering.

In the grayness just before dawn, their tall forms came like smoke out of the gray and smoking wind, to take on solidity and detail. Unperturbed by wind or weather, their garments flapping in the shrieking howl of air, they stood upon the rooftop of the world and waited as their numbers grew. Steadily more powers streaked across the sky, bringing reinforcement.

The shortest of the standing figures was taller than humanity, but from the shortest to tallest, all were indisputably of human shape. The dress of most members of the assembly displayed a more than mortal elegance, running to crowns and jewels and snow-white furs; the attire of a few was, by human standards, almost ordinary; that of many was bizarre.

By an unspoken agreement amounting to tradition the deities stood in a rough circle, symbol of a rude equality. It was a mutually enforced equality, meaning only that none of their number was willing to concede pride of place to any other. When graybearded Zeus, a laurel wreath embracing his massive head, moved forward majestically as if after all he intended to occupy the center of the circle, a muttering at once began around him. The sound grew louder, and it did not subside until the Graybearded One, with a frown, had converted his forward movement into a mere circular pacing, that soon brought him back to his old place in the large circle. There he stopped. And only when he stopped did the muttering die down completely.

And still with each passing moment the shape of another god or goddess materialized out of the restless air. By now two dozen or more tall forms were in place around the circle. They eyed one another suspiciously, and exchanged cautious nods and signs of greeting. Neighbor to neighbor they muttered in near-whispers through the wind, trading warily in warnings and backbitings about those who were more distant in the circle, or still absent. The more of them that gathered, the more their diversity was evident. They were dark or fair, old-looking or young-looking. Handsome—as gods—or beautiful—as goddesses—or ugly, as only certain gods and goddesses could be.

Twice more Zeus opened his mouth as if he intended to address them all. Twice more he seemed on the verge of stepping forward, taking the center of the circle, and trying to command the meeting. Each time he did so that warning murmur swelled up into the frozen air, through the blasting wind, giving notice that no such attempt was going to be tolerated. Zeus remained silently at his own station in the ring, stamping his feet now and then and scowling his impatience.

At last the individual gossipings around the ring began to fade toward quiet, give way to silent waiting. There was some general agreement, tacitly attained, that now a quorum had been reached. There was no use trying to wait until all the gods and goddesses were here, all of them never attended a meeting at the same time. Never had they been able to agree unanimously on anything at all, not even on a place or an agenda for their arguments.

But now the assembly was large enough.

It was Mars, spear-armed and helmeted, who broke the silence; Mars speaking in a voice that smoldered and rumbled with old anger. The tones of it were like the sounds of displaced boulders rolling down a glacier.

Mars banged his spear upon his shield to get the attention of the assembly. Then he said to them: "There is news now of the Mindsword. The man that other humans call the Dark King has it. He is, of course, going to use it to try to get the whole world into his hands. What effect this will have on our own Game is something that we must evaluate for ourselves, each according to his or her own position."

It was not this news he had just announced to the assembly that was really angering Mars. Rather it was something else, something that he wanted to keep secret in his own thoughts, that made him almost choke on rage. Mars did not conceal his feelings well. As he finished speaking he used a savage gesture, a blow that almost split the air, simply to signify the fact that he was ready now to relinquish the floor to someone else.

Next to speak was Vulcan—Vulcan the Smith with the twisted leg, the armorer and Sword-forger to the gods.

"I am sorry," began Vulcan, slyly, "that my so-worthy colleague is unable to continue at the moment. Perhaps he is brooding too much about a certain setback—one might even call it a defeat—that he suffered at the hands—or should one say the paws—of a certain mortal opponent, some eight or nine years past?"

The response of Mars to this was more sullen, angry rumbling. There also was a murmuring around the circle, some of it laughter at Mars, some a denunciation of Vulcan for this obvious attempt to start an argument.

Aphrodite asked softly, "Is this what we have come here for, to have another quarrel?" Her tall body, all curves, all essence of the female, was wrapped in nothing but a diaphanous veil that seemed always on the verge of blowing away in the fierce wind but never did. She like the other deities was perfectly indifferent to the arctic cold.

Near her, Apollo's taller form appeared emphasized for a moment in a lone ray of light from the newly risen sun. The Sun's bright lance steadily pierced the scudding clouds for just as long as it took the god to speak, and held his body in its light. Apollo demanded, "I take it that we are all agreed upon one thing at least?"

Someone else was cooperative enough to ask Apollo: "What?"

The tall god replied, "That Hermes has not come

back from his mission to gather up the Swords again. That he is never going to come back."

"That's two things," another member of the group objected.

Apollo took no notice of such carping. "That our divine Messenger, who no doubt thought himself as secure in his immortality as most of us still think we are in ours, has now been for four years *dead*?"

That word, of all words, had power to jolt them all. Many faced it bravely. Some tried to pretend that it had not been spoken, or if spoken certainly not heard. But there was a long moment in which even the wind was voiceless. No other word, surely, could have brought the same quality and duration of silence to this assembly.

It was the relentless voice of Apollo that entered into this new silence and destroyed it, repeating: "*For four years dead.*"

The repetition provoked not more silence, but the beginning of an uproar of protest; still the voice of Apollo overrode the tumult even as it swelled.

"Dead!" he roared. "And if Hermes Messenger can be slain by one of the Swords, why so can we. And what have we done about it, during these past four years? Nothing! Nothing at all! Wrangled among ourselves, as always—no more than that!"

When Apollo paused, Mars seized the chance to speak. "And there is the one who forged those Swords!" The God of War pointed with his long war-spear, and aimed an angry stare at the crippled Smith. "I tell you, we must make him melt them down again. I've said all along that the Swords are going to destroy us all, unless we are able to destroy them first!"

Leaning awkwardly on his lame leg, Vulcan

turned at bay. "Don't blame me!" Wind whipped at his fur garments, his ornaments of dragon-scale clashing and fluttering in the gale. But his words ate through the windstorm plainly, suffering no interference from mere physical air. "The blunder, if there was one, was not mine. These very faces that I see all about me now spoke urging me, commanding me, to forge the Swords."

He turned accusingly from one to another of his peers. "We needed the Swords, we had to have them, you all told me, for the Game. The Game was going to be a great delight, something we hadn't tried before. You said the Swords must be distributed among the humans, who in the Game would be our pawns. Now what kind of pawns have they turned into? But no, you all insisted on it, no matter how I warned you—"

Again an uproar of protest was breaking out, and this time it was too loud for any one voice to overcome. Objectors were shouting that, on the contrary, *they* had been the ones against the whole idea of the Swords and the Game from the very start.

Naturally this provoked a strong counterreaction from others present. "What you mean is, you've been against the Game ever since you started losing in it! As long as you thought that you were winning, it was a great idea!"

One of the graybeard elder gods, not Zeus, put in: "Let's get back to our immediate problem. You say that the man they call the Dark King has the Mindsword now. Well, that may be good or bad news for some of us in terms of the Game, but does it matter beyond that? The Game is only a game, and what real difference does it make?"

"You fool! Are you incapable of understanding?

This Game, that you're so proud of winning—it got out of hand long ago. Haven't you been listening? Did you hear nothing that Apollo just said about the death of Hermes?"

"All right. All right. Let's talk about Hermes Messenger. He had supposedly gone to collect all the Swords again, to get them out of human hands, because some of us were getting worried. But do you think he would really have destroyed the Swords, once he had them all collected? I don't think so."

That suggestion was greeted by a thoughtful pause, a general silence.

And that silence broken by a slow and thoughtful voice: "Besides, are we *really* sure that Hermes is dead? What solid evidence do we have?"

Now even Apollo the reasoner felt compelled to howl his rage at such thickheadedness. "One of the Swords killed Hermes! Farslayer, hurled from the hands of a mere human!"

Apollo got a venomous retort. "How can we be *sure* that that's what really happened? Has anyone seen the Sword Farslayer since then? Did any one of us see Hermes fall?"

At this moment, Zeus once more stepped forward. He conveyed the impression of one who had been waiting for the exactly proper instant to take action. And it seemed that he had at last timed an attempt correctly, because for once he was not howled down before he could begin to speak.

"Wisdom comes with experience," Zeus intoned, "and experience with age. To learn from the past is the surest way to secure the future. In peace and wisdom there is strength. In strength and wisdom there is peace. In wisdom and—"

No one howled him down this time, but after the first dozen words hardly any of his fellow deities were still listening. Instead they resumed their separate conversations around the circle, taking time out from the general debate while they waited for Zeus to be finished. This treatment was even deadlier than the other. Zeus soon realized what was happening. He retreated again to his own place in the ring, and there withdrew into a total, sulky silence.

Now at another place along the ring there was a stirring and a swirling movement among the snow and rocks. Attention became focused on this spot, just as a new member joined the company there. Rather than coming out of the sky as the others had, this god emerged up out of the Earth. The form of Hades was indistinct, all dimness and darkness, a difficult object even for the faculties of another deity to comprehend.

Hades in his formless voice said that yes, Hermes was certainly dead. No, he, Hades, hadn't actually seen the Messenger fall, or die. But he had been with Hermes shortly before what must have been the moment of that death, when Hermes was engaged in taking some Swords away from some humans. It was Hades' opinion that Hermes had been acting in good faith in his attempt to collect the Blades, though unfortunately they had been lost again.

Now another side discussion was developing. What about that offending human, the one that had apparently thrown Farslayer at Hermes and brought him down? The awful hubris that could strike a god, any god, to earth cried out to heaven for vengeance. What punishment had been dealt to the culprit? Surely someone had already seen to it that some special and eternal retaliation had been inflicted?

The same thought had already occurred, long ago, to certain other members of the group. Alas, they had to report now that when they first heard of the offending human he was already beyond the reach of even divine revenge.

"Then we must exact some sort of retribution from humanity in general."

"Aha, now we come to it! Just which part of humanity do you propose to strike at? Those who are your pawns in the Game, or those I claim as mine?"

Apollo's disgust at this argument was beyond all measure. "How can you fools still talk of pawns, and games? Do you not see—?" But words failed him for the moment.

Hades spoke up again, this time with his own suggestion for the permanent disposal of the Swords. If all those god-forged weapons could somehow be collected, and delivered to him, he would see to their burial. All the other deities present could permanently cease to worry.

"We might cease doing a *lot* of things permanently, once *you* had all the Swords! Of *course* you'd be willing to accept twelve for yourself—and incidentally to win the Game by doing so! Where would that leave us? What kind of fools do you take us for?"

Hades was, or at least pretended to be, affronted by this attitude. "What do I care now about a game? Now, when our very existence is at stake. Haven't you been listening to Apollo?"

"Our very existence, bah! Tell that stuff to someone who'll believe it. Gods are immortal. We all know that. Hermes is playing dead, hiding out somewhere. It's part of a ploy to win the Game. Well, I don't intend to lose, whatever happens. Not to Hermes, and not to Apollo, and particularly not to you!''

Aphrodite, murmuring softly, announced to all who would listen that she could think up her own ideas for getting back the Swords. Those who had the Swords, or most of them anyway, were only mere men, were they not?

Apollo spoke again. This time he prefaced his remarks by waving his bow, a gesture that gained him notably greater attention. He said that if the Swords could be regathered, they should then be turned over to him, as the most logical and trustworthy of gods. He would then put an end to the threat the weapons posed, by the simple expedient of shooting them, like so many arrows, clean off the Earth.

Before Apollo had finished his short speech most of his audience were ignoring him, bow and all, even as they had ignored Zeus. Meanwhile in the background Mars was rumbling threats against unspecified enemies. Others were laughing, secretly or openly, at Mars.

Vulcan was quietly passing the word around the circle that if others were to gather up the Blades and bring them back to him, and if a majority of his peers were to assure him that that was what they really wanted, he'd do his best to melt all of the Twelve back into harmless iron again.

No one was paying the least attention to Zeus mighty sulking, and he reverted to speech in a last effort to establish some authority. "It seems to me that the Smith here incorporated far too much of humanity into the Swords. Why was it necessary to quench the Blades, when they came from the fire and anvil, in living human blood? And why were so much human sweat and human tears introduced into the process?"

Vulcan bristled defensively at this. "Are you trying to tell me my trade? What do you know about it, anyway?"

Here Mars, gloating to see his rival stung, jumped into the argument. "And then there was that last little trick you played at the forging. Taking off the right arm of the human smith who helped you— what was that all about?"

The Smith's answer—if indeed he gave one—was lost in a new burst of noise. A dozen voices flared up, arguing on several different subjects. The meeting was giving every sign of breaking up, despite Apollo's best thundering efforts to hold it together a little longer. As usual there had been no general agreement on what their common problems were, much less on any course of action. Already the circle of the gods was thinning as the figures that composed it began to vanish into the air. The wind hummed with their departing powers. Hades, eschewing aerial flight as usual, vanished again straight down into the Earth beneath his feet.

But one voice in the council was still roaring on, bellowing with monotonous urgency. Against all odds, its owner was at last able to achieve something like an attentive silence among the handful of deities who remained.

"Look! Look!" was all that voice was saying. And with one mighty arm the roaring god was pointing steadily downslope, indicating a single, simple line of markings in the snow, tracks that the mundane wind was rapidly effacing.

There could be no doubt about those markings. They were a line of departing footprints, heading straight down the mountainside, disappearing behind snow-buried rocks before they had gone more than a few meters. Though they marked strides too long and impressions too broad and deep to have been made by any human being, there was no doubt that they had been left by mortal feet.

CHAPTER 2

The one-armed man came stumbling along through midnight rain, following a twisted cobblestone alley into the lightless heart of the great city of Tashigang. He was suffering with fresh wounds now—one knife-gash bleeding in his side and another one in his knee—besides the old maiming loss of his right arm. Still he was better off than the man who had just attacked him. That blunderer was some meters back along the twisted alley, face down in a puddle.

Now, just when the one-armed man was about on the point of going down himself, he steered toward a wall and leaned against it. Standing with his broad back in its homespun shirt pressed to the stone wall of somebody's house, he squeezed himself in as far as possible under the thin overhang of roof, until the eaves blocked at least some of the steady rain from hitting him in the face. The man felt frightened by what had happened to his knee.

From the way the injured leg felt now when he tried to put his weight on it, he wasn't going to be able to walk much farther.

He hadn't had a chance yet to start worrying about what might have happened when the knife went into his side.

The one-armed man was tall, and strongly built. Still, by definition, he was a cripple, and therefore the robber—if that was all he had been—might have taken it for granted that he'd be easy game. Even had the attacker guessed that his intended victim carried a good oaken cudgel tucked into his belt under his loose shirt, he could hardly have predicted how quickly his quarry would be able to draw that club and with what authority he'd use it.

Now, leaning against the building for support, he had tucked his cudgel away in his belt again, and was pressing his fingers to his side under his shirt. He could feel the blood coming out, a frighteningly fast trickle.

Except for the rain, the city around him was silent. And all the windows he could see through the rain were dark, and most of them were shuttered. No one else in the huge city appeared to have taken the least notice of the brief clash he had just survived.

Or had he survived it, after all? Real walking, he had to admit, was no longer possible on his damaged knee. For the present, at least, he could still stand upright. He thought he must be near his destination now, and it was essential that he reach it. Pushing himself along the wall that he was leaning on, and then the next wall, one stone surface after another, he stumbled on, hobbled on.

He remembered the directions he had been given,

and he made progress of a sort. Every time his weight came on the knee at all he had to bite back an outcry of pain. And now dizziness, lightheadedness, came welling up inside his skull. He clenched his will like a fist, gripping the treasure of consciousness, knowing that if that slipped from him now, life itself was likely to drain quickly after it.

His memorized directions told him that at this point he had to cross the alley. Momentarily forsaking the support of walls, divorcing his mind from pain, he somehow managed it.

Leaning on another wall, he rested, and rebuilt his courage. He'd crawl the rest of the way to get there if he had to, or do what crawling he could on one hand and one knee. But once he went down to try crawling he didn't know he'd ever get back up on his feet again.

At last the building that had been described to him as his goal, the House of Courtenay, came into sight, limned by distant lightning. The description had been accurate: four stories tall, flat-roofed, half-timbered construction on the upper levels, stone below. The house occupied its own small block, with streets or alleys on every side. The seeker's first view was of the front of the building, but the back was where he was supposed to go in order to get in. Gritting his teeth, not letting his imagination try to count up how many steps there might be yet to take, he made the necessary detour. He splashed through puddles, out of one alley and into an even narrower one. From that he passed to one so narrow it was a mere paved path, running beside the softly gurgling, stone-channeled Corgo. The surface of the river, innocent now of boats, hissed in the heavier bursts of rain.

The man had almost reached the building he wanted when his hurt knee gave way completely. He broke his fall as best he could with his one arm. Then, painfully, dizzily, he dragged himself along on his one arm and his one functioning leg. He could imagine the trail of blood he must be leaving. No matter, the rain would wash it all away.

Presently his slow progress brought him in out of the rain, under the roof of a short, narrow passage that connected directly with the door he wanted. He crawled on and reached the narrow door. It was of course locked shut. He propped himself up in a sitting position against it, and began to pound on the door with the flat of his large hand. The pounding of his calloused hand seemed to the man to be making no noise at all. At first it felt like he was beating uselessly, noiselessly, on some thick solid treetrunk . . . and then it felt like nothing at all. There was no longer any feeling in his hand.

Maybe no one would hear him. Because he was no longer able to hear anything himself. Not even the rain beating on the flat passage roof. Nor could he see anything through the gathering grayness. Not even his hand before his face. . . .

At a little after midnight Denis the Quick was lying awake, listening to the rain. That usually made him sleepy, as long as he knew that he was securely warm and dry indoors. But tonight he was having trouble sleeping. The images of two attractive women were coming and going like provocative dancers in his imagination. If he tried to concentrate on one, then the other intruded as if jealous.

He knew both women in real life, but his real-life problem was not that he had to choose between them. No, he was not so fortunate, he told himself, as to have problems of just that kind.

Denis was well accusomed to the normal night sounds of the house. The sound he began to hear now, distracting him from the pleasant torment of waking dreams, was certainly not one of them. Denis got up quickly, pulled on a pair of trousers, and went out of his small bedchamber to investigate.

His room on the ground floor of the house gave almost directly on the main workshop, which was a large chamber now illumined faintly by a sullen smoldering of coals banked in the central forge. Faint ghost-gleams of firelight touched tools around the forge and weapons racked on the walls. Most of the work down here was on some form of weaponry.

Denis paused for a moment beside the fire, intending to light a taper from its coals. But then he changed his mind, and instead reached up to the high wall niche where the Old World light was kept.

The back door leading into the shop from outside ground level was fitted with a special peephole. This was a smooth little bulge of glass, cleverly shaped so that anyone looking through it from inside saw out at a wide angle. Another lens, set into the door near its very top, was there to let the precious flameless torch shine out. Denis now lifted the antique instrument into position there and turned it on; immediately the narrow passage just outside the door was flooded with clear, brilliant light. And even as Denis did this, the sound that had caught his attention came again, a faint thumping on the door itself. Now through the fish-eye lens he could see the one who made the sound, as a slumped figure somewhat blurred by the imperfect lens. The shape of the fallen figure suggested the absence of an arm.

With the flameless light still glowing in his hand, Denis stepped back from the door. The House of Courtenay generally contained some stock of the goods in which its owners dealt, including the fancy weapons that were the specialty of the house. Also there was usually a considerable supply of coin on hand. The place was a natural target for thieves, and for any member of the household to open any exterior door to anyone, particularly at night, was no trivial matter. The only thing for Denis to do now was to rouse the household steward, Tarim. and get his orders as to what to do next.

Crossing the workshop, Denis approached the door to the ascending stair that led to the next highest level of the house; Tarim slept up there, along with most of the rest of the resident staff. Denis opened the door—and stopped in his tracks.

Looking down at him from the top of the first flight, holding a candle in her small, pale hand, was one of the characters from his recent waking dream, the Lady Sophie herself, mistress of this house. Denis's surprise was at seeing the lady there at all. Family quarters were located on the upper levels of the house, well above the noise and smoke and smell of the shop when it was busy, and of the daytime streets. Her tiny but shapely body was wrapped in a thick white robe, contrasting sharply with her straight black hair. It was hard to believe that any faint sound at the back door could have roused the lady from her bed.

The mistress called down: "Denis? What is it?" He thought she sounded nervous.

Denis stood there hugging his bare chest. "There's someone at the back door, Mistress. I could see only one man. Looked like he was hurt, but I didn't open."

"Hurt, you say?"

It looked and sounded to Denis almost as if the lady had been expecting someone to arrive tonight, had been waiting around in readiness to receive them. Denis had heard nothing in particular in the way of business news to make him expect such a visitor, but such a nocturnal arrival in itself would not be very surprising. As the headquarters of a company of traders, the house was accustomed to the comings and goings of odd people at odd hours.

Denis answered, "Yes, Ma'am, hurt. And it looked like he only had one arm. I was just going to arouse Tarim . . ."

"No." The mistress was immediately decisive. "Just stand by there for a moment, while I go get the master."

"Yes, Ma'am." It was of course the only answer Denis could give, but still it was delayed, delivered only to the lady's already retreating back. Denis was puzzled, and a moment later his puzzlement increased, for here, already fully awake and active too, came Master Courtenay himself. Courtenay was a moving mountain of a man, his great bulk wrapped now in a night robe of a rich blue fabric. With a lightness and quickness remarkable for his size, the master came almost skipping down the stairs, his lady just behind him.

Arriving on the ground floor, the master of the house faced Denis directly. The two were almost of a height, near average, though Courtenay weighed easily twice as much as his lean employee, and was possibly three times as massive as his small wife. Courtenay was not yet thirty, as nearly as Denis could judge, and very little of his bulk was fat, though in his robe he looked that way. Nor could he be described as stupid, as Denis had realized on his own first day here, despite what a first glance at Courtenay's face suggested—of course he could hardly be unintelligent and have prospered as he evidently had.

The master brushed back his almost colorless hair from his uninviting face, a gesture that seemed more one of worry than of sleepiness. In his usual mild voice he said, "We'll let the rest of the household go on sleeping, Denis." Behind the master, his lady was already closing the door to the ascending stair. "The three of us will manage," Courtenay went on. "The man's hurt, you say?"

"Looks like it, sir."

"Still, we'll take no chances more than necessary. Help yourself to a weapon, and stand by."

"Yes sir." In the year and a half that he had been at the House of Courtenay, Denis had learned that there were stretches of time in which life here began to seem dull. But so far those stretches had never extended for any unbearable length of time.

Over on the far side of the shop, the mistress was lighting a couple of oil lamps. And when she brought her hands down from the lamp shelf and faced around again, Denis thought that he saw something trailing from her right hand. He caught only a glimpse of the object before it vanished between folds of her full robe. But, had he not been convinced that Mistress Sophie was only a delicate little thing who loved her luxury, he would have thought that she was holding the leather thongs of a hunter's or a warrior's sling.

The more recent years of Denis's young life had been generally peaceful, first as an acolyte of Ardneh in the White Temple, then here in the House of Courtenay as apprentice trader and general assistant. But he had spent the longer, earlier portion of his existence serving a different kind of apprenticeship. That had been in the slum streets of Tashigang, and it had left him indelibly familiar with the more unpeaceful side of life. So now he was reasonably calm as he moved to the display of decorative weapons that occupied a good part of one side of the large room. There he selected an ornate battle-hatchet, a weapon of antique design but sharp-edged and of a pleasantly balanced weight. With this in hand, Denis nodded that he was ready.

Master Courtenay, already standing by the back door, returned the nod. Then he turned to the door and made use of the peephole and the Old World light. In the next moment Courtenay had unbarred the door and yanked it open. The crumpled body that had been sitting against it on the outside came toppling softly inward.

Denis sprang forward, quickly closed the door and barred it up again. Meanwhile the master of the house had stretched the unconscious man out full length on the floor, and was examining him with the aid of the Old World light.

The mistress, one of the more conventional lamps in her hand, had come forward to look too. Quickly she turned to Denis. "He's bleeding badly. You were a servant of Ardneh, see what you can do for him."

Denis was not usually pleased to be asked to administer medical treatment; he knew too well his own great limitations in the art. But his urge to please his mistress would not let him hesitate. And he knew that his years in Ardneh's service had left him almost certainly better qualified than either of his employers. He nodded and moved forward.

The man stretched out on the floor was not young; his unconscious face was weatherbeaten over its bloodless pallor, and the hair that fanned out in a wild spread on the flat stones was gray. Standing, he would have been tall, with a well-knit, sturdy body marred by the old amputation.

"His right arm *is* gone." That was the mistress, speaking thoughtfully, as if she were only musing to herself.

Denis heard her only absently; the man's fresh wounds were going to demand a healer's full attention. A lot of blood was visible, darker wetness on the rainsoaked clothing.

Quickly Denis began to peel back clothes. He cut them away, when that was easier, with a keen knife that the master handed him. He also tossed aside a mean-looking cudgel that he found tucked into the victim's belt.

"I'll need water, and bandages," he announced over his shoulder. There were two wounds, and both looked bad. "And whatever medicines we have to stop bleeding." He paused to mumble a minor spell for that purpose, learned in his days as Ardneh's servitor. It was about the best that Denis could do in the way of magic, and it was very little. Perhaps it brought some benefit, but it was not going to be enough.

"I'll bring you what I can find," replied the mistress of the house, and turned away with quick efficiency. Again Denis was surprised. He had long ago fixed her image in his mind as someone who existed to be pampered . . . could that really have been a sling he'd seen her holding?

But now the present task demanded his full attention. "We ought to put him on my bed," said Denis. And Courtenay, strong as a loadbeast and disdaining help, scooped up the limp heavy form as if it had been that of a small child, and held it patiently while Denis maneuvered first the door to his room and then the coverings on his bed.

The hurt man's eyelids fluttered just as he was being put down on the bed, and he muttered a few words. Denis heard something like: "Ben of Purkinje," which certainly sounded like a name. That of the victim himself? No use asking. He was out cold again.

Soon the mistress was back, with such useful items as she had been able to lay her hands on quickly, water and clean cloth. She had also brought along a couple of medicine jars, but nothing that Denis thought was likely to help. While Denis went to work washing and bandaging, the master picked up the sodden clothing that had been stripped away, and went quickly through the pockets. But whatever Courtenay was looking for, he apparently did not find it. With a sigh he threw the garments back on the floor and asked: "Well, Denis, what about him?"

"He's lost a lot of blood, sir. And, where the

wounds are, the bleeding's going to be hard to stop.
I've packed this hole in his side as best I can." As he
spoke Denis was still pressing a bandage into place.
"We could use spider webs, but I don't know where
to get a bunch of 'em quickly. His knee isn't bleeding so much now, but it looks nasty. If he lives, he
won't be walking for a while."

The Old World light had been replaced in its customary wall niche, and the mistress had now
brought one of the better ordinary lamps into
Denis's room. By the lamplight she and her husband were staring at each other with what struck
Denis as curious expressions.

"Knife wounds, I think," said Master Courtenay,
shifting his gaze at last back to Denis.

"Yes sir, I would say that's what they are."

"He couldn't have come very far in that condition."

"I'd have to agree with that, sir."

The master nodded, and turned and walked out
of Denis's room, leaving the door open behind him.
He didn't say where he was going, and nobody
asked. The mistress lingered. Denis, observing the
direction of her gaze, wondered what it was about
the patient's arm-stump that she found so
fascinating.

Having been a member of the household for a
year and a half now, Denis was—sometimes,
almost—treated like one of the family. Now he
made bold to ask, "Do you recognize him, Mistress?"

"I've never seen him before," the lady answered,
which to Denis sounded like the truth used as an
evasion. She added: "Will he live, do you think?"

Before Denis had to try to make a guess sound

like an expert opinion, there came again the sounds of someone at the back door of the shop. The sounds were different this time: demanding shouts, accompanied by a strong and determined hammering.

Following his mistress out into the shop's main room, Denis shut the door of his own room behind him. The master, Old World light in hand again, was once more approaching the back door. Even as Courtenay turned on the light and peered out through the spy-lens, the pounding came again. This time it was accompanied by a hoarse voice, somewhat muffled by the door's thickness: "Ho, in the house, open for the Watch! In the Lord Mayor's name, open!"

The master of the house continued to peer out. "Three of 'em," he reported in a low voice. "No lights of their own. Still, it's the real Watch—I think."

"Open!" the smothered roaring voice demanded. "Open or we break it down!" And there came a *thump thump thump*. But they were going to have to thump harder than that before this door would take them seriously.

Quietly the mistress said to her husband: "We don't want to . . ." She let the statement trail off there, but Denis listening had the strong impression that her next words would have been: *arouse suspicion*.

Whatever meaning the master read into her half-voiced thought, he nodded his agreement with it. Looking at Denis, he ordered: "Say nothing to them about our visitor. We've seen no one tonight."

"If they want to search?"

"Leave that to me. But pick up your hatchet again, just in case."

When all three of the people inside were ready, Courtenay undid the bars and opened the door again. In the very next instant he had to demonstrate extraordinary agility for a man of his weight, by jumping back out of the way of a blow from a short sword.

The three men who had come bursting in, dressed though they were in the Lord Mayor's livery of gray and green, were plainly not the Watch. Denis with his hatchet was able to stand off the first rush of one of them, armed with a long knife in each hand. Another of the intruders started toward Lady Sophie. But her right arm rose from her side, drawing into a whirling blur the sling's long leather strands. Whatever missile had been cradled in the leather cup now blasted stone fragments out of the wall beside the man's head, giving him pause, giving her the necessary moment to reload her weapon.

"Ben of Purkinje!" cried out the third invader, hacking again at Master Courtenay with his sword. "Greetings from the Blue Temple!" This attacker was tall, and looked impressively strong.

Master Courtenay, after advising Denis to be armed, had himself been caught embarrassingly unarmed on the side of the room away from the rack of weapons. He had to improvise, and out of the miscellany of tools around the forge grabbed up a long, iron-handled casting ladle. It was a clumsy thing to try to swing against a sword, but the master of the house had awesome strength, and now demonstrated good nerves as well. For the time being he was holding his own, managing to protect himself.

The man who had started after the Lady Sophie

now turned back, indecisively, as if to give the swordsman aid. It was an error. In the next instant the second stone from the sling hit him in the back of the head and knocked him down. The sound of the impact and the way he fell showed that for him the fight was over.

Denis was distracted by the lady's achievement— unwisely, for a moment later he felt the point of one of his opponent's long knives catch in the flesh of his forearm. The hatchet fell from Denis's grip to the stone floor. Scrambling away from the knives, clearing a low bench in a somersaulting dive, Denis the Quick lived up to his nickname well enough to keep himself alive.

He heard one of the bigger workbenches go over with a crash, and now he saw that Master Courtenay had somehow managed to catch his own attacker by the swordarm—maybe the fellow had also been distracted, dodging feints of a slung stone. Anyway it was now going to be a wrestling match—but no, it really wasn't. In another instant the swordsman, bellowing his surprise, had been lifted clean off his feet, and in the instant after that Denis saw him slaughtered like a rabbit, his back broken against the angle of the heavy, tilted table.

The knife-wielder who had wounded Denis had now changed his strategy and was scrambling after the lady. Suddenly bereft of friends, he needed a hostage. Denis, reckless of his own safety, and wounded as he was, threw himself in the attacker's way before the man could come within a knife-thrust of the mistress. Denis had one quick glimpse of the lady, her white robe half undone, scooting successfully on hands and knees to get away.

And now Denis was on his back, and the knife was coming down at him instead—but before it reached him, the arm that held it was knocked aside by a giant's blow from the long ladle. The iron weight brushed aside the barrier of an arm to mash into the knifer's cheekbone, delivering most of its energy there with an effect of devastation. Denis rolled aside, paused to look back, and allowed himself to slow to a panting halt. The fight was definitely over.

In the workshop, only three sets of lungs were breathing still.

The lady, pulling her robe around her properly once more (even amid surrounding blood, terror, and danger, that momentary vision of her body was still with Denis; he thought that it would always be.) Now she let herself slide down slowly until she was sitting on the floor with her back against one of the upset benches. Evidently more angered then terrified by the experience, she said to her husband acidly, "You are quite, quite sure, are you, that they represent the Watch?"

Coutenay, still on his feet, looking stupid, breathing heavily, could only mumble something.

Once more there came the sound of pounding on a door, accompanied by urgent voices. But this time the noise was originating within the house. The door that closed off the ascending stair was being rattled and shaken, while from behind it a man's voice shouted: "Mistress! Master! Denis, are you all right? What's going on?"

The master of the house cast down his long iron ladle. He stood for a moment contemplating his own bloodied hands as if he wondered how they might have got that way. Denis saw an unprecedented tremor in those hands. Then Courtenay drew a deep breath, raised his head, and called back, almost calmly, "It's all right, Tarim. A little problem, but we've solved it. Be patient for a moment and I'll explain."

In an aside he added: "Denis, help me get these . . . no, you're hurt yourself. Sit down first and bind that up. Barb, you help me with these visitors. Drag 'em around behind that bench and we'll throw a tarp over 'em."

Denis, in mild shock now with his wound, took a moment to register the unfamiliar name. Barb? Never before had he heard the master, or anyone else, call the lady that . . . it wasn't going to be easy, he realized, to bind up his own arm unaided. Anyway, the wound didn't look like it was going to kill him.

Courtenay, while keeping busy himself, was still giving orders. "Now close the street door." He dropped a dead man where he wanted him, and pulled out a heavy tarpaulin from its storage. "No, wait, let Tarim see it standing open. We'll say some brigands got in somehow, and . . ."

Tarim and the other awakened staff were presently allowed to come crowding in. Whether they fully believed the vague story about brigands or not, they took their cue from their master's manner and were too wise to question it. The outer door was closed and barred. Tarim himself had to be dissuaded from standing watch in the workshop for the rest of the night, and eventually he and all the others were on their way back to bed.

Alone in the workshop again, the three who had done the fighting exchanged looks. Then they got busy.

Courtenay began a preliminary clean-up, while the mistress applied a bandage to Denis's forearm, following his directions. Her small fingers, soft, white, and pampered, did not shrink from bloody contact. They managed the bandaging quite well, using some of the cloth that had been brought for the first patient.

When the job was done, her fingers held his arm a moment more. Her dark eyes, for the first time ever (he thought) looked at him with something more than the wish to be pleasant to a servant. She said, very quietly but very seriously, "You saved my life, Denis. Thank you."

It was almost as if no woman had ever touched him or spoken to him before. Denis muttered something. He could feel the blood flowing back into his face. What foolishness, he told himself. He and this lady could never . . .

A quick look at the stranger now occupying Denis's bed showed that the fight in the next room had not disturbed him. He was still unconscious, breathing shallowly. Denis, looking at him, came round to the opinion that nothing was likely to disturb this man again. With two wounded men now on hand, the mistress announced that she was going upstairs to search more thoroughly for medical materials.

The master said to his lady, "I'll come up with you, we have to talk. Denis can manage here for a few moments."

The two of them climbed in thoughtful silence, past the level where Tarim and other workers slept, past the next floor also. Reaching the topmost level of the house, they passed through another door and entered a domain of elegance. This began with a wood-paneled hall, lit now by the flame of a single candle in a wall sconce. Here the lady turned in one direction, going to rummage in her private stocks for medical materials. The master turned down the hall the other way, heading for a closet where he expected to find a fresh, unbloodied robe.

Before he reached the room that held the closet, he was intercepted by the toddling figure of a kneehigh child, an apparition followed almost immediately by that of an apologetic nurse.

"Oh sir, you're hurt," the nurse protested. She was a buxom girl, almost a grown woman now. And at the same time the child demanded: "Daddy! Tell story now!" At the age of two and a half, the little girl fortunately already showed much more of her mother's than her father's looks. Brazenly wide awake, as if something about this particular night delighted her, she waited in her silken nightdress, small stuffed toy in hand.

The man spoke to the nursemaid first. "I'm all right, Kuan-yin. The blood is nothing. I'll put Beth back to bed; you go see if you can help your mistress find what she's looking for."

The nurse looked at him for a moment. Then, like the other employees, wise enough to be incurious tonight, she moved away.

The huge man, who for the past four years had been trying to establish an identity as Master Courtenay, wiped drying gore from his huge hands onto a robe already stained. With hands now steady, and almost clean, he bent to carefully pick up the living morsel he had discovered he valued more than his own life.

Carrying his daughter back to the nursery, he passed a window. Through genuine glass and rainy night he had a passing view of the high city walls some hundreds of meters distant. The real watch were keeping a fire burning atop the wall. Another light, smaller and steadier, was visible in a slightly different direction; one of the upper windows glowing in the Lord Mayor's palace. It looked as if someone was having a busy night there too; the observer could only hope that there was no connection.

Fortune was smiling on the huge man now, for he was able to remember the particular story that his daughter wanted, and to get through the telling of it with reasonable speed. The child had just gone back to sleep, and the father was just on his way out of the nursery, shutting the door with infinite care behind him, when his wife reappeared, still wearing her stained white robe.

"We have a moment," she whispered, and drew him aside into their own bedroom. When that door too had been softly closed, and they were securely alone, she added: "I've already taken the medicine downstairs to Denis. He thinks that the man is probably going to die . . . there's no doubt, is there, that he's the courier we're expecting?"

"I don't suppose there's much doubt about that, no."

The lady was slipping out of her bloodied robe now, and throwing it aside. In the very dim light that came in through the barred window from those distant watchfires, her husband beheld her shapely body as a curved warmed silver candlestick, a pale ghost hardly thickened at all by having borne one child. Once he had loved this woman hopelessly, and then another love had come to him, and gone again, dissolved in death. Sometimes he still saw in dreams a cascade of bright red hair . . . his love for his darkhaired wife still existed, but it was very different now.

As she dug into a chest to get another robe, she told him calmly, "One of those we killed tonight cried out, something like: 'Greetings to Ben of Purkinje, from the Blue Temple.' I'm sure that Denis heard it too."

"We're going to have to trust Denis. He's proved tonight he's loyal. I think he saved your life."

"Yes," the lady agreed, in a remote voice. "Either trust him—or else kill him too. Well." She dismissed that thought, though not before taking a moment in which to examine it with deliberate care. Then she looked hard at her husband. "And you called me Barb, too, once, down there in his hearing."

"Did I?" He'd thought he'd broken himself long ago of calling her that. Ben—he never really thought of himself as "of Purkinje"—heaved a great sigh. "So, anyway, the Blue Temple has caught up with me. It probably doesn't matter what Denis overheard."

"And they've caught up with me, too," she reminded him sharply. "And with your daughter, whether they were looking for us or not. It looked like they were ready to wipe out the household if they could." She paused. "I hope they haven't located Mark."

Ben thought that over. "There's no way we can get any word to him quickly. Is there? I'm not sure just where he is."

"No, I don't suppose we can." Barbara, tightening the belt on her clean robe, shook her head thoughtfully. "And they came here right on the heels of the courier—did you notice that? They must have been following him somehow, knowing that he'd lead them to us."

"Too much of a coincidence otherwise."

"Yes. And the alliance still holds, I suppose, between Blue Temple and the Dark King."

"Which means the Dark King's people may know about the courier too. And about what we have in our possession here, that the courier was going to take away, if the rest of the shipment ever arrives." He heaved another sigh.

"What do we do, Ben?" His wife spoke softly now, standing close to him and looking up. At average height he towered over her.

"At the moment, we try to keep the courier alive, and see if he can tell us anything. About Denis— we're just going to have to trust him, as I say. He's a good man."

He was about to open the bedroom door, but his wife's small hand on his arm delayed him. "Your hands," she reminded him. "Your robe."

"Right." He poured water into a basin and quickly washed his hands, then changed his robe. Half his mind was still down in the workshop, reliving the fight. Already in his memory the living bodies he had just broken were taking on the aspects of creatures in some awful dream. Te knew they were going to come back later to assail him. Later perhaps his hands would shake again. It was always like this for him after a fight. He had to try to put it out of his mind for now.

While he was getting into his clean robe, Barbara said, "Ben, as soon as I saw that the man had only one arm, you know what I thought of."

"Mark's father. But Mark always told us that his father was dead. He sounded quite sure of it."

"Yes, I remember. That he'd seen his father struck down in their village street. But just suppose—"

"Yes. Well, we've got enough to worry about as it is."

In another moment they were quietly making their way downstairs together. The house around them was as quiet now as if everyone were really sleeping. Ben could picture most of his workers lying awake, holding their breaths, waiting for the next crash.

In Denis's room on the ground floor they found the young man, his face pale under his dark hair, sitting watch over a stranger who still breathed, but barely. The mistress immediately went to work, improving on her first effort at bandaging Denis's arm. Ben thought he could see a little more color coming slowly back into the youth's cheeks.

And now, for the third time since midnight, a noise at the back door. This time a modest tapping.

Something in Ben wanted to react with laughter "Gods and demons, what a night. My house has turned into the Hermes Gate to the High Road."

And now, for the third time, after making sure that his wife and his assistant were armed and as ready for trouble as they could get, Ben maneuvered light and lenses to look out into the narrow exterior passage. This time, as he reported to the others in a whipser, there were two human figures to be seen outside. Both appeared to be men, and both were robed in white.

"It looks like two of Ardneh's people. One's carrying a big staff that . . ." Ben didn't finish. Barbara caught his meaning.

Those outside, knowing from the light that they were under observation from within, called loudly: "Master Courtenay? We've brought the wooden model that you've been waiting for."

"Ah," said Ben, hearing a code that gave him reassurance. Still he signed to his companions to remain on guard, before he cautiously opened the door once more.

This time the opening admitted neither a toppling body nor an armed rush. There was only the peaceful entry of the two in white, who as Ardneh's priests saluted courteously first the master of the house and then the people with him. Denis, this time holding his hatchet left-handed, was glad to be able to lower it again.

White robes dripped water on a floor already freshly marked by rain and mud and blood. If the newcomers noticed these signs of preceding visitors, they said nothing about them.

Instead, as soon as Ben had barred up the door again, the older of the two whiteclad priests offered him the heavy, ornate wooden staff. It was obviously meant to be a ceremonial object of some kind, too large and unwieldy to be anything but a burden on a march or a hike. Tall as a man, cruciform in its upper part, the staff was beautifully carved out of some light wood that Denis could not identify. The uppermost portion resembled the hilt of a gigantic wooden sword, with the heads and necks of two carved dragons recurving upon themselves to form the outsized crosspiece.

"Beautiful," commented Denis, with a sudden dry suspicion. "But I wonder which of Ardneh's rites requires such an object? I saw nothing at all like it in the time I spent as acolyte."

The two white-garbed men looked at Denis. Then they turned in silent appeal to the man they knew as Master Courtenay. He told them tiredly, "You may show us the inside of the wooden model too. Denis here is fully in my confidence, as of tonight. He's going to have to be."

Denis stared for a moment at his master, who was watching closely what the priests were doing. The younger priest had the staff now, and was pressing carefully with strong fingers on the fancy carving. In a moment, the wood had opened like a shell, revealing a velvet-lined cavity inside. Hidden there, straight iron hilt within wooden crosspiece, was a great Sword. The plain handle, of what Denis took to be some hard black wood, was marked in white with a small symbol, the outline of an open human hand. The Sword was in a leather sheath, that left only a finger's-breadth of the blade visible, but that small portion of metal caught the eye. It displayed a rich mottling, suggesting centimeters of depth in the thin blade, beneath a surface gleam of perfect smoothness. Only the Old World, or a god, thought Denis, could have made a blade like that . . . and Denis had never heard of any Old World swords.

"Behold," the elder priest of Ardneh said, even as the hand of the younger drew forth the blade out of its sheath. "The Sword of Mercy!"

And still Denis needed another moment—but no more than that—to understand fully what he was being allowed to see. When understanding came, he first caught his breath, and then released it in a long sigh. By now almost everyone in the world had heard of the Twelve Swords, though there were probably those who still doubted their reality, and most had never seen one. The Swords had been forged some twenty years ago, the more reliable stories had it; created, all the versions of the legend agreed, to serve some mysterious role in a divine Game that the gods and goddesses who ruled the world were determined to enjoy among themselves.

And if this wonderous weapon were not one of those twelve Swords, thought Denis . . . well, it was hard to imagine what else it could be. In his time at the House of Courtenay he had seen some elegant and valuable blades, but never before anything like this.

There were twelve of them, all of the stories agreed on that much. Most of them had two names, though some had more names than two, and a few had only one. They were called Wayfinder, and Farslayer, and the Tyrant's Blade; there were the Mindsword, and Townsaver, and Stonecutter, called also the Sword of Siege. There were Doomgiver, Sightblinder, Dragonslicer; Coinspinner and Shieldbreaker and the Sword of Love, that last thrice-named, also as Woundhealer and the Sword of Mercy.

And, if any of the tales had truth in them at all, each Sword had its own unique power, capable of overwhelming all lesser magics, bestowing on its owner some chance to rule the world, or at least to speak on equal terms with those who died. . . .

The older priest had carefully accepted the naked Sword from the hands of the younger, and now Denis observed with a start that the old man was now approaching him, Denis, with the heavy weapon held out before him. Half-raised as if in some clumsy system of attack, it wobbled slightly in the elder's hands.

Even in the mild lamplight the steel gleamed breathtakingly. And Denis thought that a sound was coming from it now, a sound like that of human breath.

Whether he was commanded to hold out his wounded arm, or did so automatically, Denis could not afterwards remember. The room was very quiet, except for the faint slow rhythmic hiss that the Sword made, as if it breathed. The old man's thin arms, that looked as if they might never have held a weapon before in all his life, reached out. The blade, looking keener than any razor that Denis had ever seen, steadied itself suddenly. It moved now as if under some finer control than the visibly tremulous grip of the old priest.

And now the broad point had somehow, without even nicking flesh, inserted itself snugly underneath the tight bandage binding Denis's forearm. The bloodstained white cloth, cut neatly, fell away, and the Sword's point touched the wound directly. Denis, expecting pain, felt instead an intense moment of—something else, a sensation unique and indescribable. And then the Sword withdrew.

Looking down at his arm, Denis saw dried blood, but no fresh flow. The dried, brownish stuff brushed away readily enough when he rubbed at it with his fingers. Where the dried blood had been, he saw now a small, fresh, pink scar. The wound looked healthy, easily a week or ten days healed.

It was at this moment, for some reason, that Denis suddenly remembered something about the man who, the legends said, had been forced to assist

Vulcan in the forging of the Swords. The stories said of that human smith that as soon as his work was done he had been deprived of his right arm by the god.

"It is shameful, of course," the elder priest was saying, "that we must keep it hidden so, and sneak through the night with it like criminals with their plunder. But if we did not take precautions, then those who would put Woundhealer to an evil use would soon have it in their possession."

"We will do our best," the lady of the house assured him, "to keep it from them."

"But at the moment," said the master, "we have a problem even more immediate than that. Sirs, if you will, bring the Sword this way with you, and quickly. A man lies dying."

Denis led the way, and quickly opened the door to his own room. The master stepped in past him, and indicated the still figure on the bed. "He arrived here not an hour ago, much as you see him. And I fear he is the courier who was to have carried on what you have brought."

The two priests moved quickly to stand beside the bed. The young one murmured a prayer to Draffut, God of Healing. The first quick touch of the Sword was directly on the wound still bleeding in the side of the unconscious man. Denis, despite his own experience of only moments ago, could not keep from wincing involuntarily. It was hard to imagine that that keen, hard point would not draw more blood, do more harm to human flesh already injured. But the slow red ooze from the wound, instead of increasing, dried up immediately. As the Sword moved away, the packing that Denis had put into the wound pulled out with it. The cloth hung there, stuck by dried blood to the skin.

Feeling a sense of unreality, Denis passed his hand over his eyes.

Now the Sword, still in the hands of Ardneh's elder servant, moved down to touch the wound on the exposed knee. This time when the bare metal touched him, the man on the bed drew in his breath sharply, as if with some extreme and exquisite sensation; a moment later he let out a long sigh, eloquent of relief. But his eyes did not open.

And now the tip of the Sword was being made to pass back and forth over his whole body, not quite touching him. It paused again, briefly, right above the heart. Denis could see how the arms of the old priest continued to tremble, as if it strained them to hold this heavy weapon—not, Denis supposed, that this Sword ought to be called a weapon. He wondered what would happen if you swung it against an enemy.

The tip of the blade paused just once more, when it reached the scarred stump of the long-lost arm. There it touched, and there, to Denis's fresh surprise, it did draw blood at last, a thready red trickle from the scarred flesh. Again a gasp came from the unconscious man.

The bleeding stopped of itself, almost as quickly as it had started. The old priest now slid the blade back into its sheath, and handed it to his assistant, who enclosed it once again within the staff of wood.

The elder's face was pale now, as if the healing might have taken something out of him. But he did not pause to rest, bending instead to examine the man he had been treating. Then he pulled a blanket up to the patient's chin and straightened.

"He will recover," the elder priest announced, "but he must rest for many days; he was nearly dead before the Sword of Mercy reached him. Here you can provide him with the good food he needs; even so his recovery will take some time."

Master Courtenay told the two priests of Ardneh softly, "We thank you in his name—whatever that may be. Now, will you have some food? And then we'll find you a place to sleep."

The elder declined gravely. "Thank you, but we cannot stay, even for food." He shook his head. "If this man was to be the next courier, as you say, I fear you will have to find a replacement for him."

"We will find a way," the lady said.

"Good," said the elder, and paused, frowning. "There is one thing more that I must tell you before we go." He paused again, a longer time, as if what he had to say now required some gathering of forces. "The Mindsword has fallen into the hands of the Dark King."

An exhausted silence fell over the people in the workshop. Denis was trying desperately to recall what the various songs and stories had to say about the weapon called the Mindsword.

There was, of course, the verse that everyone had heard:

The Mindsword spun in the dawn's gray light
And men and demons knelt down before
The Mindsword flashed in the midday bright
Gods joined the dance, and the march to war
It spun in the twilight dim as well
And gods and men marched off to—

"Gods and demons!" Master Courtenay swore loudly. His face was grave and gray, with a look that Denis had never seen on it before.

Moments later, having said their last farewells, the two white-robed men were gone.

Denis closed and barred the door behind them, and turned round. The master of the house was standing in the middle of the workshop, with one hand on the wooden Sword-case that stood leaning there against the chimney. He was looking it over carefully, as if it were something that he might want to buy.

The lady was back in Denis's room already, looking down at the hurt man on the bed. Denis when he came in saw that the man was now sleeping peacefully and his color was a little better already.

Out in the main room of the shop again, Denis approached his master—whose real name, Denis was already certain, was unlikely to be Courtenay. "What are we going to do with the Sword now, sir? Of course it may be none of my business." It obviously had become his business now; his real question was how they were going to deal with that fact.

His master gave him a look that said this point was appreciated. But all he said was: "Even before we worry about the Sword, there's another little job that needs taking care of. How's your arm?"

Denis fixed it. There was a faint residual soreness. "Good enough."

"Good." And the big man walked around behind the big toppled workbench, and lifted the tarpaulin from that which had been concealed from Ardneh's priests.

It was going to be very convenient, Denis thought, that the house was so near the river, and that the night was dark and rainy.

CHAPTER 3

The chase under the blistering sun had been a long one, but the young man who was its quarry foresaw that it was not going to go on much longer.

Since the ambush some twenty kilometers back had killed his three companions and all their riding beasts, he had been scrambling on foot across the rough, barren country, pausing only at intervals to set an ambush of his own, or when necessary to gasp for breath.

The young man wore a light pack on his back, along with his longbow and quiver. At his belt he carried a small water bottle—it was nearly empty now, one of the reasons why he thought that the chase must soon end in one way or another. His age would have been hard to judge because of his weathered look, but it was actually much closer to twenty than to thirty. His clothes were those of a hunter, or perhaps a guerrilla soldier, and he wore his present trouble as well and fittingly as he wore his clothes. He was a tall and broad-shouldered young man, with blue-gray eyes, and a light, short beard that until a few days ago had been neatly trimmed. The longbow slung across his back looked eminently functional, but at the moment there were only three arrows left in the quiver that rode beside it.

The young man had fallen into a kind of pattern in his movement. This took the form of a trot, a pause to look back over one shoulder, another scramble, a quick walk, and then a look back over the other shoulder without pausing.

According to the best calculation he could make, which he knew might very easily be wrong, he still had one more active enemy behind him than he had arrows. Of course the only way to make absolutely sure of the enemy's numbers would be to let them catch him. They might very well do that anyway. They were still mounted, and would easily have overtaken him long ago, except that his own ambushes set over the past twenty kilometers had instilled some degree of caution in the survivors. These high plains made a good place for ambush, deceptively open-looking but cut by ravines and studded with windcarved hills and giant boulders that looked as if some god had scattered them playfully about.

By this time, having had twenty kilometers in which to think it over, the young man had no real doubt as to who his pursuers were. They had to be agents of the Blue Temple. Any merely military skirmish, he thought, would have been broken off long before this. Any ordinary patrol from the Dark King's army would have been content to return to camp and report a victory, or else proceed with whatever other business they were supposed to be about. They would not have continued to risk their skins in the pursuit of one survivor, not one as demonstrably dangerous as himself, and not through this dangerous terrain.

No, they knew who they were after. They knew what he had done, four years ago. And undoubtedly they were under contract to the Blue Temple to bring back his head.

The young man was finding time in his spare moments, such as they were, to wonder if they were also closing in on Ben, his friend and his companion of four years ago. Or if perhaps they had already found him. But he was not in a position right now to do anything for Ben.

The youth's flight had brought him to the edge of yet another ravine, this one cutting directly across his path. To the left of where the young man halted on the brink, the groove in the earth deepened rapidly, turning into a real canyon that wound its way off to the east, there presumably to join at some point a larger canyon that he had already caught sight of from time to time. In the other direction, to the young man's right, the ravine grew progressively shallower; if he intended to cross it, he should head that way.

From where he was standing now, the country on the other side of the ravine looked if anything flatter than the plain he had been crossing, which of course ought to give a greater advantage to the mounted men. If he did not cross, he would go down into the ravine and follow it along. He could see that as it deepened some shelter appeared along its bottom, provided by rough free-standing rock formations and by the winding walls themselves. If he went that way he would be going downhill, and for that reason might be able to go faster.

It was the need for water that made his choice a certainty. The big canyon ought to be no more than a few kilometers away at most, and very probably it had water at its bottom.

He was down in the bottom of the ravine, making good time along its deepening trench, before one of his over-the-shoulder looks afforded him another glimpse of the men who were coming after him. Three heads were gazing down over the rocky rim, some distance to his rear. It looked as if they had been expecting him to cross the ravine, not follow it, and had therefore angled their own course a little toward its shallower end. He had therefore gained a little distance on them. The question now was, how would they pursue from here? They might all follow him down into the ravine. Or one of them might follow him along the rim, ready to roll down rocks on him when a good chance came. Or, one man might cross completely, so they could follow him along both walls and down the middle too.

He had doubts that they were going to divide their small remaining force.

Time would tell. He was now committed, anyway, to following the ravine. Much depended on what sort of concealment he could find.

So far, things were looking as good as could be expected. What had been a fairly simple trench at the point where he entered it was rapidly widening and deepening into a complex, steep-sided canyon. Presently, coming to a place where the canyon bent sharply, the young man decided to set up another ambush, behind a convenient outcropping of rock. Lying motionless on stovelike rock, watching small lizards watch him through the vibrating air, he had to fight down the all-too-rational fear that this time his enemies had outguessed him, and a couple of them were really following him along on the high rims. At any moment now, the head of one of them ought to appear in his field of vision, just about *there*. From which vantage point it would of course be no trick at all to roll down a deadly barrage of rocks. If they were lucky his head would still be recognizable when they came down to collect it.

Enough of that.

It was a definite relief when the three men came into sight again, all trailing him directly along the bottom of the canyon. They were walking their mounts now, having to watch their footing carefully on the uneven rock. As their quarry had hoped, at this spot they had no more than half their visual attention to spare in looking out for ambush.

The young man waiting for them already had an arrow nocked. And now he started to draw it, slowly taking up the bowstring's tension. He realized that at the last instant, he'd have to raise himself up into full view to get the shot off properly.

The moment came and he lifted his upper body. The bow twanged in his hands, as if the arrow had made its own decision. The shot was good, but the man who was its target, as if warned by some subtle magic, begun to turn his body away just as the shot was made. The arrow missed. The enemy, alarmed, were all ducking for cover.

The marksman did not delay to see what they might be going to do next. Already he was on his feet and running, scrambling, on down the canyon. Only two arrows left in his quiver now, and still he was not absolutely sure that there were no more than three men in pursuit.

He hurdled a small boulder, and kept on running. At least he'd slowed his pursuers down again, made them move more cautiously. And that ought to let him gain a little distance.

And now, suddenly, unexpectedly, he had good luck in sight. As he rounded a new curve of the canyon there sprang into view ahead of him a view into the bigger cross-canyon that this one joined. Ahead he saw a narrow slice of swift gray water, with a luxuriant border of foliage, startlingly green, all framed in stark gray rock.

A little farther, and he would have not only water and concealment, but a choice of ways to turn, upstream or down. The young man urged his tired body into a faster run.

In his imagination he was already tasting the cold water. Then the tree-tall dragon emerged from the fringe of house-high ferns and other growth that marked the entrance to the bigger canyon. As the young man stumbled to a halt the beast was looking directly at him. Its massive jaw was working, but only lightly, tentatively, as if in this heat it might be reluctant to summon up the energy for a hard bite or even a full roar.

The young man was already so close to the dragon when he saw it that he could do nothing but freeze in his tracks. He knew that any attempt at a quick retreat would be virtually certain to bring on a full charge, and he would have no hope of outrunning that.

Nor did he move to unsling his bow. Even his best shot, placed perfectly into the eye, the only even semi-vulnerable target, might do no more than madden a dragon of the size of this one before him. His best hope of survival lay in standing still. If he could manage to do that, there was a bare chance that his earlier rapid movement would be forgotten and he would be ignored.

Then something happened that surprised the young men profoundly, so that now it was astonishment more than either terror or conscious effort that kept him standing like a statue.

The dragon's vast mouth, scarred round the lips with its own quondam flames, opened almost delicately, revealing yellowed and blackened teeth the size of human forearms. From that mouth emerged a voice, a kind of cavernous whisper. It was perfectly intelligible, though so soft that the motionless man could scarcely be sure that he was really hearing it.

"Put down your little knife," the dragon said to him. "I will not hurt you."

The man, who had thought he was remaining perfectly motionless, looked down at his right hand. Without realizing it he had drawn the dagger from his belt. Mechanically he put the useless weapon back into its sheath.

Even as the man did this, the dragon, perhaps three times his height as it stood tall on its hind legs, moved closer to him by one great stride. It reached out for him with one enormous forelimb, armed at the fingertips with what looked like pitchfork tines. But that frightening grip picked up the man so gently that he felt no harm. In a moment he had been lifted, tossed spinning in the air, and softly, safely, caught again. At this moment, that seemed to him certain to be the moment of his death, he felt curiously free from fear.

Death did not come, nor even pain. He was being tossed and mauled quite tenderly. Here we went up again, propelled with a grim playfulness that tended to jolt the breath out of his chest, but did him no real damage. In one of these revolving airborne jaunts, momentarily facing back up the side canyon, he got his clearest look yet at the whole small gang of his surviving human pursuers. They had been even closer behind him than he had thought, but now with every instant they were meters farther away. The three of them, two look-ing forward and away, one looking back in terror, were astride their riding beasts again, and never mind the chance that a mount might stumble here. All three in panic were galloping at full stretch back up the barren floor of the side canyon.

The dragon roared. The tossed man's own whirl-ing motion whirled the riders away, out of his field of vision. He felt his flying body brush through a fringe of greenery. His landing was almost gentle, on shaded ground soft as a bed with moss and mois-ture. He lay there on his back, beneath great danc-ing fronds. This position afforded him a fine view of the dragon's scaly green back just as, roaring like an avalanche, it launched a charge after the three riders.

In another moment the riders were completely out of sight around the first curve of the side can-yon. The dragon at once aborted its charge and ceased its noise. It turned, and with an undragonly air of calm purpose came striding back to where the man lay. He just lay there, watching its approach. The creature hadn't killed him yet, and anyway he could never have outrun it even had his lungs been full of breath.

Once more the huge dragon gently picked him up. It carried him carefully for a little distance, deeper into the heavy riverside growth of vegetation. Through the last layer of branches ahead the man could plainly see the swift narrow stream that threaded the canyon's floor.

The dragon spoke above the endless frantic murmur of the water. "They will never," it told the man in its sepulchral voice, "come back and follow a dragon into this thicket. Instead they will return to their masters and report that you are dead, that with their own eyes they saw you crushed and eaten." Saying this, the dragon again deposited the man on soft ground, this time very gently.

Then the dragon took a long step back. Its image in the man's eyes flickered, and for one moment he had the definite impression that the huge creature was wearing a broad leather belt around its scaly, bulging midsection. And there was a second, momentary impression, that from this belt there hung a scabbard, and that the scabbard held a sword.

The belt and Sword were no longer visible. Then they reappeared. The man blinked, he shook his head and rubbed his eyes and looked again. Some kind of enchantment was in operation. It had to be that. If it—

The Swordbelt, now unquestionably real, was now hanging looped from a great furry hand—it was undeniably a hand, and not a dragon's forefoot. The fur covering the hand, and covering the arm and body attached, was basically a silver gray, but it glowed remarkably with its own inner light. As the man watched, the glow shifted, flirting with all the colors of the rainbow.

The enormous hand let the belt drop.

Standing before the youth now was a furred beast on two legs, as tall and large as the dragon had been, but otherwise much transformed. Claws had been replaced by fingers, on hands of human shape. There were still great fangs, but they were bone-white now, and the head in which they were set no longer had anything in the least reptilian about it. Although the figure was standing like a man, the face was not human. It was—unique.

The great dark eyes observed with intelligence the man's reaction to the transformation.

The young man's first outward response was to get back to his feet, slowly and shakily. Then he walked slowly to where the belt and Sword were lying, on shaded moss. Bending over, he observed that the jet-black hilt of the Sword was marked with one small white symbol; but, though the man dropped to his knees to look more closely, he was unable to make out what that symbol was. His eyes for some reason had trouble getting it into clear focus. Then he reached out and put his fingers on that hilt, and with that touch he felt the power he had expected enter into him. Now he was able to see the symbol plainly. It was the simple outline of an observant human eye.

Turning his head to look up at the waiting giant, the young man said: "I am Mark, son of Jord." As he spoke he got to his feet, and as he stood up he drew the Sword. His right hand held up that bright magnificence of steel in a salute.

The giant's answer came in an inhumanly deep bass, quite different from the dragon's voice: "You are Mark of Arin-on-Aldan."

The youth regarded him steadily for a moment.

Then he nodded. "That also," he agreed. Then, lowering the Sword, he added, "I have held Sightblinder here once before."

"You have held others of the Swords as well. I know something of you, Mark, though we have not met. I am Draffut, as you must have realized by now. The man called Nestor, who was your friend, was also mine."

Mark did not answer immediately. Now that he was holding the Sword of Stealth, some inward things about the being he was looking at had become apparent to him. Just how they were apparent was something he could not have explained had his life depended on it; but across Draffut's image in Mark's eyes some part of Draffut's history was now written, in symbols that Mark would not be able to see, much less interpret, once he put down the Sword again.

Mark said, "You are the same Draffut who is prayed to as the God of Healing. Who knew Ardneh the Blessed, as your living friend two thousand years ago . . . but still I will not call you a god. Lord of Beasts, as others name you, yes. For certainly you are that, and more." And Mark bowed low. "I thank you for my life."

"You are welcome . . . and Beastlord is a title that I can at least tolerate." Actually the huge being seemed to enjoy it to some extent. "With Sightblinder in your hand I am sure you can see I am no god. But I have just come from an assembly of them."

Mark was startled. "What?"

"I say that I have just come from an assembly of the gods," Draffut repeated patiently. "And I had Sightblinder in my own hand as I stood among them so each of them saw me as one of their own number . . . and I saw that in them which surprised me, as I stood there and listened to them argue."

"Argue . . . about what?"

"In part, about the Swords. As usual they were able to agree on nothing, which I count as good news for humanity. But I heard other news also, that was not good at all. The Dark King, Vilkata, has the Mindsword now. How and when he got it, I do not know."

For a long moment Mark stood silent. Then he muttered softly, "Ardneh's bones! The gods were saying that? Do you believe it?"

"I am glad," said Draffut, "that you understand that what the gods tell us is not always true. But in this case I fear it is the truth. Remember that I held the Sword of Stealth in my own hands then, and I looked at the speakers carefully as they were speaking. They were not telling deliberate lies; nor do I think they were mistaken."

"Then the human race is . . ." Mark made a gesture of futility. ". . . in trouble." Looking down at the blade he was still holding, he swung it lightly, testing how it felt in his grip. "If the question is not too impertinent, how did you come to have this? The last time I saw it, it was embedded in the body of a flying dragon."

"It may have fallen from the creature in flight. I found it in the Great Swamp."

"And—again if you do not mind my asking—how did you come to be spying on the gods?"

Draffut rested one of his enormous hands on a treetrunk that stood beside him. Mark thought he saw the bark change color around that grip. It even moved a little, he thought, achieving a different tempo in its life. Many were the marvelous tales told of Draffut. Now the Beastlord was speaking.

"Once I had this Sword in my hand, I decided that I would never have a better chance to do something that I had long thought about—to find the Emperor, and talk to him face to face."

"You did not go first to find the gods?"

"I had met gods before," Draffut ruminated. In a moment he went on. "The Emperor is not an easy man to locate. But I have some skill in discovering that which is hidden, and I found him. I had been for a long time curious."

Mark had sometimes been curious on the same subject, but only vaguely so. He had grown up accepting the commonly held ideas about the Emperor: a legendary trickster, perhaps invented and unreal. A practical joker, a propounder of riddles, a wearer of masks. A sometime seducer of brides and maidens, and the proverbial father of the poor and the unlucky. Only in recent years, as Mark began to meet people who knew more about the world than the name of the next village, had he come to understand that the Emperor might have a real importance.

Not that his curiosity on the subject had ever occupied much of his time or thought. Still, he now asked Draffut, "What is he like?"

"He is a man," said Draffut firmly, as if there had been some doubt of that. But, having made that point, the Beastlord paused, as if he were at a loss as to what else to say.

At last he went on. "John Ominor, the enemy of Ardneh, was called Emperor too." At this offhand recollection of the events of two thousand years past, Mark could feel his scalp creep faintly. Draffut continued. "And then, a little later, some called Prince Duncan, a good man, by that title."

Draffut fell silent. Mark waited briefly, then pursued the subject. "Has this man now called the Emperor some connection with the Swords? Can he be of any help to us against Vilkata?"

Draffut made a curious two-handed gesture, that in a lesser being would have suggested helplessness. When he let go of the treetrunk its surface at once reverted to ordinary bark. "I think that the Emperor could be an enormous help to us. But how to obtain his help . . . and as for the Swords, I can tell you this: I think that Sightblinder did not deceive him for a moment, though I had it in my hand as I approached."

"It did not deceive him?"

"I think he never saw me as anything but what I am." The Beastlord thought for a moment, then concluded: "Of course it was not my intention to deceive him, unless he should mean me harm—and I do not believe he did."

The speaker's intense, inhuman gaze held Mark's eyes. "It was the Emperor's suggestion that I take this Sword and use it to observe the councils of the gods. And he told me something else: that after I had heard the gods, I should bring Sightblinder on to you."

Mark experienced an inward chill, a feeling like that of sudden fear, but with a spark of exhilaration at the core of it. To him both emotions were equally inexplicable. "To me?" he echoed stupidly.

"To you. Even the Sword of Stealth cannot disguise me well enough to let me pass for human, or for any type of creature of merely human size. At a distance, perhaps. But I cannot enter the dwellings of humans secretly, to listen to their secret councils."

"You say you're able to spy on the gods, though. Isn't that even more important?"

The Beastlord was shaking his head. "The war that is coming is going to jar the world, as it has not been jarred since the time of Ardneh. And the war is going to be won or lost by human beings, though the gods will have a role to play."

"How do you know these things?"

Draffut said nothing.

"What can we do?" Mark asked simply.

"I am going, in my own shape, to try to influence the actions of the gods. As you may know, I am incapable of hurting humans, whatever happens. But against *them* I can fight when necessary. I have done as much before, and won."

Again Mark could feel his scalp creep. He swallowed and nodded. Apparently there was some basis of truth for those legends that told of Draffut's successful combat against the wargod Mars himself.

Draffut added: "I am going to leave the Sword with you."

Again to hear that brought Mark a swift surge of elation, an emotion in this case swiftly dampened by a few memories and a little calculation.

"Sir Andrew, whom I serve, has sent me on a mission to Princess Rimac—or to her General Rostov, if he proves easier to find. I am to tell them certain things . . . of course, I can take the Sword of Stealth along with me. And I suppose I could give it to them when I get there . . . but what did the Emperor have in mind for me to do with it? Do you trust him?"

Questions were piling up in his mind faster than he could ask them.

"I have known and dealt with human beings for more than fifty thousand years," said Draffut, "and I trust him. Though he would not explain. He said only that he trusts you with the Sword."

Mark frowned. To be told of such mysterious trust by an apparently powerful figure was somehow more irritating than pleasing. "But why me? What does he know about me?"

"He knows of you," said Draffut immediately, in a tone of unhelpful certainty. "And now, I must be on my way." The giant turned away, then back again to say, "The Princess's land of Tasavalta lies to the east of here, along the coast, as I suppose you know. As to where Rostov and his army might be at the moment, you can probably guess as well as I."

"I'll take the Sword on with me, then, to the Princess." Mark raised his voice, calling after the Beastlord; Draffut, moving at a giant's walk considerably faster than a human run, was already growing distant. Mark sighed, swallowing more questions that were obviously not going to be answered now.

Splashing through the shallow river, Draffut turned once more, for just long enough to wave farewell. Then he began to climb the far wall of the great canyon. He climbed like a mountain goat, going right up the steep rocks. Mark thought he could see the rock itself undergoing temporary change, wherever Draffut touched it, starting to flow with the impulses of life.

Then Draffut was gone, up and over the canyon rim.

Left alone, Mark was suddenly exhausted. He

stared for a long moment at the Sword left in his hands. Then he bent to enjoy, at last, the drink he needed from the river, whose name he did not know. He cooled himself with splashing. Then he stretched himself out on a shady moss, with Sightblinder tucked under his head, and slept securely. Any enemy coming upon him now would not see him, but instead some person or thing that they loved or feared, or at any rate would not harm. Of course there might come a sudden thunderstorm upstream, a canyon flood, and he'd be drowned; but he had lived much of his life with greater risks than that.

Mark did not awake until the sun had dropped behind the high stone western wall and it was nearly dark. Before the light had faded entirely, he managed to get a rabbit with one of his two remaining arrows. He even managed to retrieve the arrow undamaged, which convinced him that his luck was definitely improving. After cooking his rabbit on a small fire, he devoured most of it and slept again.

It was deep night when he awoke the second time, and he lay looking up at the stars and wondering about Draffut. The Beastlord was a magnificent and unique being, and it was small wonder that most folk thought he was a god. His life had begun so long ago that even Ardneh's struggle with the demon Orcus was recent by comparison. Mark, holding the Sword of Stealth while he looked at Draffut, had seen that that was true.

The Sword had allowed Mark to see something more wonderful still.

He had seen, very plainly, though only for a moment, and in a mode of seeing impossible to explain, that the Beastlord had begun his long life as a dog. A plain, four-footed dog, and nothing more.

That was a mystery beyond wondering about. Mark slept yet again, and awoke beneath turned stars. Just after his eyes opened he saw a brilliant meteor, as if some power had awakened him to witness it.

He lay awake for some time, pondering.

Who, after all, was the Emperor? And why and how did the Emperor come to be aware of Mark, son of Jord? Of course Mark's late father was himself a minor figure in legends, through his unwilling conscription by Vulcan to help in the forging of the Swords. And Mark had taken part in the celebrated raid of four years ago on the Blue Temple treasury. But why should either of those dubious claims to fame have caused the Emperor to send him a Sword?

All the stories agreed that the Emperor liked jokes.

Mark was no closer to an answer when he once more fell asleep.

In the morning he was up and moving early. Soon he found a side canyon that appeared passable, and led off to the east. He refilled his water bottle before leaving the river, then followed the side canyon's gradually ascending way. When, after some kilometers, the smaller canyon had shallowed enough to let him climb out of it easily, he did so. Now eastern mountains, blue as if with forests, were visible in the distance. Tasavalta, he thought. Or somewhere near to it.

He was a day closer to those mountains when he

saw the mounted patrol. He was sure even at a considerable distance that these riders were the Dark King's soldiers. He had fought against such often enough to be able to distinguish them, he thought, by no more than the fold of a distant cloak, the shape of a spearhead carried high. The patrol was between him and his goal, and was heading almost directly toward him, but he did not think that they had seen him yet.

Mark had automatically taken concealment behind a bush at his first sight of the riders, and he continued watching them from hiding. He was planning, almost unthinkingly, how best to remain out of their sight as they passed, when he recalled what Sword it was that now swung at his side. He had used Sightblinder once before, and he trusted its powers fully.

Boldly he stood up, hand on the hilt of the Sword, feeling a stirring of its power as he approached his enemies, he marched straight toward the oncoming riders. But before the patrol saw him they altered course slightly, perversely turned aside. Mark muttered oaths. If he had been helpless and endeavoring to hide, he thought, they would have stumbled over him without trying.

They were completely out of sight when he reached their trail, but he followed it into the setting sun, blue mountains now at his back. His messages for Princess Rimac were really routine. His soldier's instincts told him that here he might have an excellent target of opportunity.

An hour or so later he found the patrol, a dozen tough-looking men, gathered by their evening fire, which was large enough to show that they had no particular fear of night attack. The hilt of Sightblinder was vibrating smoothly in Mark's hand as he strode into the firelight to stand before them.

They looked up at him, and they all sat still. Hard warriors though they were, he could see that they were instantly afraid. Of what, he did not know, except that it was some image that they saw of him. Looking down at his own body, he saw, as he had known he would, himself unchanged.

Mark left it to them to break the silence. At last one who was probably their sergeant stood up, bowed, and asked him: "Lord, what will you have of us?"

"In what direction do your orders take you?" Mark's voice, to his own ears, sounded no different than before.

"Great Lord, we are bound for the encampment of the Dark King himself. There we are to report to our captain the results of our patrol."

Mark drew in a deep breath. "Then you will take me with you."

CHAPTER 4

Jord scratched delicately at his itching arm-stump, then grimaced at the unaccustomed soreness there. He rubbed at the place, more delicately still, with a rough fingertip. There was some kind of minor swelling, too.

Not that he was complaining. On the contrary. He was lying on a soft couch covered with fine fabric, in morning sunshine. Birds sang pleasantly nearby. Otherwise he was alone on the elegant rooftop terrace, largely a garden of plants and birds, fresh from last night's rain. The terrace covered most of the flat roof of the House of Courtenay. A plate of food, second helpings that Jord had been unable to finish, rested on a small table at his side. He was wearing a fine white nightshirt, of a material strange to him, that felt as what he supposed silk must feel. Well, he'd obviously and very fortunately reached wealthy and powerful friends, so none of these details were really all that surprising.

What did surprise him—what left him in fact

almost numb with astonishment—was what had happened to his wounds.

The husky men, obviously some kind of servants, who had carried Jord up here to the terrace this morning had told him that he'd arrived here at the House of Courtenay only last night. Jord hadn't questioned the servants beyond that, because he wasn't sure how much they knew about their master's secret affairs, and about who he, Jord, really was, in terms of his business here.

Jord's last memories from last night were of being afraid of bleeding to death, and of trying to pound on the back door of his house, knowing that if he fainted before he got help he'd likely never to wake up. Well, he must have fainted. And he had certainly awakened, feeling almost healthy, ravenously hungry—and with his wounds well on the way to being completely healed.

The sun, rising higher now, would have begun to grow uncomfortably hot, but at just the proper angle a leafy bower now began to shade the couch. The noise of the city's streets was increasing, but it was comfortably far below. Jord had learned enough about cities to live in them when he had to, but he felt really at home only in a village or small town.

The trellises that shaded him, he noticed now, also screened him well from observation from any of the city's other tall buildings nearby. Meanwhile the interstices of latticework and leaves afforded him a pretty good outward view. Slate rooftops, like trees in a forest, stretched away to the uneven horizon formed by the city's formidable walls. Tashigang was built upon a series of hills, with the Corgo, here divided into several branches, flowing between some of them. The House of Courtenay, practically at riverside, was naturally in one of the lowest areas. The effect was that some of the sections of wall, and the hilltop buildings in the distance, loomed to what seemed magical height, becoming towers out of some story of the Old World.

"Good morning." The words breaking in upon Jord's thoughts came in a female voice that he did not recognize. He quickly turned back from peering through the trellis. She was young and small, really tiny, and black-haired; dressed in white, she was obviously a lady. A young nursemaid and a small child were visible in the background, out of easy earshot along a graveled path that helped make the rooftop look like a country garden.

"Good morning, Lady." In the past ten years or so Jord had been often enough in cosmopolitan society that now he could feel more or less at ease with practically anyone. "The men who brought me up here told me that I was in the house of Mistress and Master Courtenay."

"So you are; I am the mistress of this house. Gods and demons, don't try to get up. And you are Jord."

Jord abandoned his token effort to rise. "I am Jord, as you say. And I thank you for your help."

"Is the food not to your taste?"

"It's very good. Only they gave me more than enough."

The lady was looking at him thoughtfully. There were chairs nearby but just now she evidently preferred standing. "So, the Princess Rimac sent you to us. As courier, to carry two Swords back to her."

Jord tried to flex his wounded knee a little, and

grimaced at the sensation. "I seem to have failed in that task before it was fairly started." It was said matter-of-factly. "Well, I'll do as best I can with whatever comes next. It seems I'll need to heal before I can do much at all."

The lady continued to regard him. It appeared that for some reason she was strongly interested. Presently she said "The servants—all except Denis, who's really more than that—think that you are simply a fellow merchant, who's had an encounter with thieves and is in need of help. Such things are all too common in our business."

"And in mine, unhappily. Again I thank you for saving my life." Jord paused. "But tell me something. Those who carried me up here said that I arrived only last night. But . . ." He gestured in perplexity toward his wounds.

"One of the blades that you were going to take to Princess Rimac is the Sword of Mercy."

"Ah." Jord, who had been supporting himself on his elbow, lay back flat again. "That explains it."

The lady had turned her head away. The little child was babbling somewhere on the other side of the roof. But someone else, a huge man of about the lady's own age, was approaching around a corner of trellis. Birds flew out of his way. "My husband," she explained.

Again Jord raised himself on his elbow. "Master Courtenay. Again my thanks."

The big man smiled, an expression that made his face much more pleasant in appearance. "And you are welcome here, as I expect my wife has already told you."

Jord's hosts seated themselves together on a bench nearby, and asked to hear from him about last night's attack that had left him wounded. Both appeared relieved when he told them he had dispatched his lone assailant before he had collapsed himself.

The master of the house informed him, "A few more of those who were following you arrived a little later. But we managed to dispose of them."

"Following me? More of them?" Jord swore earthily, calling upon various anatomical features of several gods and demons. "I feared as much, but I saw nothing of 'em." He groaned his worry.

Master Courtenay's thick hand made a gesture of dismissal; there was nothing to be done about that now. Then Coutenay glanced at his wife, a look transmitting some kind of signal, and she faced their guest with the air of someone opening a new subject.

"Jord," she asked him, "what village do you come from?"

It had been years since that question had surprised him. "Why, you're quite right, Ma'am, I'm a village man, not of the cities. And I've lived in a good many villages."

"But twenty years ago you were living in Arin-on-Aldan, weren't you? And still there, up to about—ten years ago?"

Jord nodded, and sighed faintly. "Like a lot of other villages, Lady, it's not there any longer. Or so I've heard. Your pardon, gentlefolk, but most who start asking me about my village have an earlier one than that in mind. Treefall, the place that Vulcan took me from to help him forge the Swords. Yes, I'm that Jord. Not too many Jords in the world with the right arm missing. Often I use another name, and I put most people off when they start asking where I'm from. But you of course I'll answer gladly. Whatever you'd like to know."

"We," said the huge, broad man, "are no more gentlefolk than you. The name I was born with is nothing like Courtenay, but simply Ben. That was in a poor village too, where one name was enough. Ben of Purkinje, some call me now. You've heard that somewhere, most likely, within the past four years. I'm the Ben who robbed the Blue Temple, and they're out to hunt me down. I'm pretty sure it was their people who followed you here last night."

"And my name is really Barbara," the lady said simply. She moved one small pale hand in a gesture that took in the luxury of the terrace, her whole house. "This is all Blue Temple wealth, or was. A single handful of their chests and baskets full of jewels."

"Ah." Jord nodded. "I've heard of the man called Ben who robbed those robbers. That story has gone far and wide—"

The lady interrupted him, eagerly. "Since you've heard the stories, you must have heard that a man named Mark was in on the raid with Ben, here." Here Barbara really smiled at Jord for the first time. "And you have a grown son named Mark, don't you?"

"Yes," said the man on the couch. "It's a common enough name. Why?"

"Because it is the same Mark," the lady said. "And we are his good friends, though we have not seen him for a long time. He took no wealth for himself from the Blue Temple. He's still out there soldiering, in Sir Andrew's army. And I'm afraid he thinks that you are dead."

"Ah," said their visitor again. He lay back flat,

and closed his eyes, and clenched his fist. His lips moved, as if he might be praying. Then he opened his eyes and once more raised himself a little on his elbow.

He spoke to his hosts now almost as if he were their prisoner and they his judges. "Mark had to run away from the village, that day ... is it ten years now? Almost. He had to take Townsaver and get away with it. Yes, he saw me struck down. He must have been thinking ever since that I'd been killed. He wasn't able to come back, nor we to find out where he was. So much happened, we had to leave the village. We never had any news ..."

Jord's voice changed again, happily this time. "Tell me about him. Still soldiering, you say? What—?" He obviously had so many questions that he didn't know where to start.

Again someone was arriving on the rooftop. Jord heard a door close, and footsteps came crunching lightly along the graveled path. A pause, and a few words in what sounded like the nursemaid's voice. Then the footsteps resumed. This time there appeared a slender, dark-haired youth who was introduced to Jord as Denis, nicknamed the Quick. He greeted the older man courteously, and stood there rubbing his forearm through its long sleeve as if it might be sore.

Jord rubbed his arm-stump again. Already it seemed that the swelling, where the Sword had touched him, was a little greater.

Ben asked the new arrival, "What news from the streets?"

"None of the local people on our payroll noticed anything out of the way around midnight. It was a good night to be staying in."

"Denis," said Ben, "sit down." And he indicated an unoccpuied chair nearby. Then he turned his head and called: "Kuan-yin? Take the baby downstairs, would you?"

Presently a door closed again. Four people looked solemnly at one another. Ben said to his young employee, "There's one thing we've not told you about Jord yet. His reason for coming here." And at that point Ben paused, seemingly not knowing quite what to say next.

His wife put in, "You must know by now, Denis, where our political sympathies lie."

"The same as mine, Mistress," the young man murmured. "Or, indeed, I wouldn't be here now." But he knew that was not true; he would have stayed anyway, to be near her. Might he have stayed to be near Kuan-yin? That was more problematical.

Ben said to him, "You also know that our guest here is a secret courier, if not the details. And, as you can see, someone else is now going to have to do the job. It can't wait, and Jord can't walk."

Jord was listening silently, frowning but not interfering.

"I can't leave town right now, nor can Barbara. It'll be a well-paid job, Denis, if you'll do it."

"Please do it," the lady of the house urged softly.

Denis could feel his cheeks changing color a little. He indicated agreement, almost violently. "I'll need no special pay, sir, mistress."

Jord was still frowning at Denis intently.

Barbara, correctly interpreting this look, hasted to reassure the older man. "Denis came to us a year and a half ago, on the recommendation of the White Temple. We had gone to them and told them we were looking for a likely, honest prospect to be trained to help us in our business. A lot of people recruit workers there, you know."

Jord asked Denis: "How long were you there, at the White Temple?"

"Three years, a little more."

"And why were you ready to leave?"

Denis shrugged. "They were good people, they saved my life. And it was good to serve Ardneh for a time. But then ..." He made a gesture, of something fading, falling away.

"You must have been only half grown when you went to them."

"And half dead also. They picked me up out of the street after a gang fight, and brought me back to life. I owed them much, but I think I repaid their help in the time that I was there. We parted on good terms."

"Ah," said Jord. He appeared to have relaxed a little. He looked at Ben, and said, "Well sir, the matter's in your hands, not mine. Maybe sending this lad is the best choice now."

Ben cast a cautious look around, though he must have been already certain that they were secure against being overheard. Then he said quietly to Denis, "You'll be carrying two Swords."

' "Two," said Denis, almost inaudibly, and he swallowed.

"Yes. They're both here in the house now, and I think we must get them away as quickly as we can, since we must assume now that the enemy are watching the house. The city authorities are disposed to be friendly to me; but of course the Lord Mayor is ultimately responsible to the Silver Queen as his overlord. And she, as we all know, is at least sometimes an ally of Vilkata, and of the Blue Temple too. So we cannot depend with any certainty on the Lord Mayor's friendship, or even on his looking the other way as we do certain things."

"I'll do my best. I'll get them there safely," said Denis suddenly. He looked at Barbara as he said it. And she, smiling her approval, could see a pulse beating suddenly in his lean throat.

"Good," said Ben. "You're not going to take them to the Princess, though. You'll take them in the other direction, to Sir Andrew. I fear someone's already waiting to waylay you on the road to Princess Rimac. After what happened here last night I can almost feel it."

Jord nodded agreement, slowly and reluctantly. "We must get the Swords into action somewhere. And Sir Andrew's a good man, by all I've heard about him."

"And your son serves him," Barbara reminded her guest.

"Aye, Lady. Still . . . I know that Rostov was counting on the Swords. Well, the responsibility's yours now. I failed early on."

A little later, Denis and Jord were both watching while Ben dug out from its hiding place the second of the two Blades that Denis was to carry. The three men were down on the ground floor of the house now, in a little-traveled area behind the main shop, inside a storeroom that was usually kept closed with a cheap lock. None of the miscellaneous junk readily visible inside the shed appeared to be worth anyone's effort to steal.

Ben was bent over, rummaging in a pile of what looked like scrap metal, consisting mainly of swordblades and knifeblades, bent or broken or rusted, in all cases long disused. Denis could not remember when he had seen any of the metalworkers actually using this stuff.

From near the bottom of this pile of the treacherously sharp edges, Ben carefully brought out, one at a time, two weapons—the blades of both were long, blackened, but unbent. And these two also had hilts, which a majority of the others did not.

Before wiping the two blades clean, Ben held them out to Jord. The older man put out his hand, hesitated, and then touched a hilt, all of its details invisible under carefully applied oil and grime.

"Doomgiver," said the only human who had ever handled all the Twelve. "There's not one of them I'd fail to recognize."

The remainder of the day and much of the night had passed before Denis was ready to depart. He was not allowed one thing he asked for: a private good-bye with young Kuan-yin, the nursemaid— Ben said they would tell her that Denis had had to leave suddenly on a business trip of an indefinite duration. That had happened before, and Kuan-yin should not be too surprised.

Denis got in some sleep also. There were instructions to be memorized, which took a little time. He dressed in white, in imitation of a lone Ardneh-pilgrim, for his departure. Ben gave him some money and some equipment. And Denis also had a private conference with Jord.

When it was time to go, in the hour before dawn, Denis was surprised not to be conducted to the back door, where Jord had come in. Instead the master, Old World light in hand, led Denis down a flight of stairs into a place that Denis knew as nothing more than a cramped basement storeroom. The place smelled thickly of damp. There were the scurrying sounds of rats, evidence that the creatures somehow defied the anti-rodent spells and poisons that were both periodically renewed.

The master used his strength to shift a heavy bale out of position. Then it turned out that one of the massive stones that made up this chamber's floor could be tilted up. Looking down into the cavity thus created, Denis was surprised when the light showed him a steady current of water of unknown depth, scarcely a meter below his feet. Even though he knew how close the house was to the river, he had never suspected.

The man who Denis was now beginning to know as Ben bent down and caught hold of a thin chain within the opening. Then he tugged until the white prow of a well-kept canoe appeared, bobbing with the water's motion.

"I loaded her up this afternoon," Ben grunted, "while you were sleeping. Your cargo's under this floorboard here. The two Swords, wrapped in a blanket so they won't rattle. And sheathed, of course. They may get wet but they won't rust." Ben spoke with the calm authority of experience. "There's a paddle, and I think everything else that you're going to need."

Denis had used canoes a time or two before, on trading missions for the House of Courtenay. He could manage the craft well enough. But it wasn't obvious yet how he was going to get this one back to the river.

Ben gave him directions. You had to crouch down low in the boat at first, to keep from banging your

head on the low ceiling of the secret waterway.
Then you moved the craft forward through the narrow channel by pushing and tugging on the stone-
work of the sides. There was not far to go,
obviously, to reach the river.

There were no markings on the white canoe,
Denis observed as he lowered himself carefully
aboard. There was nothing in it, or on Denis, to connect the canoe or him to the House of Courtenay.
Once Denis was on his way, the plan called for him
to play the role of a simple Ardneh-pilgrim; his
White Temple experience would fit him well for
that. As a pilgrim, it was relatively unlikely that
he'd be bothered by robbers. Everyone had some
interest in the availability of medical care, and
therefore in the wellbeing of those who could provide it. A second point was that Ardneh's people
were less likely than most to be carrying much of
value. In the third place, Ardneh was still a
respected god, even if the better-educated insisted
that he was dead, and a good many people still
feared what might happen to them if they offended
him.

Last farewells were brief. Only the mistress of the
house, to Denis's surprise, appeared at the last
moment, to press his hand at parting. The warmth
of her fingers stayed with his, like something sealed
by magic. He could not savor it now, nor get much
of a last look at her, because it was time to crouch
down in his canoe, to give his head the necessary
clearance. Somebody released the chain for him,
and he began to pull the light craft forward, working hand over hand against the rough wall of the
narrow subterranean passage. He was propelling
himself against the current, and away from the

light. Darkness deepened to totality as the floor-stone was lowered crunching back into place.

Denis pulled on. Presently a ghost of watery light reached his eyes from somewhere ahead. He managed to see a low stone lintel athwart his course, and to bend his head and body almost completely down under the gunwales to get himself beneath the barrier.

His craft had now emerged into a larger chamber, and one not quite as completely dark. There was room enough for Denis to sit up straight. In a moment he realized that there were timbers about him, rising out of the water in a broad framework, and supporting a flat wooden surface a meter of so above his head. Denis realized that he was now directly underneath a riverside dock.

There were gaps between pilings large enough for the canoe to pass, and leading to the lesser darkness of the open, foggy night. Emerging cautiously from underneath the dock, using his paddle freely now, Denis found himself afloat upon a familiar channel of the river. Right there was the house he had just left, all windows darkened as if everyone inside were fast asleep. If there was other traffic on the river tonight, he could not see or hear it in the fog. At this hour, he doubted that there was.

Denis turned the prow of his canoe upstream, and paddled steadily. The first gleams of daylight were already becoming visible in the eastern sky, and he wanted to reach the gate in the city walls at dawn, when it routinely opened for the day. There would probably be a little incoming traffic, produce barges and such, waiting outside; the watch ought to pass him out promptly, and most likely without paying much attention to him.

This channel of the river took him past familiar sights of the great city. Most people Denis had met said that it was the greatest in the world, but who knew the truth of that? Here on the right bank were the cloth-dyers, as usual starting their work early, already staining the water as they rinsed out the long banners of their product. And on the other bank, one of the fish-markets was opening.

Now through thinning fog there came into Denis's sight the city walls themselves, taller than all but a very few of the buildings they protected, and thick as houses for most of their height. They were build of almost indestructible stone, hardened, the stories had it, by the Old World magic called technology. They were supported at close intervals by formidable towers of the same material. Tested over five hundred years by scores of sieges (so it was said), threatened again and again by ingenious engines of attack, and various attempts at undermining, they still stood guard over a city that since they were built had never fallen to military attack. Kings and Queens and mighty generals had raged impotently outside those walls, and would-be conquerors had died there at the hands of their own rebellious troops. Siege, starvation, massacre, all had been threatened against Tashigang, but all in vain. The Corgo flowed year-round, and was always bountiful with fish. The prudent burghers and Lords Mayor of the city had a tradition of keeping good supplies of other food on hand, and—perhaps most important of all—of choosing their outside enemies and allies with the greatest care.

Now the gate that closed the waterway was going up, opening this channel of the river for passage.

The river-gate was a portcullis built on a titanic scale, wrought by the same engineering genius as the city walls. Its movement was assisted by great counterweights that rode on iron chains, supported by pulleys built into the guard-towers of the wall. The raising made a familiar city-morning noise, and took some little time.

There was another huge iron chain spanning the channel underwater, as extra proof against the passage of any sizeable hostile vessel. But Denis did not have to wait for that to be lowered into the bottom mud. With a wave of his hand that was casually answered by the watch, he headed out, plying his paddle energetically.

He went on up the river, now and again looking back. With the morning mist still mounting, the very towers of Tashigang seemed to be melting into it, like some fabric of enchantment.

CHAPTER 5

In Mark's ears was the endless sound of hard, hooflike footpads beating the earth, of moving animals and men. Day after day in the sun and dust, night after night by firelight, there was not much in the way of human speech. He and the patrol of the Dark King's troops escorting him entered and traversed lands heavily scarred by war and occupation, a region of burned-out villages and wasted fields. With each succeeding day the devastation appeared more recent, and Mark decided that the army that had caused it could no longer be far away. The only human inhabitants of this region clearly visible were the dead, those who had been impaled or hanged for acts of resistance perhaps, or perhaps only on a whim, for a conqueror's sport.

At first Mark had known faint doubts about where he was being taken. These now disappeared. It was his experience that all armies on the march caused destruction, but only the Dark King's forces moved with this kind of relentless savagery. A few

of the human victims on display wore clothing that
had once been white; evidently not even Ardneh's
people were being spared by Vilkata now.

Even animal life was scarce, except for the omni-
present scavenger birds and reptiles. As the patrol
passed, these sometimes rose, hooting or cawing,
from some hideous feast near roadside. Once a live
and healthy-looking goat inspected the men
through a gap in a hedge as they went cantering by.

Mark's escort had never questioned his right to
give them orders, and they got on briskly with the
business of obeying the one real order he had so far
issued. Familiar as he was with armies and with
war, he considered these to be well-disciplined and
incredibly tough-looking troops. They spoke the
common language with an accent that Mark found
unfamiliar, and they wore Vilkata's black and gold
only in the form of small tokens pinned to their hats
or vests of curly fur.

One more thing about these men was soon just as
apparent as their discipline and toughness: they
were for some reason mightily afraid of Mark. In
what form they perceived him he could only guess,
but whatever it was induced in them quiet terror
and scrupulous obedience.

In Mark's immediate presence the men rarely
spoke at all, even to each other, but when they were
at some distance he saw them talking and gesturing
freely among themselves. Occasionally when they
thought he was not watching one of them would
make a sign in his direction, that Mark interpreted
as some kind of charm to ward off danger. Gradually he decided that they must see him as some
powerful and dangerous wizard they knew to be in
Vilkata's service.

Upon recovering from their first surprise at his approach, they had been quick to offer him food and drink, and his pick of their riding beasts for his own use—they had been traveling with a couple of spare mounts. Each night when they halted, Mark built his own small fire, a little apart from theirs,. He had soon decided that they would feel somewhat easier that way, and in truth he felt easier himself.

The country grew higher, and the nights, under a Moon waxing toward full, grew chill. Using the blanket that had been rolled up behind the saddle of his borrowed mount, Mark slept in reasonable comfort. He slept with one hand always on the hilt of Sightblinder, though he felt confident that the mere presence of the Sword in his possession would be enough to maintain his magical disguise. He was vaguely reassured to see that the patrol always posted sentries at night, in a professional manner.

The journey proceeded swiftly. On the afternoon of the fourth day after Mark had joined them, the patrol rode into sight of Vilkata's main encampment.

As the riders topped a small, barren rise of land, the huge bivouac came into view a kilometer ahead, on slightly lower ground. The sprawling camp was constructed around what looked to Mark like a large parade ground of scraped and flattened earth. The camp appeared to be laid out in good order, but it was not surrounded by a palisade or any other defensive works. Rather it sprawled arrogantly exposed, as if on the assumption that no power on earth was going to dare attack it. Mark considered gloomily that the assumption was probably correct.

As he and his escort rode nearer to the camp, he realized that it probably contained not only more human troops than he had ever seen in one place before, but a greater variety of them as well, housed in a wild assortment of tents and other temporary shelters. The outer pickets of the camp, men and women patrolling with leashed warbeasts, made no attempt to challenge Mark and his escort as they approached. And Mark observed that when the human sentries were close enough to get a good look at him, they, like his escort originally, shrank back perceptibly.

He had to wonder again: Who, or what, did they see? And who or what would Vilkata see when Mark entered his presence, if Mark succeeded in pushing matters that far? It was hard for Mark to imagine that there could be anyone the Dark King either feared or loved.

Only now, at last, did Mark clearly consider that he might be headed for a personal encounter with the Dark King. He had first approached the patrol with no more than a vague idea of eavesdropping on the enemy's secret councils, just as Draffut said he had moved unrecognized among the gods. Now for the first time Mark saw that it might be his duty to accomplish something more than that. The thought was vastly intriguing and at the same time deeply frightening, and he did not try now to think it through to any definite conclusion.

He rode on, still surrounded by his escort, until they were somewhere deep inside the vast encampment. There the patrol halted, and its members began an animated discussion among themselves, in some dialect that Mark could not really follow. Judging that the debate might be on how to separate themselves from him as safely and properly as possible, he took the matter into his own hands by dismounting, and then dismissing both his steed and his escort with what he hoped looked like an arrogantly confident wave of his hand.

Turning his back on the patrol then, Mark stalked away on foot, heading for a tall flagpole that was visible above the nearby tents. The pole supported a long banner of black and gold, hanging limp now in the windless air. Mark hoped and expected that this flag marked the location of some central headquarters. As he walked toward it he saw the heads of soldiers and camp-followers turn, their attention following him as he passed; and he saw too that some people either speeded up or slowed their own progress, in order not to cross his path too closely.

Now he had to detour around some warbeasts' pens, the smell and the mewing of the great catlike creatures coming out of them in waves. Now he was in sight of one corner of the vast parade ground. From the farther reaches of its expanse, somewhere out of Mark's sight, there sounded the chant and drumbeat of some hapless infantry unit condemned to drilling in the heat. Looking across the nearest corner of the field, he could now see the tall flagpole at full length. There was a wooden reviewing stand beside the flagpole, and behind the stand a magnificent pavilion. This was a tent larger than most houses, of black and gold cloth.

Mark stalked directly toward the great pavilion, considering that it had to be the Dark King's headquarters. His right hand, riding on the hilt of sheathed Sightblinder, could feel a new hum of power in the Sword; perhaps there were guardian spells here that had to be overcome.

The front of the reviewing stand displayed another copy of Vilkata's flag, this one stretched out to reveal the design, a skull of gold upon a field of black. The eyesockets of the skull stared forth sightlessly, twin windows into night.

Again Mark had to make a small detour, round more low cages that he at first thought held more warbeasts. But the wood-slatted cages looked too small for that. All but one of them were empty, and that one held ... the naked body confined inside was human.

Abruptly something shimmered in the air above Mark's head, broadcasting torment. As Mark moved instinctively to step aside, this presence moved with him. Only at this moment did he realize that it was sentient.

And only a moment after that did he realize that he was being confronted by a demon.

And the demon was addressing him, demanding something of him, though not in human speech. Whether its communication was meant for his ears or to enter his mind directly he could not tell. Nor could he grasp more than fragments of the meaning. It was basically a challenge: *Why was he here? Why was he here now, when he ought to be somewhere else? Why was he as he was?*

He realized with a shock that he was going to have to answer it, to offer something analogous to a password before it would allow him to pass this point, or even release him. What image it saw when it looked at him evidently did not matter. Here, approaching the pavilion, everyone must be stopped. And he doubted there was anything, or anyone, that this demon feared or loved.

Mark could no more answer the demonic voice

intelligently, in its own terms, than he could have held converse with a bee. He knew fear, exploding into terror. He ought to have foreseen that here there might be such formidable guardians, here at the heart of Vilkata's power and control; the Dark King himself was most likely in that huge tent ahead. Here, perhaps, they had even been able to plan defenses against the Sword of Stealth. Here its powers were not going to be enough—

Only moments had passed since the demon had first challenged him, but already Mark could sense the creature's growing suspicion. Now it sent an even more urgent interrogation crashing against Mark's mind. Now it was probing him, searching for evidence of the signs and keys of magic that he did not possess. In a moment it would be certain that he was some imposter, not a wizard after all.

In his desperation Mark grasped at a certain memory, four years old but still vivid. It was the recollection of his only previous close encounter with a demon, in the depths of the buried treasure-vaults of the Blue Temple. Now, in desperate imitation of what another had done then, Mark gasped out a command into the shimmering air:

"In the Emperor's name, depart and let me pass!"

There was a momentary howling in the air. Simultaneously there came a tornado-blast of wind, lasting only for an instant. Mark caught a last shred of communication from the thing that challenged him—it was outraged, it had definitely identified him as an imposter. But that did not matter. The demon could do nothing about it, for in the next instant it was gone, gone instantaneously, as if yanked away on invisible steel cables that extended to infinity.

Now the air above Mark was quiet and clear, but moments passed before his senses, jarred by the encounter, returned to normal. He realized that he had stumbled and almost fallen, and that his body was bent over, hands halfway outstretched in front of him, as if to avoid searing heat or ward off dreadful danger. It had been a very near thing indeed.

Hastily he drew himself erect, looking around carefully. Wherever the demon had gone, there was no sign it was coming back. A few people were standing, idly or in conversation, near the front of the pavilion, and he supposed that at least some of them must have noticed something of the challenge and his response. But all of them, as far as Mark could tell, were going on about their business as if nothing at all out of the ordinary had taken place. Maybe, he thought, that was the necessary attitude here, in what must be a constant center of intrigue.

Mark walked on. Having now passed the prison cages and the reviewing stand, he was within a few paces of the huge pavilion, by all indications the tent of Vilkata himself. Having come this far, Mark swore that he was going forward. Two human sentries flanked the central doorway of the huge tent, but to his relief these only offered him deep bows as he approached. Without responding he passed between them, and into a shaded entry.

Cool perfumed air, doubtless provided by some means of magic, wafted about him. Mark paused, letting his eyes adjust to the relative gloom, and he had a moment in which to wonder: How could any spell as simple as the one he had just used, recited by a mundane non-magician like himself, repel even the weakest demon? And what a repulsion! Repulsion was the wrong word. It had been instant banishment, as if by catapult.

His puzzlement was not new; essentially the same question had been nagging at him off and on for the past four years, ever since a similar experience in the Blue Temple treasure vaults. Mark had recounted that event to several trusted magicians in the meantime, and none had given him a satisfactory explanation, though they had all found the occurrence extremely interesting.

He was not going to have time to ponder the matter now.

From just inside the inner doorway of the tent he could hear voices, five or six of them perhaps, men's and women's mixed, chanting softly what Mark took to be words of magic. The voices came wafting out with the cool air and the perfume, some kind of incense burning. There was another odor mingled with it now, one not intrinsically unpleasant; but when Mark thought that he recognized it, the strength seemed to drain from his arms and legs, making it momentarily impossible to go on. He thought that he could recognize the smell of burning human flesh.

Ardneh be with me, Mark prayed mechanically, and wished even more ardently that living, solid Draffut could be with him also. Then he put back a heavy curtain with his hand, and made himself walk forward into the next chamber of the tent. A moment later he wished that he had not.

The human body fastened to the stone altar-table was not dead, for it still moved within the limits of its bonds, but it had somehow been deprived of the power to cry out. Yesterday it had probably been young; whether it had then been male or female was no longer easy to determine, in the dim light of the smoking lamp that hung above the altar. Around the altar half a dozen magicians of both sexes were gathered, various implements of torture in their hands. There was a lot of blood, most of it neatly confined to the altar itself, where carved troughs and channels drained it away. Near the altar stood a small brazier, with the insulated handles of more torture-tools protruding from the glow of coals.

Mark had seen bad things before, in dungeons and in war; still he had to wait for a moment after entering. He closed his eyes, gripping tightly the hilt of Sightblinder, cursing the Sword for what it had let him see when he looked at the victim. He knew a powerful urge to draw the Sword, and slaughter these villains where they stood. But a second thought assured him that it would not be easy to accomplish that. The air in here was thick with familiars and other powers, so thick that even a mundane could hardly fail to be aware of them. Those powers might now be deceived about Mark, but let him draw a sword and they would take note, and he thought they would not permit their human masters to be slaughtered.

And there was something more important, he was beginning to realize, that he must accomplish here before he died.

The half dozen who were gathered around the altar-table, garbed and hooded in various combinations of gold and black, paid little attention to Mark when he entered. One of their number did glance in the newcomer's direction, taking a moment from the chant between the great slow pulse-beats of its hideous magic in the air.

"Thought you were off somewhere else," a man's voice casually remarked.

"Not just now," said Mark. He exerted a great effort trying to make his own voice equally casual. Whatever the other heard from him was evidently acceptable, for the man with a brief smile under his hood turned back to his foul task.

Mark stood waiting, praying mechanically for a sign from somewhere as to what he ought to do next. He did not want to retreat, and he hesitated to move on into the interior doorway he saw at the other side of the torture chamber. And he continued to wish devoutly that he could somehow get out of sight of what was on this table.

Presently one of the women in the group turned her face toward him. She asked, in a sharp, businesslike voice: "This area is secure?"

Not knowing what else to do, Mark answered affirmatively, with a grave inclination of his head.

The woman frowned at him lightly. "I thought I had detected some possible intrusion, very well masked . . . but you are the expert there. And I thought also that our next subject, the one still in the cage outside, possesses some peculiar protection. But we shall see when we have her in here." Briskly the woman turned back to her work.

Mark, with only a general idea of what she must be talking about, nodded again. And again his answer appeared to be acceptable. Whoever they took him for, none of these people seemed to think it especially odd that he should continue to stand there, watching them or looking away. He continued standing, waiting for he knew not what.

Quite soon another one of the men turned away from the altar, as if his portion of the bloody ritual were now complete. This man left the group and approached a table near Mark, there to deposit his small bloodstained knife in a black bowl of some liquid that splashed musically when the small implement went in.

Then, standing very near Mark and speaking in a low voice, this man asked him, "Come, tell me— why did he really summon you back here?" When there was no immediate reply, the man added, in a voice suddenly filled with injured pride, "All right then, be silent, as befits your office. Only don't expect those you keep in the dark now to be eager to help you later, when—"

The man broke off abruptly at that point. It was as if he had been warned of something, by some signal that Mark totally failed to perceive. The man turned his face away from Mark, and toward the doorway that Mark had supposed must lead into the inner chambers of the pavilion.

Meanwhile one of those still at the altar warned, in a low voice: "The Master comes." All present— except of course the sacrificial victim—fell to their knees, Mark moving a beat behind the rest.

It was Vilkata himself who emerged a moment later through the curtains of sable black. Mark had never laid eyes on the Dark King before, but still he could not doubt for an instant who this was.

The first impression was of angular height, of a man taller than Mark himself, robed in a simple cloth of black and gold. The hood of the garment was pulled back, leaving the wearer's head bare except for a simple golden circlet, binding back long ringlets of white hair. The exposed face and hands of the Dark King were very pale, suggesting that the whiteness of the hair and of the curled beard resulted from some type of albinism rather than from age.

The second impression Mark received was that some of the more horrible tales might be true, for the Dark King was actually, physically blind. Under the golden circlet, the long-lashed lids sagged over what must be empty sockets, spots of softness in a face otherwise all harsh masculine angles. According to the worst of the stories, this man in his youth had put out his own eyes, as part of some dreadful ritual necessary to overpower his enemies' magic and gain some horrible revenge.

Looped around Vilkata's lean waist was a sword-belt of black and gold, and in the dependent sheath there rode a Sword. Even in the dim light Mark could not fail to recognize that plain black hilt, so like the one he was now clasping hard in his own sweaty fist. And Mark, his own vision augmented in some ways by Sightblinder, could not miss the small stylized white symbol of a banner that marked Vilkata's Sword.

It was of course the Mindsword, just as Draffut had warned. Mark was struck with the instant conviction that what he had to do now was to get the Mindsword out of Vilkata's possession, prevent his using it to seize the world. The decision needed no pondering, no consideration of consequences.

Vilkata's blind face turned from left to right and back again, as if he might be somehow scrutinizing his assembled magicians carefully. Mark could read no particular expression on the harsh countenance of the Dark King. Then one large, pale hand extended itself from inside Vilkata's robe, making a lifting gesture, a signal to his counselors that they might stand. Would the King have known, Mark wondered, if they had all been standing instead of kneeling as he entered? But then there would not have been this faint robe-rustle sound of rising.

Mark held his breath as the blind face turned once more toward him, and this time stayed turned in his direction. Behind those eyelashes, white and grotesquely long, the pale collapsed lids were as magnetic as any stare. Something about them was perversely beautiful.

There was a tiny almost inaudible humming, a miniature disturbance in the air near the Dark King's head. Some demonic or familiar power was communicating with him—so Mark perceived, watching with Sightblinder's handle in the grip of his hand.

The Dark King seemed about to speak, but hesitated, as if he were magically aware that something was wrong, that matters here in this innermost seat of his power were not as they should be. Still the blind face confronted Mark, and Vilkata whispered a soft question into the air. A humming answer came. Mark could feel the power of the sheathed Sword at his own side suddenly thrum more strongly.

When Vilkata did speak aloud, Mark was surprised at the sound of his voice, smooth, deep, and pleasant.

"Burslem, I am surprised to see you here. I take it that the task I sent you on has been completed?"

Burslem. To Mark the name meant nothing. "It is indeed, my lord. My head on it."

"Indeed, as you say ... now all of you, finish quickly what you are about in here. I want you all at the conference table as quickly as possible. The generals are waiting." And Vilkata and his half-visible familiar vanished, behind a sable swirl of draperies.

One wizard, a junior member of the group perhaps, stayed behind briefly to settle whatever still remained to be settled upon their ghastly altar. The others, Mark among them, filed through the doorway where Vilkata had disappeared. They passed through the next chamber, which was filled with what looked like draped furniture, and entered the next beyond that.

The room was larger, and somewhat better lighted. It contained a conference table large enough to accommodate in its surrounding chairs all of the magicians and an approximately equal number of military-looking men and women, who as Vilkata had said were already seated and waiting. The military people wore symbolic scraps of armor, though as Mark noted none of them were visibly armed there in the presence of their King. Vilkata himself, predictably, was seated in a larger chair than the others, at one end of the table. Behind him a map on a large scale, supported on wooden poles, bore many symbols, indicating among other things what appeared to be the positions of several armies. There was Tashigang, near the center of the map, there the winding Corgo making its way northward to the sea. There was the Great Swamp. . . .

Mark was making a hasty effort to memorize the types and positions of the symbols on the map, but the distractions at the moment were overpowering. The magicians were taking their places at the table, and fortunately there seemed to be little ceremony about it. But again Mark had to delay marginally, to be able to make a guess as to what place Burslem ought to take. He was not sure whether to be relieved or not, when he found himself pulling out the last vacant chair, some distance down the table from the King.

As the faint noise of people seated themselves died out, a silence hold upon the room, and stretched. As Vilkata sat on his raised chair, the hilt of the Mindsword at his side was plainly visible to the rest of the assembly. And the humming presence above the King's head came and went, all but imperceptibly to the others in the room.

"I see," the Dark King said at last—and if there was irony in those two words, Mark thought that it was subtly measured—"that none of you are able to tear your eyes away from my new toy here at my side. Doubtless you are wondering where I got it, and how I managed to so without your help. Well, I'll give you all a close look at it presently. But first there's a report or two I want to hear."

Again the blind face turned back and forth, as if Vilkata were seeking to make sure of something. A faint frown creased the white brow, otherwise youthfully unlined. "Burslem," the Dark King added in his pleasant voice, "I want to hear your report in private, a little later. After you have seen my Sword."

"As you will, Lord," Mark said clearly. In his own ears, his voice still sounded like his own. The others all heard it without noticing anything amiss. But whatever Vilkata heard did not erase his faint suspicious frown.

Now some of the magicians and generals, following an order of precedence that Mark could not identify, began to make reports to the King and his council, each speaker in turn standing up at his or her own place at the table. The unsuspected spy was able to listen, half-comprehending, to lists of military units, to descriptions of problems in levying troops and gathering supplies, to unexpected difficulties with the constructions of a road that would be needed later to facilitate the unexplained movement of some army. It seemed to Mark that invaluable facts, information vital for Sir Andrew and his allies, were marching at a fast pace into his ears and out again. Listen! he demanded of himself in silent anguish. Absorb this, retain it! Yet it seemed that he could not. Then there came a relieving thought. When he saw Dame Yoldi again, she would be able to help him recapture anything that, he heard now; he had seen her do as much for others in the past.

If he ever got to see Dame Yoldi's beautiful face again. If he ever managed to leave this camp alive.

There was the monstrous Sword at Vilkata's side, and here was Vilkata himself, seated within what looked like easy striking distance of Mark's own Sword, or of his bow—Mark still had his two arrows left. More important by far, thought Mark, than any mere information that could be collected, would be to deprive the Dark King of the Mindsword, and, if possible, of his own evil life as well.

Mark knew of no way by which the Mindsword, or any of its eleven peers, could be destroyed. The only way he could deprive the enemy of its use would be by capturing it himself, and getting away with it. There was a chance, he told himself, maybe even a good chance, that Sightblinder could disguise and preserve him against demonic and

human fury while he did so. Against demons he had
a new hope now, hope in the inexplicable power of a
few simple words.

It seemed likely that he would have to kill Vilkata
to get the Mindsword from him. And that would be
a good deed in itself. Yes, he would kill Vilkata . . . if
he could. If the evil magicians in the outer chamber
had had magical defenses, how much stronger, if
less obvious, would be those of the Dark King himself?

To strike at Vilkata successfully, he would have
to choose his moment with great care. Bound into
his own thoughts by calculation and fear, Mark lost
touch with the discussion that was going on around
the table. Presently, with a small shock, he realized
that the Dark King was now addressing his assembled aides, and had been speaking for some time.
All of them—including Mark himself, half consciously—were answering from time to time with
nods and murmurs of agreement. Probably Mark
had been roused to full attention by the fact that the
voice of the Dark King was now rising to an orator-
ical conclusion:

"—our plan is war, and our plan goes forward
rapidly!"

There was general applause, immediate and
loud. The first to respond in a more particular way
was a bluff, hearty-looking military man, who wore
a scrap or two of armor to indicate his status. This
man leaped to his feet with apparently spontaneous
enthusiasm, and with a kind of innocence in his
face.

There was a tone of hearty virtue in his voice as
well. "Who are we going to hit first, sir?"

Vilkata paused before he turned his blind face

toward the questioner, as if perhaps the Dark King had found the question none too intelligent. "We are going to hit Yambu. She is the strongest—next to me—and therefore the most dangerous. Besides, I have just received disturbing news about her . . . but of that I will speak a little later."

Here Vilkata paused again. The almost inaudible humming, almost invisible vibration, continued to perturb the air above his head. "I see that most of you are still unable to keep from staring at my plaything here," he said, and put his pale right hand on his Sword's hilt. "Very well. Because I want you, later, to be able to concentrate upon our planning—I will demonstrate it *now!*"

The last word burst in a great shout from the Dark King's throat, and in the same moment he sprang to his feet. And Mark thought that the Mindsword itself, as the King drew and brandished it aloft, made a faint roaring noise, like that of many human voices cheering at a distance.

Even here, in the dim smoky interior of this tent, the flourished steel flashed gloriously, seeming to stab at the eyes with light. Mark had never seen, nor ever imagined that he would see, anything so beautiful. Like all the others round the table he found himself on his feet, and he was only dimly aware of his chair toppling over behind him.

At that moment, Sightblinder, with Mark's hand on its hilt, came leaping by itself halfway out of its own sheath, as if it were springing to accept the challenge of its peer.

But Mark could not tear his eyes free of the Mindsword. The terrible force of it was tugging at him. Wordlessly it demanded that he throw his own Sword down at Vilkata's feet, and himself after it, pledging eternal loyalty to the Dark King. And already, only half realizing what he did, Mark had gone down on his knees again, amid a small crowd of wizards who were doing the same thing.

The cheering roar of the Mindsword drowned all other sound, the glitter of its blade filled every eye.

Mark wondered why he had come here to this camp, why he had entered this tent . . . but whatever the reason, it hardly mattered now. All that mattered now was that instantly, instantly, he should begin a new lifetime of service to Vilkata. That flashing steel thing told him that he must, that glorious Blade that was the most beautiful thing under the heavens or in them. Nothing that it told him could possibly be wrong.

He stood somehow in danger, danger of being left behind, left out, if he did not swear his fealty at once, as the other kneeling shapes around him were doing now. Voices that in the outer chamber had sounded cynical were now hoarse with fervor, gabbling the most extravagant oaths. What was it that made him, Mark, delay? Something must be wrong with him, something about him must be unforgivably different.

He was groveling on the floor with the others, mouthing words along with them, but he knew his oaths meant nothing, they were not sincere. Why was he hesitating? How could he? He must, at once, consecrate himself body and soul to the Dark King. How glorious it would be to fight and conquer in that name! And how perfect would be a death, any form of death, attained in such a cause! There was nothing that a man need fear, as long as that glittering Sword led him. Or, there was but one thing fearful only—the chance that such a glorious opportunity might somehow be missed—that death might come in some merely ordinary way, and so be wasted.

So why, then, did he delay?

Mark's mind swayed under the Mindsword's power, but did not yield to it entirely. A stubborn core of resistance remained in place. He was not carried into action, beyond the meaningless imitative oaths and grovelings. Part of his mind continued to understand that he must resist. His right hand still clutched Sightblinder's hilt, and he thought that he still drew power from it. Inside the core of his mind that was still sane, he could only hope and trust in the existence of some power that might save him—even though he could no longer remember clearly just why he needed saving.

Cowering on his knees like those around him, Mark watched the Mindsword flash on high. From that beautiful arc emanated a droning roar, as of many voices raised in praise, voices that never stopped to breathe. Against the background of that sound, the voice of the Dark King was rising and falling theatrically, like that of some spellcaster in a play. Vilkata was reciting and detailing now all of the malignant and detestable qualities that marked the Queen of Yambu as a creature of special evil. One accusation in particular, that the voice emphasized, caught at and inflamed Mark's imagination, stinging him with the unimaginable foulness that it represented. Even among her other shameless deeds this one stood out: Not only did she possess the Sword called Soulcutter, but she intended to begin to use it soon. And to use it against the blessed Dark King, the savior of the world!

In spite of himself, Mark groaned in rage. He

found himself imagining his hands locked on the throat of the Silver Queen, and strangling her. Other groaning, outraged voices joined around him, until the pavilion sounded like the torture chamber that it truly was.

And when the Dark King paused, the voices rose up even louder, crying aloud their heartfelt protest against Yambu. That she should so plot to warp their minds with Soulcutter's foul magic, that she should even for a moment contemplate such a thing, was a sin crying to the gods for her to be wiped out, expunged from the Earth's face, at once and without mercy!

Vilkata had lowered the blade a little now, holding the hilt no higher than his shoulders. But still the steel kept twinkling above them like a star. As far as Mark could tell, there was no resistance at all in any of the audience except himself. And how much was left in him, he did not know.

One of the wizards, he who had whispered conspiratorially to Mark in the outer chamber, now abandoned himself entirely. With a great frenzied howl he sprang up on the conference table, his arms outstretched to gather that glorious Blade to his own bosom. But the Dark King withdrew the weapon out of the wizard's reach, and with a lunge the magician fell on his face among the tipped and scattered chairs.

It seemed a signal for general pandemonium. Men and women rolled back and forth on the tent floor. They scrambled to stand on furniture, they danced and sang in maddened cacophony. Cries and grunts came jolting out of them, until the council chamber looked and sounded lik a small battlefield.

The sounds of a more familiar danger helped Mark regain some small additional measure of control. He huddled almost motionless on the floor, trying to remember where he was, and who he had been before that Sword appeared.

Now the Dark King flourished his Sword above his head in a new gesture, like a field commander's signal to advance. And now Vilkata, guided by the humming presence that hovered always near him, was moving in long, sure strides around the conference table, passing through the litter of chairs and humanity that almost filled the room. He was heading for the front entrance of the pavilion.

Mark, caught up in the rush of people following the King, was jostled against the torture-altar when passing through the outer chamber. He felt something sticky on his hand, gazed at it dumbly and saw blood. It was frightening, but he could not understand. . . .

Exiting from the pavilion's front door, Vilkata strode forth into the sun, whose light exploded from the Sword he carried into a thousand piercing lances. His little mob of followers, including Mark, accompanied him out into the glare, leaping and chanting with a look of ecstasy. At once their numbers were augmented by those who happened to be near when the Dark King emerged with glory in his hands. The air above the swelling crowd was wavering, as if with the heat of a great fire; familiar powers and small demons were moving in concert with their magician masters, and sharing their excitement, whether in joy or fear Mark could not tell.

The Mindsword swung in Vilkata's grip. It shattered the bright sun into lightning, whose bolts struck left and right. The hundreds who were near, and then the thousands only a little farther off, gaped in surprise, and then were caught up in the savage enthusiasm.

Vilkata marched on without hesitation, heading for the reviewing stand. The crowd surging around him was growing explosively, and already seemed to number in the thousands. Men and women, caught by curiosity, by the attraction of the growing crowd itself, came running through the camp from all directions, to be captured at close range by the sight of the blinding Blade. Again and again, through the waves of merely human cheering, Mark thought that he could hear the surf like oar of the Sword itself, grown louder in proportion to the crowd it led.

Now, somewhere out on the parade ground, beyond the cages for prisoners and beasts, an enormous drum began to bang. The growling and snarling of the caged warbeasts went up, to challenge in its volume the whole mass of human voices.

Now, across the whole vast reach of the parade ground, humans and trained beasts alike were demonstrating spontaneously at the sight of the Blade that waved above Vilkata's head. The cry of his name went up again and again, each time louder than the last. A thousand weapons were being brandished in salute.

Now the Dark King had reached the reviewing stand, and now he mounted quickly. His closer followers, Mark still with them, swarmed up onto the platform too. Immediately the stand was overcrowded, and people near the edges were jostled off. A small clear space—more magic?—remained around the person of the King. All around the base of the platform and across its surface where they had room, grand military potentates and dreaded wizards were prancing and gesturing like demented children. The aged and dignified abased themselves like dogs at one moment, and in the next leaped howling for the sky. And the very sky was streaked by demons, speeding, whirling in a pyrotechnic ecstasy of worship.

Grimly Mark held on to the small margin of self-awareness and self-control that he had regained in the pavilion. He thought that he would not be able to hold onto it for very long—but perhaps for long enough. He remembered now who he was, and what goal he had determined to accomplish. He still held Sightblinder's hilt in his right hand. But . . . to strike at Vilkata, possessor of the Mindsword . . . how could anyone do that? Or even plan to do it?

To strike at one who held the Mindsword might well be more than any mere human will could manage. If once Mark summoned up the will to try, and failed, he was sure that he could never try again.

Even to work his way through the press of frenzied bodies on the platform, to get himself close enough to the Dark King to strike at him, was going to be difficult. Get close to the Dark King, he ordered himself, forget for the moment why you are trying to get close. He almost forgotten his bow, still slung in its accustomed place across his back. And there were two arrows left . . . he groped with a trembling hand, and found that there were none. Spilled somehow in the jostling? Or had some enthusiast's hand snatched them away?

He was going to have to strike with Sightblinder, then. Even had his mind been clear, entirely his own, it would not have been easy. Most of the people on the platform were also struggling to get closer to the Dark King, to touch him if possible; the ring of those who were closest, constrained to do all they could to protect the Mindsword's master, were striving to hold the others back. Their task was perhaps made easier by the fact that Vilkata was swinging the Sword more wildly now, inspiring fear as well as ecstasy in those near enough to stand in some danger from the Blade. There was still a cleared space of several meters directly around the king.

Mark elbowed room enough to let him draw Sightblinder—no one, he thought, was able to see that he was holding it, no magical guardians struck at him yet.

The small crowd atop the reviewing stand surged again, chatocially, as more people kept trying to climb on. Inevitably at one edge, more people were pushed off.

Mark forced himself a little closer to Vilkata, but then was stopped, pushed back again. *This is impossible*, he thought. *I cannot fail simply because I can't get through a crowd.* Still he dared not use the Sword to hack bodies out of his path; surely if he did that the magical defenses of the King would be triggered, and he would have no chance to strike the blow that really counted.

He had to get closer without killing. He gritted his teeth and closed his eyes, and blindly bulled his way ahead. His Sword, invisible to the people in his way, he held raised awkwardly above the jostling bodies that would otherwise have carved themselves on it.

But even as Mark scraped up new determination

and tried again, the crowd surged against him, and its hundred legs effortlessly bore him even a little farther away. The cause of this last surge was one of Vilkata's sweeps with the Mindsword. Mark exerted one more great effort, and forced his way through, or almost through, but was deflected in the process to a place precariously near the platform's edge.

Now, one more effort ... but the Blade in the Dark King's hand came swinging heedlessly past, and grazed Mark's forehead. The Dark King was laughing thunderously now, to see his courtiers duck and dodge in terror, and at the same time come pressing helplessly forward all the same.

Those next to Mark in the crush violently shoved back. Tangled with others, he fell over the edge of the platform, others falling with him. The distance to the ground was no more than a man's height, and the ground below was soft. Mark landed with a shock, but without further injury. By some miracle none of those falling with him had impaled themselves on Sightblinder, which lay on the soft earth under his hand.

He had failed, not heroically, but as by some demonic joke. He grabbed up his Sword and got to his feet again. Then he understood that he was hurt more than he had thought at first by Vikata's accidental stroke. He could see blood, feel it and taste it, his own blood running down from his gashed forehead into his left eye. A centimeter or two closer to the Mindsword's swing and it would have killed him.

The fall had taken him out of reach of the Dark King; but at least it had also broken his direct eye contact with that flashing, hypnotic Blade. Now, with freedom roaring louder than the Mindsword in his mind, Mark looked up to catch a glimpse of Vilkata's back on the high platform. The monarch was turned away from Mark at the moment, facing out over the excited masses of the crowd at its front edge.

He must be struck down, Mark repeated grimly to himself, *And I must do it, do it now, no matter what, and get his Sword.*

He tore himself free of a fresh tangle of frenzied bodies on the ground. Shoving people out of his way with one hand, holding Sightblinder uplifted in the other, he ran along his side of the reviewing stand and then along its front. The pain in his wounded forehead savaged him, made him yearn to strike out at those villainous legs of officers and sorcerers that danced and pushed for advantage on the platform before him at eye level. But he held back his blow, grimly certain that he would be able to strike no more than once.

Blood bothering his eyes, pain nailing his head, Mark looked up trying to locate Vilkata again. It seemed hopeless. The sun was dazzling. The Mindsword flashed in it, and flashed again. Only in surrender to it was there hope. Mark had to look away, bend down his neck to get away from it. He could not let his eyes and soul be caught by it again—

As he turned his gaze away from the platform, there came into his vision the vast expanse of the parade ground and its howling mob of people. Sightblinder made two details stand out in rapid succession, each so strongly that they were able to distract him even now.

The first, astonishingly for Mark, was the prison cage with its lone occupant, even though he could glimpse it only intermittently now through the swirl of ecstatic bodies. He had encountered the sentry demon beside that cage, and he remembered, or almost remembered, something else, something that one of the magicians had said inside about the prisoner—

And then the second distracting detail captured Mark's attention even from the first. He saw a small gray cloud, rolling in a very uncloudlike way down the steep flank of a distant mountain. Inside that cloud Mark's sharpened perception could pick out half a dozen living beings, all apparently of human shape.

Already, as he watched, the cloud reached the comparatively level land at the mountain's foot. Now it rolled closer rapidly, directly approaching the encampment, moving independently of any wind. It was traveling with deceptive speed, outracing wind, traversing kilometers in mere moments.

Some of the people on the platform above Mark had now become aware of the cloud as well. The uproar immediately surrounding the Dark King had abated somewhat. Mark cast a quick look toward Vilkata, and saw that the King was lowering his own Sword, giving the approaching cloud his full attention.

A shrieking in the air passed rapidly overhead. A flight of the airborne demons, acting either on their own or at some direct command from their human masters, had melded themselves into a tight formation and were flying directly at the approaching cloud, intent on investigation and perhaps attack. But just before they reached the cloud their formation recoiled and burst, its members scattering. Mark had the impression that they had been brushed aside like so many insects, by some invisible power.

In a flash understanding came. The gods were coming to take charge. Through his pain and blood and fear Mark gasped out a sob of deep relief. Humanity had hope of being saved, by the beings who had made the Swords, from powers that were too much for it to manage. He had seen gods handle savage and rebellious men before. Vilkata, shrunken to the stature of a noxious insect in their presence, might be crushed before his horror could reach over the whole human world. Mark's own Sword might be taken from him too, but on the scale of these events that would make little difference.

The cloud, no longer serving any purpose of concealment, was being allowed to dissipate, and it vanished quickly. The handful of beings who had ridden it were walking now, already entering the parade ground at its far side, and approaching quickly. The sea of humans occupying the open space parted at the deities' approach. Four gods and one goddess, each tall as Draffut, came striding forward without pause, and Mark got the impression that they would have stepped on people without noticing had any remained in their way.

Towering taller and taller as they drew near, the five advanced, marching straight for the reviewing stand. Mark thought that now he could recognize some of them individually. Four were attired with divine elegance, wearing crowns, tunics, robes ablaze with color, gold, and gems. But one, who limped as he strode forward, was clad in simple furs.

Again Mark glanced back quickly at the platform.

Vilkata was out of striking range, and still closely surrounded by his people and his magical attendants.

The Dark King had sheathed the Mindsword now, and was issuing terse orders to certain of his wizards. In the next instant one of these magicians gave a convulsive leap that carried him clear off the platform. He fell more heavily than Mark had fallen, and lay writhing helplessly on the ground. Mark could guess that some protective spell of this man's had somehow impeded the divine progress; and that when the spell was snapped, like some ship's hawser in the docks, he who had been holding it was flattened by the recoil.

Whatever magic had been in their path, spells perhaps triggered automatically by their intrusion, the gods had broken their way through it; they were irritated, Mark thought, looking at them, like adults bothered by some maze of string set up by children.

At last the four gods and one goddess halted their advance. They stood on the parade ground only a score of meters from the platform, their heads still easily overtopping that of the Dark King who faced them from his elevation. Everyone else on the platform was kneeling, Mark realized, or had thrown themselves face down in abject panic, and everyone near him on the ground also. He and the Dark King were the only two humans within a hundred meters still on their feet. How curious, Mark wondered distantly. The only other time in his life when he had seen deities as close as this, why that time too he had been able to remain standing, while around him other humans knelt or huddled in collapse. . . .

The limping god was moving forward. In the

silence that lay over the whole camp, his ornaments of dragon-scale could be heard clinking as he lurched to within one great stride of the platform. That is Vulcan the Smith, thought Mark, staring up at the fur-garbed titan—he who took off my father's arm. Vulcan paid no attention to Mark, but was looking at Vilkata. As far as Mark could tell, Vilkata did not flinch, though when the god halted he was close enough to the platform to have reached forth one of his long arms and plucked Vilkata from it.

Wind came keening across the camp, blowing out of the bare, devastated lands surrounding it. Otherwise there was silence.

A silence abruptly broken, by the voice of Vulcan that boomed forth at a volume appropriate for a god. "What madness is this that you fools of humans are about? Do you not realize that the Swordgame is over?"

Vilkata summoned up his best royal voice to answer. "I am the Dark King—" It was no surprise at all to Mark that the King's voice should quaver and falter and quit on him before the sentence ended. The only wonder was that the man could stand and speak at all in such a confrontation.

Vulcan was neither impressed nor pleased. "King, Queen, or whatever, what do I care for all that? You are a human and no more. Hand over that tool of power that you are wearing at your side."

Vilkata did not obey at once; instead he dared to answer once more in words. Mark did not hear the words exactly, for his attention had once more been distracted by something in the distance. This was another cloud, and it looked as unusual as the first.

This cloud was not rolling down a mountainside,

only drifting through the air, but its path was at a right angle to those of other clouds and the wind. Now the strange cloud was hovering, hesitating in its slow passage. It appeared to be maintaining a certain cautious distance from the scene on the parade ground. With Sightblinder still in hand, Mark could perceive in this second cloud also the presence of figures of human shape but divine dimensions. There was one, a perfect essence of the female, that he thought could be only Aphrodite. He could see none of the others so clearly as individuals, though all of their faces seemed to be turned his way.

The distraction had been only momentary. Now Vulcan, made impatient by even a moment's temporizing on the part of this mere human king, thundered out some oath, and stretched forth his arm toward Vilkata. With a swift motion the Dark King drew the Mindsword from its sheath—but not to hand it over in surrender. Instead he brandished it aloft.

Vulcan cried out once, a strange, hoarse tone, like masses of metal and rock colliding. The lame god threw up a forearm across his eyes. He reeled backward, and fell to one knee. Mark could feel in the ground under his own feet the impact of that fall.

Just behind the Smith, the four other deities who had come out of the cloud with him were kneeling also.

Once again a long moment of silence held throughout the camp. The distant airborne cloud was moving faster now, departing at accelerated speed. Mark gazed after it numbly for a moment. The gods had failed. The thousands of human

beings massed around him were cheering once
again.

Now Vilkata was speaking again. After Vulcan's
thunder the King's voice sounded puny, but it was
triumphant and confident once again as he shouted
an order to the kneeling gods, their heads still
higher than his own. "Follow me! Obey!"

"We hear." The ragged chorus rolled forth. The
wooden stand, the earth, vibrated with it. "We follow, and obey."

The huge wardrum boomed to life again, and
from the crowd went up the loudest roar yet. The
mad celebration resumed, twice madder than
before.

The gods on the parade ground were climbing
ponderously back to their feet. "Surely this is
Father Zeus!" Vulcan cried out, pointing with a
tree-sized arm at the Dark King. "He who has been
playing that role among us must be an impostor!"

The Smith's divine companions roared approval
of this statement, and launched themselves spontaneously into a dance, that looked at once ponderous
and uncontrolled. The ground shook; Mark could
see the tall flagpole swaying in front of the King's
pavilion. The crowd of humans in the vicinity of the
reviewing stand began to thin, with everyone who
was anywhere near the dancing gods being eager to
move back. Yet they remained under the Mindsword's spell, and many joined the dance.

Mark stood drained, exhausted, leaning on his
own Sword. With pain stabbing at his forehead,
and blood still trickling into his eye, he watched the
maddened gods and had the feeling that he was
going mad himself. But surely he ought to have
expected something like this. If one of the Swords

could kill a god—and with his own eyes Mark had seen Hermes lying dead, the wound made by Farslayer gaping in the middle of the Messenger's back—then why should not another Sword have power to make slaves of other gods?

What power had Vulcan called upon to forge them, that was greater than the gods themselves?

And was he, Mark, the only being here still capable of resistance?

With his pain, with the drip of his own blood that seemed now to burn like poison, he could no longer think. But maybe he could still act.

He gripped Sightblinder in his two hands, and moved for the third time to try to kill Vilkata.

If the crowd on the ground was moving more wildly now, it was thinner, and that helped. But when Mark raised his eyes to the Dark King, who still stood on the platform, the Mindsword dazzled him again, sent splintering shafts of poisoned light into his brain. He was stumbling toward the sun in glory, and it was unthinkable for anyone to try to strike the sun.

Vilkata, the god! Holder of the Mindsword, he who must be adored!

Mark lifted his own Sword in both arms. Then he realized that he was not going to strike, he was going to cast down Sightblinder as an offering. It was all he could do to tear himself free. Still desperately holding onto his own Sword, lurching and stumbling, he fled the platform, his back to the glory that he dared no longer face. It tugged him and tore at him and urged him to turn back. He knew that if he turned for an instant he was lost.

The prisoner's cage loomed up ahead of him. Someone in the crowd jostled Mark, turning him slightly sideways so that he saw the cage and its inmate quite clearly.

With no consciousness of making any plan, acting on impulse, Mark raised the Sword of Stealth high in a two-handed grip, and brought it smashing down against the wooden door and its small lock. The Sword's magic did nothing to aid the blow, but its long weight and keen edge were quite enough. The cage had not been built to sustain any real assault. Mark struck again and the door fell open. Amid the pandemonium of jumping, screaming bodies and brandished weapons, no one paid the least heed to what he was doing. The earth still shook under the tread of the bellowing, dancing gods.

He sheathed his weapon and reached in with both hands to grasp the helpless prisoner. The body he drew forth was that of a young woman, naked, bound with both cords and magic. The cords fell free quickly, at a touch of Sightblinder's perfect edge. But the magic was more durable.

One arm about the prisoner, half carrying and half pulling her through the frenzied crowd, Mark headed straight away from the reviewing stand, still not daring to look back. Whatever the people around saw when they looked at him now, it made them draw back even in their frenzy, leaving his way clear.

There seemed no end to the parade ground, or to Vilkata's maddened army. With each retreating step the pressure of the Mindsword eased, but only infinitesimally. Steps added up, though. Now Mark could begin to think again, enough to begin to plan. There, ahead, a little distance in the crowd, were two mounted men who looked like minor magicians of some kind. Mark set his course for them, dragging the still stupefied young woman along.

The magicians, looking half stupefied themselves with their participation in the Mindsword's glamor, paid no attention as Mark approached. These two, Mark hoped, did not rate guardian demons. He desperately needed transportation.

Sightblinder obtained it for him, quickly and bloodily, working with no more magic than a meataxe. Again, in the general surrounding madness, no one appeared to notice what was happening.

Mark wrapped the girl in a cloak of black and gold that one of the magicians had been wearing, and got her aboard one of the riding beasts, and got himself aboard the other. Once in the saddle, he could only sit swaying for a moment, afraid that he was going to faint, watching his own blood drip on his hands that held the reins.

Somehow he got moving, leading the girl's mount. No one tried to interfere with them as they fled the camp. No one, as far as Mark could tell, even took notice.

The booming of the wardrum and the roaring of the gods followed them for a long time, pursuing them for kilometers of their flight across high barren lands.

CHAPTER 6

A kilometer or two upstream from Tashigang, before the Corgo split itself around the several islands that made parts of the city, the current was slow enough that Denis the Quick could make fairly good time paddling his light canoe against it. Here it was possible to seek out places in the broader stream where the surface current was slower still, with local eddies to make the paddler's task less difficult. This made it easy for Denis to stay clear of the other river traffic, which in early morning was mostly barges of foodstuffs and other commerce coming downstream. There were also some small fishing craft out on the river, and one or two light sailboats that appeared to be out purely for pleasure. Here above the city there were no ships of ocean-going size, such as plied the reaches downstream from Tashigang to the sea.

Two kilometers upstream from the walls, Denis reached the first sharp upstream bend of the Corgo and looked back again, ceasing to paddle as he sought a last glimpse of the high towers. Visible above the morning mist that still rose from the river, the lofty walls and battlements caught rays of the early morning sun. Here and there upon the venerable masses of brown or gray stone, glass or bright metal sparkled, in windows, ornaments, or the weapons of the Watch. On several high places the green and gray of the city's own colors were displayed. Upon the highest pole, over the Lord Mayor's palace, a single pennant of black and silver acknowledged the ultimate sovereignty of Yambu.

As he paddled farther upstream, Denis's canoe passed between shores lined with the villas of those wealthy citizens who felt secure enough about the prospects of long-term peace to choose to live outside the city walls. These were impressive houses, each fortified behind its own minor defenses, capable of holding off an occasional brigands' raid.

Independent villas soon gave way to suburbs of somewhat less impressive houses, built together behind modest walls; and these in turn to farms and vineyards. These lands like Tashigang itself were tributary to the Silver Queen, though enjoying a great measure of independence. Yambu in her years of domination had maintained general peace and order here, and had wisely been content to levy no more than moderate tribute and to allow the people to manage their own affairs for the most part. Tribute flowed in regularly under such a regime, and the Queen built a fund of goodwill for herself. Meanwhile she had been busy venting her aggressive energies elsewhere.

Pausing once to eat and reat, Denis made an uneventful first day's journey up the river. By evening he was far enough from the city's center of population to have no trouble in locating a small island that offered him a good spot to camp. He even succeeded in catching a suitable fish for his dinner, and was rather pleased with this success in outdoor skills.

On the second day he got an early start again. He had a worker's calloused hands and did not mind the constant paddling overmuch; the healed wound in his forearm did not trouble him at all. This day he kept a careful eye out for certain landmarks, as Ben had instructed him. Around noon he was able to identify without any trouble the tributary stream he wanted, a small river that entered the Corgo on a winding course from the northeast. This smaller river, here called the Spode, drained a portion of the Great Swamp—it did not, unfortunately, lead directly to the part where Sir Andrew and his army were likely to be found. To reach that, Denis would have to make a portage later.

The voyager passed three or four more days in similarly pleasant journeying. Each day he saw fewer people, and those he did see usually greeted the acolyte of Ardneh with friendly waves. Some offered him food, some of which he graciously accepted.

Denis spent much of his mental time in wondering about his hidden cargo. He knew something now at first hand about the Sword of Mercy. But what exactly did the Sword of Justice do? Denis had not wanted to ask, lest they believe he was pondering some scheme of running off with it. (The treacherous thought had crossed his mind, in the guise of yet another delicious daydream. So far—so far—his other, fiercer feelings had kept him from being really tempted by it.)

And Ben had not thought it necessary to discuss the qualities of the Sword of Justice with Denis at any length. The master of the House of Courtenay had said only one thing on the subject.

"Denis, if it does come down to your having to fight someone on the way, I'd recommend you get Doomgiver out and use it, if you have the chance. Don't try to fight with Woundhealer, though. Not if your idea is to carve up someone instead of making him feel good."

But so far there had not been the remotest danger of a fight. So far the journey's only physical excitement had been provided by occasional thunderstorms, threatening the traveler with lightning and drenching white robes that had not been waterproofed.

On Denis's fifth day out he passed through calm farm country, in lovely weather. That night he again made camp on a small island.

And dreamed, as he often did, of women. Kuanyin, the governess he had embraced in real life, and thought of marrying, beckoned to him. And tonight he dreamed also of the mistress of the House of Courtenay, who in real life had never touched him except to bind his wounded arm. Denis dreamed that she who he had known as the Lady Sophie had come to visit him in his room beside the workshop. She sat on his cot there and smiled, and held his hand, and thanked him for something he had done, or was perhaps about to do. Her white robe was in disarray, hanging open, but incredibly she seemed not to notice.

The dream was just approaching its moment of greatest tension, when Denis awoke. He lay in warm moonlight, with the sense that the world to

which he had awakened was only a perfected
dream. There was a scent in the air—of riverside
flowers?—incredibly sweet and beautiful, too subtle to be called perfume.

And there was in the air also—something else. A
fearless excitement. Denis's blood throbbed with
oneiric anticipation, of he knew not what. Yet he
knew that he was wide awake.

He looked along the river, his gaze caught by the
path of reflected moonlight. He saw a shadow, as of
some drifting boat, enter upon that path. It was
some kind of craft—a barge, he thought—speckled
with its own small lights, and moving in perfect
silence. Almost perfect. A moment more, and Denis
could hear the gentle splash and drip of oars.

As the barge drew closer, he could see that it was
larger than he had thought at first, so large that he
wondered how it managed to navigate the narrower places in this small river. The lights along its
low sides were softly glowing amber lamps, as
steady as the Old World light that Denis was familiar with, but vastly subtler.

Denis was on his feet now. He still had no doubts
that he was awake, and he was conscious of being—
more or less—his ordinary self. Whatever was happening to him now was real, but he had no sense of
danger, only of thrilling promise. He moved a step
closer to the bank, the water murmuring like lovers' laughter at his feet. He stood there leaning on
the upended bottom of the canoe that he had prudently pulled out of the river before retiring.

As the barge drew closer still, Denis could see
that it bore amidships a small house or pavilion,
covered by an awning of some fine cloth. Just forward of this there was a throne-like chair or lounge,

all centered between two rows of strangely silent and briefly costumed young women rowers.

A woman was reclining upon the lounge, in the middle of a mass of pillows. With only the Moon behind her, and the dim lamps on her boat, Denis could see her at first only by hints and outlines. At first his heated imagination assured him that she was wearing nothing at all. But presently his eyes were forced to admit the fact of a garment, more shimmering mist and starlight, it seemed, than any kind of cloth. Most of the woman's body was enclosed by this veil, though scarcely any of it was concealed.

Denis's heart lurched within him, and he understood. A name sprang into his mind, and he might have spoken it aloud, but just at that moment he lacked the breath to say anything at all. He had never seen a god or goddess in his life before, and had never really expected to see one before he died.

In response to some command unseen and unheard by Denis, the inhumanly silent rowers stopped, in unison. He was vaguely aware, even without looking directly at them for a moment, of how comely they all were, and how provocatively dressed. With the Goddess of Love herself before his eyes, he could not have looked at any of them if he had tried.

The barge, under a control that had to be more than natural, came drifting very slowly and precisely toward Denis on the island. From inside the cabin—he thought—there came a strain of music, lovely as the perfume, to waft across the small width of water that remained. Every note was framed in perfect silence now that the silvery trickle from the oars had stopped.

With an undulating movement Aphrodite rose from her couch, to stand in a pose of unstrained grace.

"Young man?" she called to Denis softly. The voice of the goddess was everything that her appearance had suggested it might be. "I must speak with you."

Denis started toward her and stumbled. He discovered that it was necessary to make his way around some large and unfamiliar object—oh yes, it was his canoe—that somehow happened to be right in his path.

"Lady," he choked out, "I am yours to command. What would you have of me?" At this point he became aware that he had just fallen on his knees with a loud squelching sound, right in the riverside mud. This would not have mattered in the least, except that it might tend to make the goddess think that he was clumsy; and when he got up, she was sure to see how muddy his white robes had got, and he feared that she might laugh.

So far, thank all the gods and goddesses, she was not laughing at him.

"Young man," said Aphrodite, "I know that you are carrying two Swords with you. I understand that one of them is the one that heals. And the other . . . well, I forget at the moment what they told me about the other. But that doesn't matter just now. I want you to hand both of them over to me at once. If you are quick enough about it I will perhaps allow you to kiss me." The goddess paused for just a moment, and gave Denis a tiny smile. "Who knows what I might allow, on such a romantic night as this?"

"Kiss me," Denis echoed vacantly. Then, giving a

mad bound, he was up out of the mud and on his feet, stumbling and splashing about. He had to find the two Swords she was talking about—where were they, anyway?—and give them to her. What else was he going to do with them, anyway?

They were in the canoe . . . where was the canoe?

He tripped over it and almost tumbled himself back into the mud before he really saw it. Then he broke a fingernail getting the craft turned rightside up.

Aphrodite encouraged him in a friendly way. "That's it. They're hidden right in the bottom of your little boat or whatever it is there—but then I suppose you know that." The goddess sounded mildly impatient with his clumsiness—how could she not be? But she did not yet sound angry; Denis silently offered thanks.

He thought he was going to lose another finger-nail getting the trick board pried up. Then he real-ized that he would do a lot better prying with a knife instead.

Aphrodite slowly approached the near side rail of her luxurious barge. Gracefully she knelt there upon a small mound of silken cushions, between two of her inhumanly beautiful rowers. They paid her no attention.

"Be quick, young man! I need what you are going to give me." The goddess beckoned with one hand, and her voice, melded with her laughter, stretched out in silken double meaning. Her laughter, Denis desperately assured himself, was not really meant to be unkind. Yet still it somehow wounded him.

He pried with his knife, and the small nails hold-ing the board came squeaking out. The hidden compartment lay open, its contents exposed to moonlight.

Aphrodite, to get a better look, gave a pert little kneeling jump, a movement of impossible grace that made the softer portions of her body bounce. What color was her hair? Denis asked himself desperately. And what about her skin? In the moonlight he could not tell, and anyway it did not matter in the least. And was she really tall or short, voluptuous or thin? From moment to moment all those things seemed to change, with only the essence of her sex remaining constant.

Now she was standing at the rail of her craft. The barge continued to drift minutely in toward shore, ignoring the current even though the oars were raised and idle.

"Be quick, young man, be quick." There was a hint of impatience in her voice.

Denis, groping almost sightlessly for his treasure to hand it over, felt his hand fall first upon Woundhealer. Somehow he could identify the Sword from its first touch. Humbly he brought it out, sheathed as it was, and with a kind of genuflection handed it over, hilt-first, to the goddess. She accepted it, with a sprightly one-handed gesture that showed how strong her smooth young-looking arm could be.

She held the Sword of Mercy sheathed, and said: "The other one now. And then I believe that—perhaps—you will have earned a kiss."

He fumbled in the bottom of the canoe again, and brought out Doomgiver.

This Sword he held with one hand supporting its sheathed blade, and the other holding the hilt, and through the hilt he felt a flow of strange and unfamiliar power. It gave him a sense of steady certitude. The sheath seemed to fall free of itself, the Sword was drawn.

Denis straightened up, intending to present this Sword as well to the goddess. But when his eyes fell on her he was shocked to see that she was changed.

Or was the change in him—and not in her?

Aphrodite let fall her arm that had been extended to receive the second Sword. She stepped back, her other hand still holding the sheathed Sword of Mercy.

Again Denis pondered: What does she really look like? But still the moonlight (he thought it was the moonlight) made it quite impossible to tell.

Certainly more lovely than any mortal woman could ever be. Yet now, since he had drawn the second Sword, he thought she was in some way inferior to even the least of human mortals. In some way she was—unreal.

He realized that he did not want her now.

Power was still flowing from the Swordhilt into his hand. In sudden curiosity he looked at what his fingers gripped. He saw in moonlight, without understanding, the simple hollow white circle that marked the black.

Wonder of wonders, the goddess appeared to be fighting some inner struggle with herself.

"Give me—" she began to say, in a voice that still fought to be commanding. But after those first two words her voice faltered and her speech broke off.

She sagged back from the railing of her barge (Denis was shocked to see how graceless the movement was), and stopped half-kneeling on her silken pillows once more. The cloud of her moonlit hair concealed her face.

"No," she contradicted herself, speaking now in

yet another voice, much softer. "No, do not give it to me now. I am a goddess, and I could take it from you. But I will not."

Denis's arm that held the Sword of Justice faltered, and the blade sank down slowly at his side. It hung in his hand like a dead weight, though still its power flowed. He felt an overwhelming—*pity*—for the goddess, mixed with a slight disgust.

"Do not give it to me," repeated Aphrodite, in her soft and newly thoughtful voice. "That would cause harm to you." After a pause she went on, marveling to herself. "So, this is love. I have always wondered, and never known what it was like. I see it can be terrible."

She raised her head until her wide-spaced eyes were visible under the cloud of moonlit hair. "I see . . . that your name is Denis, my beloved. And you have known a score of women before now, and dreamed of a thousand more. Yet you have never really known any of them. Nor will you, can you, ever really know a goddess, I suppose." And Aphrodite gave a sigh, her bosom heaving.

Denis could only stand there uncomfortably. He felt more pity for this lovely woman than he could bear, and he wished that she would go away. At the same time he wanted to let go of the Sword in his right hand; he wanted to throw it in the river. It seemed to him that his life had been much more intense and glorious just a few moments ago, before he had drawn Doomgiver. But the Sword would not let him throw it away just now, any more than it would allow the goddess to take it from him.

"I love you, Denis," the goddess Aphrodite said.

He made an incoherent noise of embarrassment, low down in his throat. As speech, he thought, it was inadequate, clumsy, mundane, and mean, like everything else he did. He did not love her, or even want her. He could not, and he wished that she would leave.

She said to him softly, "And the blade that you hold there, my love, is truly called Doomgiver, for I see now that it truly giveth me my doom."

"No!" Denis protested, feeling so sorry for her already, not knowing just what it was he feared.

"Ah yes. I, who have for ages amused myself with the love of men, must now feel what they have felt. And, as I love you now, I cannot take Doomgiver from you. To rob you of the Sword of Justice now, my little mortal darling, would do you much harm. As a goddess I can foresee that. But Wound-healer—it will be better if I take that with me now."

Denis wanted to tell her that he was sorry. The words stuck in his throat.

"How sweet it would be if you could tell me that you loved me too. But do not lie." And here the goddess extended her arm that still held the Sword of Love, across the narrow strip of water that still separated her from the island, and with the sheathed tip of Woundhealer touched Denis over his heart. "I could . . . but I will not. My full embrace would not be good for you—not now, not yet. Someday, perhaps. I love you, Denis, and for your sake I must now say farewell."

And the goddess leaned forward suddenly, and kissed him on the cheek.

"No . . . no." He stumbled forward, into mud. Was it only pity that he felt now?

But the marvelous barge was already shimmering away into the moonlight.

CHAPTER 7

The two riding beasts must have been well rested when Mark seized them, for they bore their riders willingly and swiftly on the first long stage of the flight from Vilkata's encampment. The young woman stayed in her saddle firmly, like an experienced rider, but instinctively, passively, and with no apparent understanding of what was happening to her now. Her blue-green eyes stared steadily out at horror, some horror that was no longer visible to Mark. Her body was thin, almost emaciated. Her face was pale under its mask of grime; her hair, colorless with filth, hung long and matted over the captured cloak that she clutched about her with one hand. Since Mark had pulled her from the cage she had not spoken a single word.

The two of them rode for a long time, side by side, over roadless and gradually rising ground, before Mark stopped the animals for a rest. He had at last been able to convince himself that there was no pursuit. Phantom echoes of Vilkata's demonic celebration had persisted in his exhausted mind and senses long after the real sounds had faded.

He was living now with ceaseless pain, and with the taste and sight and smell of his own blood, for the oozing from his forehead wound would not diminish. And Mark could not shake the feeling that there was something wrong now with his own blood, with the way it smelled and tasted, as if the Mindsword had left a shard of poisoned sunlight embedded in his brain.

Mark dismounted the first time he stopped the animals. He spoke gently to the young woman, but she only continued to sit her mount in silence, staring straight ahead, not responding to him at all. He decided not to press the matter of communication, as long as she remained docile. The all-important thing was to get farther from Vilkata.

Presently they were under way again. Now their course, aimed directly away from Vilkata's camp, took them into a range of low hills. Now the encampment, which had still been intermittently visible in the distance, dropped permanently from sight. Here in the hills the land still showed devastation wrought by the Dark King's foragers. Soon the fugitives came to a stream, and a thicket that offered shelter of a kind. Mark stopped again.

This time he employed gentle force to pry the young woman's hands from the reins, and to get her down from the saddle. Still half-supported by Mark's arm, she stood beside the animal waiting for whatever might happen to her next. Her lips were cracked, hideously dry. Mark had to lead her to the stream, and get her to kneel beside it. Still she did not appear to realize what was in front of her. Only after he had given her the first drink from his own cupped hands did she rouse from her trance enough to bend to the water for herself.

"I can stand," she announced suddenly, in a disused croak of a voice. And stand she did, unaided, a little taller than before. A moment later, her eyes for the first time fastened on Mark with full attention.

In the next instant he was startled to see joyous recognition surge up in her face. In a much clearer voice, she murmured, "Rostov . . . how did you ever manage . . . ?"

The instant after that, she fell unconscious in Mark's arms.

He caught her as well as he could, and stretched her out on the grass. Then he sat down, and, holding his own head, tried to think through his pain. Rostov was a Tasavaltan name, borne by the famed general, and, Mark supposed, by many others as well. He was still wearing Sightblinder, and the young woman had seen him as someone she knew and trusted.

Mark lay down and tried to rest, but his wound made that practically impossible. Presently he decided that they might as well go on, if he could get his companion back into the saddle. She roused herself when he tugged at her, and with his help she got mounted again. Though she appeared now to be asleep, with closed eyes, she sat steadily astride the riding beast, wrapped in the cloak of gold and black. That hateful cloak might be a help, thought Mark, if any of the enemy should see her from a distance. He himself was still protected by Sightblinder, but his companion would not be.

Still his wound throbbed mercilessly. He was sure now that the Mindsword must have had some poisonous effect, but unless he could find help somewhere there was nothing he could do about it. He rode on, side by side with his companion, Mark now and then rousing himself enough to realize that neither of them was more than half conscious. Grimly he concentrated—whenever he was able to concentrate—on maintaining a generally uphill direction; that ought to at least prevent them from riding in a circle right back to Vilkata and his captive gods.

They stopped again only when full night came, and Mark could no longer see where they were going. There was no food. Mark had lost his bow somewhere, after his last arrows were lost, and anyway he was in no condition to try to hunt. His limbs felt weak and he was shaking with chill. When the young woman had dismounted again and stood beside him, he took the cloak off her and clothed her in his own long hunter's shirt; he could feel her body shivering too, with the night's approaching cold. Then he lay down with her and huddled against her, wrapping the cloak around them both. He was too sick to think of wanting anything more from her than warmth. Feverishly he kept thinking that he ought to get up and do something to tend the animals, but he could not.

In pain and blood, Mark did not so much fall asleep as lapse into unconsciousness. He woke up, half delirious, in the middle of the night. Someone's hand had shaken him awake.

The young woman, still wearing his shirt, was sitting upright beside him. There was firelight, somehow, on her face, and under the dirt he could see a new look of alert intelligence.

"You are not Rostov. Where did he go?"

She had to repeat the question several times before Mark was able to grasp the sense of it. Yes, of course, she had seen him as someone else, when he had been wearing the Sword. When he had been—

His hand groped at his side, to find that she had disarmed him. Weakly he managed to raise his head a little. There was Sightblinder, lying just out of his reach. He could see it by the light of the small fire that his companion had somehow managed to start.

"I took it away from you, you were raving and thrashing about. Where is Rostov? Who are you?"

Mark had great difficulty in trying to talk. It crossed his mind that he was probably dying. He could only gesture toward the Sword.

She said, puzzled, "You killed him with—? But no, you can't mean that."

"No. No." He had to rest a little, to gather his strength before he spoke again. Even so the words wouldn't come out clearly. ". . . was never here."

The young woman stared at him. Her face was still haggard and worn and filthy, but inner energies were making a powerful effort to revive it. Now, as if struck by a sudden idea, she turned away to where the Sword lay, and crouched looking at it carefully. Then she extended one hand, with the practiced gesture of a sorceress, to touch the hilt.

She froze there in that position, one finger touching black.

The grimy girl was gone, and in her place Mark saw his mother, Mala, aged a decade since he had seen her last, her dark lustrous hair now broadly streaked with gray. It was Mala who knelt near the little campfire holding one finger against Sightblinder's hilt, wearing not Mark's hunting shirt but her own peasant's trousers and a patterned blouse that her son could still recognize.

Then the figure of Mark's mother blurred and shifted, became that of his sister Marian. Marian was a woman of nearly thirty now, also altered by the years that had passed since Mark had seen her last, on the day that he fled their village.

Marian turned her face to look directly at him, and now in her place Mark beheld a plump girl of the Red Temple, a girl he had encountered once, casually embraced, and then, somehow, never afterward forgotten. The Red Temple girl turned her body more fully toward Mark, letting go the Sword.

It was the young woman he had rescued from Vilkata's camp, her hair matted, her lean body clad in his dirty, tattered hunting shirt, who approached Mark and bent over him again. Above her head, above the firelight, massed clouds of stars made a great arc.

She drew a deep breath. "I should have realized which Sword that was. Though I have never seen one of them before . . . but now I am fully awake, I hope. I begin to understand. My name is Kristin. Who are you?"

"Mark."

"Well, Mark." She touched his wounded head, so gently that it barely added to the pain. When he winced she quickly withdrew her hand again. "Was it you who came into—that place—with Sight-blinder, and got me out?"

He managed a nod.

"And did you come alone? Yes, you nod again. Why? But never mind that now. I will never forget what you have done for me. You saved my life, and more . . . have we any water?''

Then she was quick to answer her own question, looking and finding Mark's water bottle. She gave him a drink, first, then took a mouthful for herself. "Ah," she said, and relaxed.

But only for a moment. "Are you expecting to meet help, here, anywhere nearby? . . . No." Again she stretched forth a gentle hand, that this time touched him painlessly and soothed his face. "Whom do you serve?"

"Sir Andrew."

"Ah. A good man, from all I've ever heard about him. We in Tasavalta honor him, though we don't know . . . but never mind. I must try to do something for that cut on your forehead."

Kristin closed her eyes, and muttered spells, and Mark could feel a shivery tugging at the wound, a quasimaterial endeavor to pull out the knife of pain. But then the knife came back, twisting more fiercely than before, and he cried out.

"At least the bleeding has stopped," Kristin muttered, with heartlessly reassuring calm. "But there's more wrong. I can do little for you here." She glanced up for a moment at the stars, evidently trying to judge her position or the time or both. "Have we any food?"

"No."

She began to move around, looking for something. She was inspecting some of the nearby plants when Mark lost consciousness again.

When he awoke again it was still night. He was shivering violently, though he alone was now wrapped twice round in the cloak of black and gold. His head was supported gently in the warmth of

Kristin's lap, and her warm magical fingers were trying to soothe his head.

But he hardly noticed any of that. Something that seemed more momentous was happening also. The tall circle of the gods had formed around them both. Once before, when he was a boy in danger of freezing to death in the high Ludus Mountains, he had seen the gods, or dreamt them, surrounding him in such a way. He tried now to call Kristin's attention to the ring of observing deities, but she was busy with her own efforts, her own spells. She raised her head once to look, and murmured some agreement, and then went back to trying to soothe and heal him.

He could tell she was not really aware of the surrounding presences. But he knew that they were there. And, just as on that other night when he had seen them in a ring about his lonely fire, they were arguing about him. Tonight what they were saying was even less clear than it had been then, nor were the faces of the gods as clearly visible tonight.

Eventually the vision passed.

Kristin's voice had a different tone now, murmuring real words, not incantations. It sounded as if she were angry with him. "I am not going to let you die, do you hear me? I will not let you die." She raised her head. "This much I can do against you, Dark One, for what you did to me. Damn you, I will not let you have this man!"

And back to Mark: "You saved my life . . . saved more than that . . . and I am not going to surrender yours to them. Poisoned wound or not, you'll live. I promise you."

The night passed for him in periods of unconsciousness, in visions and intervals of lucidity, in a struggle to breathe that at last he seemed to have won.

In the morning they moved on. There was no water where they had spent the night, and they were still uncomfortably close to Vilkata's army. Now it was Mark who needed help to get aboard his riding beast, and Kristin who led his animal as they traveled, and she who chose the route, and sometimes kept him from falling out of the saddle in his weakness. He endured the day. He chewed on roots and berries when she put them into his mouth. Again he experienced difficulty in breathing. But he stayed alive, supported by his own grim will and Kristin's magic.

Another night passed, much like the one before, and another day of traveling much like the last. After that day Mark lost count. His whole life had vanished into this hideous trek, it seemed, and often now he no longer cared whether he lived or not.

At night, every night, his fever rose, and sometimes the gods regathered round Kristin's magical little fire to taunt him and to argue among themselves. Each dawn Mark awoke to see them gone, and Kristin slumped beside him in an exhausted sleep.

A night came when his chills were more violent than ever. Kristin bundled herself with him inside the cloak. She slept, he thought, while the usual parade of deities walked through his fevered mind. He awoke again at dawn, his mind feeling clearer, and told himself he had survived another night.

And then he got a sharp shock, jolting his mind into greater clarity. This morning not all the deities were gone. A woman, statuesque, magnificent, as real as any woman he had ever seen, stood across the ashes of the fire, holding in her strong right arm a Sword.

The goddess was looking down at Kristin, who was asleep sitting beside Mark, the hunting shirt half open at her breast.

"I am Aphrodite," the goddess said to Mark. "I was called; I had to come to you, and now I see I must do something. How sweet, the mortal child, to give you everything. She is restoring your life to you, and giving you her entire life as well in the process, and I hope you appreciate it. But men never do, I suppose."

Mark said, "I understand."

"Do you? No, you don't. You really don't. But perhaps one day you will."

And the goddess approached the two of them with long unhurried steps, meanwhile raising the Sword in her right hand. Mark, alarmed, sat bolt upright. Before he could do more, the Sword in Aphrodite's hand was thrusting straight for Kristin's sleeping back.

The Sword in its swift passage made a sound like a gasp of human breath. Mark saw the wide, bright steel vanish into Kristin's back and emerge quite bloodlessly between her breasts, to plunge straight on into his own heart as he sat beside her. He cried out once, with a pang more intense than that of any wound that he had ever felt, and then he fell back dead.

But then he realized that he was only dreaming he was dead.

Actually, he thought now, he was waking up.

He was lying on his back, that much was real and certain. And the endless pain in his head was gone at last. It was too much trouble, his eyelids were much too heavy, to try to open his eyes to discover if he was asleep or dead.

With a sigh of contentment, knowing the inexpressible comfort of pain's cessation, he shifted his position slightly, and quickly fell into a natural sleep.

When Mark awoke again, he thought that daylight was fading. Had it really been dawn before, when the goddess and her Sword appeared? That might have been a dream. But this, Kristin and himself, was real. The hunting shirt was cast aside now, but she was here, inside the cloak that enfolded both of them.

It was as if her blood flowed now in his veins, giving healing, and his blood crossed into her body too, giving and receiving life.

Into her body. His own life flowing. . . .

It was morning again when he awoke, gently but at last completely, at first accepting without wonder the pressure of the warm smooth body beside his own. Then he began to remember things, and wonder rapidly unfolded.

In an instant he was sitting upright, raising both hands to his head. He was still caked with old, dried blood and dirtier even than he remembered, and he felt thirsty and ravenously hungry, but the pain and fever were entirely gone. Kristin, as grimy and worn-looking as he felt, but alive and safe and warm, was snuggled naked beside him in an exhausted sleep.

The sun was about an hour high. Nearby were the ashes of a long-dead fire. They were camped in a grove, with running water murmuring somewhere just out of sight. Mark could not recognize the place at all or remember their arriving at it.

A little distance away stood the two riding beasts, looking lean and hard-used, but at the moment contentedly munching grass. Someone had taken off their saddles and tethered them for grazing.

Mark stood up, the cape of black and gold that had been his only cover falling back. Again he raised a hand to his forehead. He dared to probe more firmly with a finger. There was no longer any trace of a wound, except for the dried blood.

Kristin stirred at his feet, and he looked down and saw that his movement had awakened her; her eyes were open, marveling at him.

"You have been healed," she said. It was as if she had been half-expecting such an outcome, but still it surprised and almost frightened her.

"Yes." He was almost frightened himself, at his own suddenly restored well-being. He was almost reluctant to move, afraid to break the healing spell. "You did it for me."

"Mark." It was as if she were trying out the name, speaking it for the first time. Then she asked a question that to Mark, at the moment, did not seem in the least incongruous: "Do you love me?"

"Yes." He gave his reply at once, gravely certain without having to think about it. But then he seriously considered the question and his answer. He knelt beside Kristin, and looked at her and touched her with awe, as if she herself were the great, true question that required his best reply.

"Yes," he repeated. "I love you more, I think, than my own life—if this that has happened to us comes from some enchantment, still it is so."

"I love *you* more than life," she said, and took his

hand and kissed it, then held it to her breast. "I thought . . ."

"What?"

She shook her head, as if dismissing something, and then sat up beside him. "I feared that my enchantment would not save you—though it was the best that I could do. I thought we were both lost."

They stared at each other. Mark broke the short silence. "I dreamed that Aphrodite was here with us."

Kristin for some reason thought it necessary to consider this statement very solemnly. It struck Mark that they were gazing at each other like two children, just beginning to discover things about the world, and both gravely shocked at what they learned. He had thought he knew something of the world before now, but evidently there was still much he did not know.

Then what Kristin was saying seized his full attention. "I dreamed, too, that *she* was here. And that she was about to kill both of us, with one of the Swords."

Mark stared at her. Then he jumped up out of the nest again, naked in the morning's chill, and went scrambling about to find Sightblinder. The Sword lay nearby, in plain view. In a moment he had it in his hands.

And froze, staring at the hilt. The little white symbol was not an eye. It was an open human hand.

Kristin was beside him, leaning on his shoulder—in a certain way it was as trusting and intimate a contact as any that had gone before. She whispered: "That's Woundhealer, isn't it?"

"Yes."

"She's left it with us."

"And taken Sightblinder in exchange." They stared at each other in wonder, in something like panic. He began a frantic search of the nearby area, but the Sword of Stealth was gone. It was an alarming thought that Woundhealer was going to be useless if Vilkata's troops encountered them.

Kristin was already pulling Mark's deteriorated shirt on over her head. The garment was dirtier than she was, and beginning to show holes. "We've got to get moving. All thanks to Aphrodite, but she's taken our protection with her."

All the dressing and packing they could do took only moments. And moments after that they had got the animals ready and were on their way.

Kristin indicated a course. "Tasavalta lies in this direction. We'll keep our eyes open as we go, and find some fruit. I've been able to gather enough food here and there to keep us going so far."

The country around them and its vegetation were changing as they progressed. The season was advancing too, more wild fruits coming into ripeness. Kristin appeared expert on the subject of what parts of what plants could be eaten; she had more lore in that subject than Mark did, particularly here close to her homeland. He commented on the fact, while marveling silently to himself that it had taken him so long to realize how beautiful she was.

"I have been trained in the white magic. Sorcery and enchantment were to have been my life."

"Were to have been?"

"I have made a different disposition of my life now." And suddenly she rode close beside him, very

close, and leaned sideways in her saddle to kiss him
fiercely.

He said, "You were a virgin, before last night—
yes, you were to have been consecrated to the white
magic, weren't you? Or to Ardneh."

Her expression told him that was so.

"I begin to understand. You have given me what
was to have gone to Ardneh." Comprehension grew
in him slowly. "That was why, how, Aphrodite
came to heal me. You summoned her."

"Goddesses go where they will. I could only try.
What else could I do? I discovered that I loved
you."

Mark put his arm around her as they rode side by
side. The embrace at first was only tender. But soon
tenderness grew violent in its own way. They
stopped the animals beside a thicket and dismounted.

When, after some little time, they were riding on
again, solemnity had given way to silliness; again
and again they had to reprove themselves for not
watching what they were about, warn themselves
to stay alert. Love had granted a feeling of invulner-
ability.

At about midday they came to a decent stream.
By now they had got pretty well beyond the worst
damage done by Vilkata's foragers, though the
countryside was still deserted, the visible houses
abandoned as far as could be seen in passing.

The stream, of clean, swift water, was a marvel,
and washing at this stage almost as great a relief as
being able to drink their fill. Kristin's hair emerged
from the worst of its covering of grime to reveal
itself as naturally fair. Whatever color had

appeared would have been, in Mark's eyes, the only perfect one.

Bathing together soon led to other activities, self-limiting in duration; there was presently a pause for more varied conversation.

Mark asked her, "How did you come to be a prisoner there?"

Kristin's blue-green eyes looked off into the distance. "A group of us were traveling, through country we thought was reasonably safe." She shrugged. "We were attacked by a patrol of the Dark King's army. What happened to the others in our party I do not know; I suppose they were all killed. The enemy had a magician with them. We had a contest, naturally, and he proved too strong for me. Except that I was able to—to hide myself, in a fashion. I knew little of what was happening to me, and my captors were able to tell little about me. They brought me back to their main encampment. What would have happened to me next—"

Mark put out a hand. "It won't happen now. You're safe."

"Thanks to you. But how did you come to be there?"

He explained his mission in broad terms, first as a diplomatic messenger for Sir Andrew, then on his own after his strange encounter with Draffut. That was a well-nigh incredible tale, he realized, but Kristin watched him closely as he spoke and he thought that she believed him. If she had ever heard of Mark, the despoiler of the Blue Temple, she did not appear to connect that person with the man before her. He sometimes thought, hearing his own name in the song of some passing stranger, that he was famous. But actually the name was common enough. And fortunately for his chances of avoiding the Blue Temple assassins, his face was not famous at all.

Before they left the stream, he tried to study his own face in the quietest available pool. "How do I look?" His fingers searched his forehead.

"There's a scar. No more than that. A simple scar, you'll still be handsome." She kissed it for him.

He sat back. "So, as you see, I was on my way to Tasavalta anyway. As a courier."

"How convenient." She kissed him again.

"Yes. What is the Princess like?"

"A few years older than I am." Kristin paused. "I can hardly claim to know her."

"I suppose not. We'd better get moving."

They were dressed, in washed garments, and packed and back on their animals heading east, before Mark resumed the conversation. "I don't know Tasavaltan customs at all well. Should I be asking you who your parents are? I mean, what is the customary way of taking a wife in your land? Who else must I talk to about it, if anyone?"

"My parents are both dead."

"Sorry."

"It was long ago. Yes, there will be people we have to see. Old Karel first, I suppose. He's my uncle, and also my teacher in magic. A rather well-known wizard. You may have heard of him?"

"No. But I've known other magicians, they don't frighten me especially. We'll see your Uncle Karel . . . by the way, will you marry me?"

Kristin appeared vaguely disappointed. "You know I will. But I am glad you thought to ask."

"Ah yes." And again there was an interval in

which no thoughtful planning could be accomplished.

The interval over, Mark said, "I gather you're not exactly looking forward to seeing your old uncle. He was intent on consecrating you as a sorceress, is that it?"

"Partly."

He felt somewhat relieved; he could have imagined worse. "Well, not all the women who are good at magic are virgins, I can assure you of that." He paused. "I mean . . ."

They cautiously approached and entered a deserted house, and then another, and helped themselves to a few items of clothing the inhabitants had not bothered to take with them when they fled. Mark wondered whether to leave payment, and decided not—the arrival of Vilkata's looters seemed likely to occur before the return of the proper owners. Feeling a shade more civilized, they rode on.

It struck Mark that Kristin was resisting making plans for their own future. She loved him, they were going to marry, that much was certain between them. But she was reluctant to go into details at all. A sense of mystery, of something withheld, persisted. Mark put it down to exhaustion. Though Woundhealer had restored them marvelously, still the journey was hard and their food meagre.

Yet it was happy, despite continued difficulties and periods of fear. And as they left the last fringes of the area already devastated by Vilkata's army, their own foraging became correspondingly easier. Farms and houses were even fewer now; this was a region sparsely inhabited in the best of times.

Mark tried to count up the days of their journey. Watching the phases of the Moon, he decided it was now almost a month since he had approached and entered Vilkata's camp.

At last there came the day when they rode into sight of a banner of blue and green, raised on a tall rustic pole. The Tasavaltan flagpole stood atop a crag that overlooked the road, just where the road entered the first pass of mountain foothills. Kristin shed tears at sight of the flag; Mark had to look at her closely to be sure that they were tears of joy.

She assured Mark that what he had been told of Tasavalta was correct, that although it was not a huge land it was certainly spectacular. In any event he could now begin to see that for himself. Kristin explained the topography in a general way: there were two main mountain ranges, one right along the coastline to the east, the other a few kilometers inland, just inside the first long line of sheltered valleys. Both these ranges were really southern extensions of the Ludus Mountains, now many kilometers to the north.

"I grew up in sight of the Ludus," Mark said. "We could see them on a clear day, anyway, from home."

Despite the southern latitude they had now reached, here in late summer there were still traces of ice and snow visible upon the highest Tasavaltan peaks ahead. The coast was deeply cut with fjords here, and cold ocean currents kept this almost tropic land in a state of perpetual spring.

Mark and Kristin pushed on, urging their tired riding beasts past that first frontier marking. Mark kept glancing at his companion. She was more often silent now, and looked more worried the farther they went.

He asked Kristin suddenly, "Still worried about

what your teacher in the white arts is going to say?"

"That's not it. Or not altogether."

Still the secrecy, and it annoyed him. "What, then?"

But she would not give him what he considered a straight answer, and his annoyance grew. Something about her family, he supposed. What they were going to say when she brought home an almost penniless foreign soldier as a prospective husband. Mark was sure by now that Kristin's family were no peasants. Well, the two of them had been traveling alone together for a month. If her people were like most of the well-to-do families that Mark had known, that would be a powerful inducement for them to give their consent. In any case he was going to marry her, he would entertain no doubt of that, and he kept reassuring himself that she showed no hesitation on that point either.

She might, he sometimes thought, be withholding information about some complication or obstacle. If she feared he might be influenced by anything like that—well, she didn't yet know him as well as she was going to.

Once they had passed that first flagpole marking the frontier, the road immediately improved. It also began a steeper climb, sometimes requiring long winding switchbacks. For the first time on this journey Mark could glimpse the sea, chewing at the feet of the coastal mountains. It was deep blue in the distance, then the color of Kristin's eyes, then as it met land frothed into white. Now, on either side of the road, there were meadows, presently being harvested of hay by industrious-looking peasants who were not shy about exchanging waves at a distance with shabbily dressed wayfaring strangers. The lifesaving cloak of Vilkata's colors had long since been rolled up into a tight black bundle and lodged behind Mark's saddle.

Now Kristin pointed ahead, to where the sun-spark of a heliograph could be seen winking intermittently from the top of a small mountain. "That may be some message about us. In times like these, the lookouts tend to take notice of every traveler."

"Do you know the code?"

"Yes—but that's not aimed in our direction. I can't see enough of it to read."

Now—oddly as it appeared to Mark—Kristin's worry had been replaced by a kind of gaiety. As if whatever had been worrying her had happened now, and all that mattered after that was to make the best of life, moment by moment. Now she was able to relax and enjoy her homecoming, like any other rescued prisoner.

He took what he saw as an opportunity to try to talk seriously to her again. "You're going to marry me, and right away, no matter what you family or anyone else says about it." He stated it as firmly as he could.

"Yes, oh darling, yes. I certainly am." And Kristin was every bit as positive as he was about it. But he could see now that her sadness, though it had been conquered, was not entirely gone.

Things of very great importance to her—whatever all the implications might be exactly—had been set aside, because it was more important to Kristin that she marry him. Mark made, not for the first time on this journey, a silent vow to see that she never regretted that decision.

He was cheered to see that happiness increasingly dominated her mood as they went on. She was coming home, she was going to see a family and friends who must at the very least be badly worried about her now, who might very possibly have given her up for dead.

The road, now well paved, rounded a shoulder of the same small mountain upon whose peak they had seen the heliograph. Then it promptly turned into a cobblestone street, as the travelers found themselves entering the first village of Tasavalta. It was, Mark decided, really a small town. He wondered what it was called. Not far ahead on the right was a small, clean-looking inn, and he suggested that they stop. He had a little money with him still, carried in an inner pocket. "If they will let us in; we do look somewhat ragged." Their scavenging through deserted houses had added to their wardrobe, but only doubtfully improved its quality.

"All right. We can stop anywhere. It makes little difference now." Kristin looked him squarely in the eye, and added warmly: "I love you."

It was something they said to each other, in endless variations, a hundred times a day. Why should the effect, this time, be almost chilling, as if she were telling him goodbye?

"And I love you," he answered softly.

She turned her head away from him, to look toward the inn, and something in her aspect froze. Mark followed her gaze. Now they were close enough to the inn for him to see the white ribbon of mourning that was stretched above the door. And there was another white ribbon, now that he looked for it, wrapped round the arch of the gate leading into the inn's courtyard from the street.

He said to Kristin: "Someone in the innkeeper's family . . ."

She had turned in her saddle again, and was looking wordlessly up and down the street. Now that they were closer to the other doors and gateways they could see the white bands plainly, everywhere. In this town the badge of mourning appeared to be universal.

"What is it, then?" The words burst from Kristin in a scream, a sound that Mark had never heard from her before. He stared at her. They had stopped, just outside the open gateway of the courtyard of the inn.

In response to the outcry an old woman in an apron, the innkeeper's wife by the look of her, appeared just inside the yard. In a cracked voice she admonished, "Where've you been, young woman, that you don't know—"

At that point the old woman halted suddenly. Her face paled as she stared at Kristin, and she seemed to stumble, almost going down on one knee. But Kristin, who had already dismounted, caught her by the arms and held her up.

And shook her, fiercely. "Tell me, old one, tell me, who is the mourning for?"

The eyes of the innkeeper's wife were pale and hopeless. "My lady, it's for the Princess . . . Princess Rimac . . . has been killed."

Again Kristin let out a scream, this one short and wordless. Mark had heard another woman scream just that way as she fell in battle. Kristin swayed but she did not fall.

He jumped off his own mount and went to her and held her. "What is it?"

She clung to him as if an ocean wave were tugging at her, sweeping her away. For just a moment her eyes, flashing with mystery and fright, looked directly into his. "My sister . . ."

She tried to add more words to those two. But Mark heard hardly any of them. He retreated, one backward step after another in the direction of the inn, until directly behind him there was an old bench, that stood close by the white-ribboned doorway. He sat down on the bench, in the partial shade of an old tree, leaning his back against the inn's whitewashed wall. Already half a dozen more townspeople had appeared from somewhere, to make a little knot around Kristin and the old woman in the courtyard, and even as Mark watched another half dozen came running. They were kneeling to Kristin, seizing her hands and kissing them, calling her Princess. Someone leaped on the back of a fresh riding beast in the courtyard and went pounding away down the street, hooves echoing for what seemed like a long time on distant cobblestones.

Mark remained sitting where he was, on the shaded bench near the worn doorway, while people rushed in and out ignoring him. Now and again through the press of bodies his eyes met Kristin's for a moment. The Sword of Love in its sheath weighed heavily at his side.

Among the other things that people were shouting at her were explanations: how Princess Rimac had ridden out carelessly as was her habit; how there had been a sudden, unexpected attack by one of the Dark King's raiding parties; how now there was going to be war. . . .

The crowd grew rapidly, and Mark's glimpses of Kristin became less frequent. At one point dozens of eyes suddenly turned his way, and there was a sudden, comparatively minor fuss that centered about him—she must have said something that identified him as her rescuer. People thronged about him. Men with an attitude between timidity and bravado beat him on the back in congratulation, and tried to press filled beer mugs into his hand. Women asked him if he were hungry, and would not hear anything he answered them, and brought him cake. Girls threw their tender arms about his neck and kissed him, more girls and young women kissing him now in a few moments than had even looked at him for a long time. One girl, pressed against him by the crowd, took his hand and crushed it against her breast. By now he had lost sight of Kristin entirely, and if it were not for the continuing crowd he would have thought that she had left the courtyard.

There was the sound of many riding beasts out in the street. Now the crowd, filling the gateway, blocking Mark's view of the street, had a growing new component. Soldiers, uniformed in green and blue. Mark supposed that the heliograph had been busy.

Someone near him said: "General." Mark recognized Rostov at once, having heard him described so often, though he had never seen the man before.

Round one thick arm in its blue-green sleeve, Rostov like the other soldiers was wearing a band of mourning white. There was one decoration on his barrel chest—Mark had no idea of what it represented. The General was as tall as Mark, and gave Mark the impression of being stronger, though he was twice Mark's age. Rostov's curly black hair was heavily seasoned with gray, and his black face marked on the right cheek by an old sword-slash. A gray beard that looked like steel fiber raggedly trimmed sprouted from cheeks and chin. His facial expression, thought Mark, would have been quite hard enough even without a steel beard.

Kristin was now coming through the crowd, and Mark from only two yards away saw how the General greeted her. He did not kneel—that appeared to be quite optional for anyone—but his eyes lit up with relief and joy, and he bowed and kissed her hand fervently.

She clung to his hand with both of hers. "Rostov, they tell me that Parliament has been divided over the succession? That they have nearly come to blows?"

"They have come very nearly to civil war, Highness." The General's voice was suitably gravelly and deep. "But, thank the gods, all that is over now. All factions can agree on you. It was only the thought that you were missing, too . . . thank all the gods you're here."

"I am here. And well." And at last her eyes turned in Mark's direction.

Now Mark and Rostov were being introduced. The General glowered at him, Mark thought; that was the way of generals everywhere, he had observed, when looking at someone of insignificance who had got in the way. Still Rostov was quick to express his own and his army's formal thanks.

A hundred people were speaking now, but one

soft voice at Mark's elbow caught his full attention. It was a woman's, and it said: "They told me that your name was Mark. And so I hurried here to see."

Mark recognized his mother's voice, before he turned to see her face.

CHAPTER 8

The scar on Denis's arm, the last trace of the wound that had been healed by the Sword of Mercy, looked faint and old already. He thought that the second touch of Woundhealer in the hand of Aphrodite had reached his heart, for there were times when he had the feeling of scar tissue forming there as well. The vision of the goddess as she had appeared to him at night on the river-island was with him still. He still felt pity for her whenever he thought of what had happened; and then, each time, fear at what might happen to a man who dared feel pity for divinity.

His emotions whipsawn by his encounter with Aphrodite, Denis sometimes felt as if years had passed in the few days since his departure from Tashigang. In the days that followed, he went on paddling his canoe into the north and east. He toyed no more with the idea of absconding with the remaining Sword; he was still in awe and shock from that demonstration of its powers, and he

163

wanted nothing but to be honorably and safely rid of it.

With that objective in mind, he tried his best to keep his attention concentrated upon practical affairs. It was necessary now to watch for a second set of landmarks, these to tell him where to leave this river and make the small necessary portage. The markers were specially blazed trees, in the midst of a considerable forest through which the little river now ran. Denis paddled upstream through the forest for a full day, looking for them. The stream he was now following grew ever younger and smaller and more lively as he got further from the Corgo, and was here overhung from both banks by great branches.

On the night that Denis left Tashigang, Ben had told him that if he saw any wild-looking people after he had come this far, they were probably Sir Andrew's. The Kind Knight's folk would escort a courier the rest of the way, or at least put him on the right track, once he had convinced them he was bona fide.

. . . and the Goddess of Love had told him, Denis, that she loved him. Even in the midst of trying to make plans he kept coming back to that, coming back to it in a glow of secret and guilty pride, guilty because he knew that it was undeserved. Was ever mortal man so blessed?

Much good had such a blessing done him. Pride came only fitfully. In general he felt scarred and numb.

He did manage to keep his mind on the job, and spot his required landmarks. The blazed trees were not very conspicuous, and it was a good thing that he had been keeping an alert eye open. Once he had found the proper place, he had to beach his canoe on the right bank, then drag it through a trackless thicket—this route was apparently not much used—and next up a clear slope, over ground fortunately too soft to damage the canoe. This brought him into a low pass leading through a line of hills that the stream had now been paralleling for some time.

After dragging his canoe for half a kilometer, lifting and carrying it when absolutely necessary, Denis reached the maximum slight elevation afforded by the pass. From this vantage point he could look ahead, over the treetops of another forest, and see in the distance the beginnings of the Great Swamp, different kinds of trees rearing up out of an ominous flatness. During the last four years that largely uncharted morass had swallowed up the larger portions of a couple of small armies, to the great discomfiture of the Dark King and the Silver Queen respectively. And neither monarch was any closer now than four years ago to their goal of slaughtering Sir Andrew and the impertinent fugitives of his own small military force.

The stream that Denis had to find now was not hard to locate. It was running in the only place nearby that it very well could run, just beyond the line of hills in the bottom of the adjoining gentle valley. After resting a little while on its bank, he launched his canoe again, and resumed paddling, once more going upstream. In this waterway the current was slower, and Denis made correspondingly better time. But this was a more winding stream, taking him back and forth on wide curves through the forest; he was going to have to paddle farther just to get from here to there.

Denis spent an entire day paddling up this stream before he was challenged. This happened at just about the point where he could see that he was entering some portion of the Great Swamp itself.

His challengers were three in number, a man and two women, one of them standing on each bank of the narrow stream and one on an overhanging bough. All three looked quite tough and capable. Their weapons did not menace but they were certainly held ready. Against this display Denis lifted his own hands, empty, in a sign of peace.

He said, "I need to see Sir Andrew, as quickly as I can. I come from a man named Ben, and I have here a cargo that Sir Andrew needs."

The three who had stopped him spoke quickly among themselves, and two of them promptly became Denis's escort. They made no comment on the fact of his empty-looking boat, as contrasted with his claim of valuable cargo. They did take from him his only visible weapon, a short knife. Then the man got into the rear seat of Denis's canoe, and took over the paddling, while one of the women oared another small craft along behind. As they glided deeper into the swamp, under the twisted limbs of giant trees festooned with exotic parasite-plants, Denis saw a small arboreal creature, of a type strange to him, headed in the same direction. It was brachiating itself along through the upper branches at a pace that soon overtook and passed the boats. He surmised it was some species of half-intelligent messenger.

Presently, after about a kilometer of paddling, Denis was delivered to a camouflaged command post, a half-walled structure made of logs and shirt-sized tree fronds, where he repeated his terse message to an officer. Again he was sent on, deeper into the swamp, this time with a different and larger escort.

This leg of the escorted journey took longer. It occupied a fair portion of the remaining daylight hours, and ended with Denis's canoe grounding on the shore of what appeared to be a sizable island of firm land that reared up out of the swamp. There were people on this island already. He estimated a score of them or more, many of them conspicuously wearing Sir Andrew's orange and black. A few tents had been set up, but the place did not have the worn look of a permanent encampment.

The people who were already gathered here appeared to be waiting for something. They were not, as it turned out, anticipating Denis's arrival, which in itself did not cause much of a stir. His canoe was beached for him, and he was at once conducted a short distance inland, toward one particular knot of people who were engaged in some serious discussion. Taking the chance to look about him from the slightly higher vantage point of this firm ground, Denis realized that this was no true island at all, or else it was a much larger island than he had first assumed. From here he could see a double track, what looked like a regular road, though a poor one, approaching through the trees to end in the small clearing where the knot of people were conversing.

The focus of that group's attention was one man, heavily built, gray-haired, and wearing clothing that might once have been fine. This man was standing with his back to Denis, but the black hilt of a Sword visible at his side convinced Denis that this must be Sir Andrew himself, who was known to hold Shieldbreaker.

Sir Andrew turned. The face of the man known as the Kind Knight showed more age than his strong body did. He was holding a book in his left hand, and had been gesturing with it to make some point, when Denis's arrival interrupted the discussion.

Standing at Sir Andrew's right hand was a woman, not young but certainly still attractive. There was much gray now in the lady's black hair, but Denis thought that in youth her face must have been extremely beautiful. He had no idea what her name might be, but at first glance he was certain she was a sorceress. Certain details of her dress gave that indication, but the impression was created chiefly by an impalpable sense of magic that hung about her. Denis could feel that magical aura, and he did not consider himself a sensitive.

Two pairs of brown eyes, the lady's younger and quicker than Sir Andrew's, studied the new arrival. Names were formally exchanged.

"And where," asked the Knight then, in his slow, strong voice, "is this cargo that you say you have for me?"

"In the canoe, sir. There's a false bottom."

"And what is the cargo? Speak freely, I have no secrets from any here."

Denis glanced around. "A Sword, sir. One of the famous Twelve, I mean. Sent from the man called Ben, in Tashigang. There were two Swords, but— something happened to me on the way."

"I can see that," the enchantress murmured. Her eyes were narrowed as she studied Denis. "Show me this remaining Sword."

They moved quickly to the waiting beached

canoe. At Denis's direction the concealing board was pried up once more. Dame Yoldi, the graying sorceress, supervised this operation carefully, and gave the exposed cargo a close inspection before she would allow Sir Andrew to approach it.

She also questioned Denis first. "You say that two Swords were sent, and one lost on the way?"

"Yes Ma'am." Denis related in barest outline, and not dwelling on his own feelings, what had happened between him and the goddess. He heard a snicker or two, and scoffing noises, in the background. But he thought the lady perhaps believed him. At least she stepped back to let Sir Andrew approach the canoe.

The Knight's right hand plucked Doomgiver from the secret compartment, and held it, still sheathed, aloft. There was a general murmur, of appreciation this time, not scoffing.

"Do you feel anything from the two Swords, Andrew?" the sorceress asked gently. "You are holding two at one time—you still wear Shieldbreaker."

He huffed and gave her a look. "I've not forgotten what I wear. No, I feel nothing in particular—you once told me that even three Swords at once would not be too many for some folk to handle."

"And I tell you again that two, in certain combinations, might do strange things to other folk. And you are sensitive."

"Sensitive! Me!" He huffed again.

Dame Yoldi smiled, and Denis could see how much she loved him. Denis wondered suddenly if he himself had actually handled the two Swords at the same time at any point. If he had, he couldn't remember feeling anything strange.

Now Sir Andrew turned back to Denis. "We must soon hear your story about the goddess, and Woundhealer, in more detail. Meanwhile we are all grateful to you for what you have brought to us. But at the moment even such a gift as the Sword of Justice must wait to have my full attention, and you must wait to get your proper thanks."

"You're quite welcome, sir."

Already Dame Yoldi had Denis by the arm and was turning him away. "At the moment you are in need of food and rest." She gestured, and a woman came to take Denis in charge.

He resisted momentarily. "Thank you, Ma'am. But there is one bit of news, bad news, that I must tell you first." That certainly got their full attention back. Denis swallowed, then blurted out the words. "The Dark King has the Mindsword in his hands. So we were told in Tashigang, by some of Ardneh's people." The source put a strong flavor of reliability upon the news.

His hearers received his announcement with all the shock that Denis had anticipated. He braced himself for the inevitable burst of questions, which he answered in the only way he could, pleading his own lack of further knowledge.

At last he was dismissed. Led away, he was given bread and wine, then shown to a tent where he stretched out gratefully upon the single cot. His eyes closed, their lids suddenly heavy, and with a swiftness that might have been genuinely magical, he plunged into a deep sleep.

Denis awoke suddenly, and feeling greatly refreshed. He was surprised to see that the pattern of tree shadows on the tent had shifted very little, and no great length of time could have passed. What had awakened him he did not know.

Listening to the silence outside the tent, he thought that there was some unusual tension in it.

He got up and left the tent. Seeing that some people were still gathered at the place where he had left Sir Andrew and Dame Yoldi, he hurried in that direction. Now, as he walked, Denis could see a few more people in orange and black approaching quickly on foot along the landward road. These were turning and gesturing, as if to indicate that someone or something of importance was coming after them. Everyone nearby was looking in that direction.

Denis halted in surprise at sight of the next two figures that appeared down the road. Both were wearing black and silver, the colors of Yambu. Both were mounted, riding freely, not at all like prisoners. Still, neither was visibly armed. One was a burly man, and the other—

With a silent gasp, Denis recognized the Silver Queen herself. He had seen her twice before, both times years ago, both times in the city of Tashigang. She, as the city's formal overlord, had been appearing then in ceremonial processions. He, then no more than a street urchin, had been clinging to precarious perches above the crowds, eager to watch.

In those processions the Queen had ridden her virtually unique mount, a superbly trained and deadly warbeast. Her steed today was less remarkable, though still magnificent, a huge riding beast matching that ridden by her companion. This burly man, her escort, as they approached Sir Andrew and the others waiting, dropped a deferential half-length behind.

The two riders halted, calmly, at a little distance from where the folk in orange and black were waiting to receive them. They dismounted there and approached Sir Andrew's group on foot, the tall Queen a pace ahead in her light silvery ceremonial armor, taking long strides like a man. Denis calculated that she must be now well into her middle thirties, though her tanned face looked younger. Her whole body was strong and lithe, and despite her stride the generously female shape of her body left no doubt at all about her sex. The Queen's nose, Denis noted now in private impertinence, was too big for her ever to be called pretty, by any reasonable usage of the word. And yet, all in all—well, if he were to meet some woman of attainable station who looked just like her, he'd not refuse a chance to know her better.

And have you forgotten me already? The voice of Aphrodite came to Denis only in his imagination. It shook him, though, in a resonance of conflicting feelings.

Sir Andrew was standing with folded arms, waiting for his visitors, as if the last thing in the world he might do would be to make any gesture acknowledging his old enemy's greater rank. But she, approaching, as if she thought he might do so and wished to forestall him, was quick to make the first gesture of greeting, flinging up her right hand in the universal gesture of peace.

"We meet again!" The Silver Queen's voice, hearty and open, neither assumed a royal superiority nor pretended a friendship that did not exist. "My honored enemy! Would that my friends and allies were half as dependable as you. So, will you take my hand? And never mind the fripperies of rank."

And when Dame Yoldi moved between them, Queen Yambu added: "Aye, lady, you may look at my hand first. I bring no poisoning, no tricks; which is not to say that none such were suggested by my magicians."

Dame Yoldi did indeed make a brief inspection of the Queen's hand. Meanwhile Denis was having to use his elbows to keep himself from being crowded back by the small but growing throng of Sir Andrew's people who wanted to observe the meeting closely. There had evidently been more than twenty on the island after all. He managed to remain close enough to see that the Queen's hand looked like a soldier's, being short-nailed, spotted with callouses—the sort that came from gripping weapons—and strong. But, for all that, it was shapely, and not very large.

The Queen's offered hand was briefly engulfed in Sir Andrew's massive paw. And then the Knight stood back again, grim-faced, arms folded, waiting to hear more.

The Queen cast a look around her. Sir Andrew's friends and bodyguard, heavily armed, most of them impressive warriors, were hovering suspiciously close to her and her companion, and looking as grim as Sir Andrew did himself.

She said to the Knight: "I do trust you, you see, and your safe-conduct guarantee. In nine years of fighting you, off and on, I've learned to know you well enough for that."

The Knight spoke to her for the first time. "And we have learned something of your character as well, Madam. And of yours, Baron Amintor. Now, what will you have of me? Why this urgent call for a meeting?''

The Baron was as big and solid as Sir Andrew, and with much the same hearty and honest look, though the Silver Queen's companion was probably the younger of the two men by some fifteen years. Both were battle-scarred, Denis observed, evidently real fighters. Amintor's eyes were intelligent, and Denis had heard that he was gifted with a diplomatic tongue when he chose to use it.

And the Queen . . . this Queen had been no more than a half-grown girl when she ascended to the throne of Yambu. Her first act afterward, it was said, had been to put to death the plotters who had murdered both her parents in an abortive coup attempt. Nor had the throne been easy for her to hold, through the twenty years that followed. Many plotters and intriguers during that time had gone the way of that first set. Ever since its shaky beginning, her reign—except in a few lucky places like Tashigang—had not been gentle. It was said that she grew ever more obsessed with the idea that there were plots against her, and that about four years ago she had sold her bastard adolescent daughter into slavery, because of the girl's supposed involvement in one. The girl, Ariane, had been her only child; everyone knew that the Silver Queen had never married formally.

Now the Queen said to Sir Andrew, "I like a man who can come straight to the point. But just one question first: are you aware that the Dark King now has the Mindsword in his possession?"

The Knight answered calmly. "We have been so informed."

Both the Queen and Baron Amintor appeared somewhat taken aback by this calm response. Yambu said, "And I thought that you were existing in a backwater here! My compliments to your intelligence service."

And Amintor chimed in: "You'll agree, I'm sure, Sir Andrew, that the fact does change the strategic situation for us all."

Sir Andrew took just a moment to consider him in silence, before facing back to the Queen. "And just what, Madam, do you expect this change to mean?"

The Silver Queen laughed. It was a pleasant, rueful sound. There was a fallen tree nearby, a twisted log that rested at a convenient height on the stubs of its own branches, and she moved a couple of steps to it and sat down.

"I foresee myself as Vilkata's first victim, unless I do something about it, quickly. I'll speak plainly—if you've begun to know me, as you say, you know that's how I prefer to speak. If Vilkata with the Mindsword in his hand falls on my army now, then unless they can withstand it somehow—and I've no reason to hope they can—then my army will at best melt away. At worst it'll join Vilkata and augment his strength, which is already greater than yours and mine combined.

"You, of course, will applaud my fall and my destruction—but not for very long."

The Knight, his aspect one of unaltered grimness, nodded. "So, Queen of Yambu, what do you propose?"

"No more than what you must have already guessed, Sir Andrew. An alliance, of course, between us two." Yambu turned her head slightly;

her noble bearing at the moment could almost turn the fallen log into a throne. "Tell him, good Dame, if you love him—an alliance with me now represents his only chance."

Neither Sir Andrew nor his enchantress gave an immediate answer. But the Knight looked so black that, had he spoken, Denis thought the conference would have ended on the instant.

Dame Voldi asked the Queen, "Suppose we should join forces against Vilkata—what then? How do you propose to fight the Mindsword, with our help or without it?"

It was the Baron who replied. "To begin with, we mean to avoid battle with Vilkata's troops unless we're sure he's not on the scene himself—he'll never turn the Mindsword over to a subordinate, you may be sure of that. Your people and ours will exchange intelligence regarding the Dark King's movements. Yes, it'll still be damned difficult even if we're allied—but if we're still fighting each other at the same time, it's going to be impossible."

Yoldi had another question. "Supposing for a moment that such an alliance could be made to work, even temporarily—what do you intend doing with the Mindsword, after the Dark King has somehow been defeated?"

Yambu smiled with what looked like genuine amusement. It made her face more attractive than before. "Why, I would leave that up to you."

"You'd turn the Mindsword over to us?" Yoldi asked the question blankly.

The Queen paused very briefly. "Why not? I can agree to that, because I think that your good Knight there is one of the few men in the world who'd never use it."

"And what of my people who are now your slaves, my lands that you have seized?" This was from Sir Andrew. He had now mastered his obvious anger, and was almost calm, as if he were only discussing some theoretical possibility.

"Why, those are yours again, of course, as soon as you and I can reach agreement. As soon after that as I rejoin my own people, I'll send word by flying beasts to all my garrison commanders there, to begin an evacuation at once."

"And in return for that, what do you want of me?"

"First, of course, immediate cessation of hostilities against my forces, everywhere. And then your full support against the Dark King, until he is brought down. Or until he crushes both of us." The Queen paused, giving an almost friendly look to Sir Andrew and his surrounding bodyguard. She added: "You really have no choice, you know."

There was a long pause, during which Sir Andrew studied the Queen even more carefully than before. At last he said, "Tell me something."

"If I can."

"Did you in fact sell your own daughter into Red Temple slavery?"

Denis saw a shadow, he thought of something more complex than simple anger, cross the Queen's face. Her voice when she replied was much less hearty. "Ah," she said. "Ah, and if I tell you the truth of that, will you believe me?"

"Why not? Apparently you expect us to believe your proposal to give us the Mindsword—perhaps at this moment you even believe that yourself. Still, I would like to hear whatever you wish to say about your daughter."

This time the pause was short. Then, with a sudden movement, the Silver Queen got up from her seat on the dead tree.

"Amintor and I will walk apart a little now, while you discuss my offer. Naturally you will want to talk to your close advisers before giving me an answer. I trust they are all here. Unfortunately—or perhaps fortunately—there isn't time for diplomacy as usually conducted. But I'll wait, while you have your discussion."

And the two visitors from Yambu did indeed walk apart, Baron Amintor apparently pointing out some curiosities of the swamp flora to the Queen, as if neither of them had anything more important than wild plants on mind.

Sir Andrew and several others were huddled together, and Denis could imagine what they were saying: About Vilkata and the Mindsword, it must be true, for now we've heard it twice. But, an alliance? With *Yambu*?

But, thought Denis, the Queen was right. He has no real choice but to accept.

CHAPTER 9

Kristin, crowned only hours ago in hurried but joyful ceremony as Princess Regnant of the Lands of Tasavalta, was alone in one of the royal palace's smaller semipublic rooms, sitting on one of her smaller thrones. She had chosen to sit on this throne at this moment because she was tired—exhausted might have been putting it mildly—and the throne was the most convenient place in the room to sit. There were no other chairs. She could willingly have opted for the floor, but the fit of her coronation gown, which had been her sister's, and today had been pressed into service hurriedly, argued against that.

She was waiting for her lover Mark to be brought to her. There were certain things that had to be said to him, and only she could say them, and only when the two of them were alone. And her impending collapse into exhaustion had to be postponed until after they had been said.

The room was quiet now, except for the distant

continuing sounds of celebration from outside. But if Kristin thought about it, she could remember other days in this room. Bright days of loud voices and free laughter, in the time when her older sister had been alive and ruling Tasavalta. And days from an earlier time still, when Kristin had been only a small girl, and there were two girls in this room with their father, a living King, who joked with them about this throne. . . .

Across the room in present time a small door was opening, quietly and discreetly. Her Uncle Karel, master of magic and teacher of magicians, looked in, saw she was alone, and gave her an almost imperceptible nod of approval. Karel was enormously fat and somewhat jolly in appearance, red cheeks glowing as usual above gray whiskers, as if he had just come in from an invigorating winter walk. As far as Kristin could tell he had not changed in the slightest from those bright days of her own girlhood. Today of course he was decked out, like herself, in full ceremonial garb, including a blue-green garland on his brow.

He reached behind him now to pull someone forward. It was Mark, dressed now in strange borrowed finery, that he thrust gently into the room where Kristin waited.

Karel said to her, in a voice that somewhat belied his jolly face; "Highness, it will look bad for you to be alone for very long with this—"

She stood up, snapped to her feet as if brought there by a spring, weary muscles energized by outrage, by the tension of all that had happened to her today. "Uncle Karel, I have been alone with him for a month already. Thank the gods! For before that I was alone with Vilkata's torturers, and *you* were not there to bring me out.''

That was unfair and Kristin knew it; her voice softened a little. ''There are important matters that I must—convey to this man. Before I dispatch him on a mission that will take him out of Tasavalta.''

Her uncle had winced at the jab about Vilkata's torturers, but his relief at her last words was evident. He bowed himself out silently, closing the door behind him.

Mark heard the same words from Kristin with muted shock, but no real surprise. It was hours now since he had opened his mouth to say a word of his own to anyone. Many had spoken to him, but for the most part only to give him directions: Bathe here, wait there, put this on and see if it fits. Here is food, here is drink, here is a razor. Stand here, wait. Now come this way. He had been fed, cleaned up, draped with robes and what he supposed were honors, then shunted aside and left to watch from an inconspicuous place during the coronation ceremony.

Now he marveled to himself: it was less than a day ago—hardly more than half a day—that this girl and I were riding alone as lovers, on the edge of the wilderness, both of us still in rags. I could have stopped my mount then, and stopped hers—yes, even in sight of that first flagpole bearing blue and green—and got down from my saddle, and pulled her down from hers, and lain with her on the ground in our rags, or out of them, and she would have loved it, welcomed it. And now. . . .

This audience chamber, in which Mark now found himself alone with Kristin, was, like the rest of the palace—like the whole domain of Tasavalta, perhaps—a larger and somehow more important place than it had appeared at first impression. It was a sunlit, cheerful room, beautiful in a high vertical way. The air moving in through the open windows smelled of flowers, of perpetual spring; drifting in with the scents of spring came the music of the dance that was still going on far below the windows, part of the coronation celebration. The dance and the music, like the rest of the day, had become to Mark something like a show to which he need only listen, and watch. As if none of it had anything, really, to do with him.

The windows of this room were equipped with heavy shutters, as was fitting in a castle constructed to withstand assault. But on this upper level of the castle, high above any possible assault by climbing troops, the windows were large, and today all the shutters had been thrown open. Framed in their casement openings, the sea and the rocky hills and the town below all appeared like fine tapestries of afternoon sunlight, thrown by some Old World magic on the walls.

Kristin had risen quickly from the throne when the door opened, and when her uncle had closed it again behind him she had moved a few paces forward, toward Mark. But now the two of them, she and Mark, were still standing a little apart, looking at each other as if they had nothing to say—or perhaps as if neither of them could manage to say anything.

But their eyes drew them together. Suddenly they were embracing, still without a word of speech. Then Kristin tore herself away.

"What is this they've given you to wear?" she asked, as if the sight of the costume they had put on him, some antique ceremonial thing, made her want to laugh and cry at once.

But still he said nothing.

She tried again, not with laughter, but now with an almost distant courtesy. How fine that he had already been reunited with his family. She'd had no idea, of course, that they'd been living here. In recent years a lot of refugees, good people, had come in. Did Mark's mother and sister know him after so long a time? How long had they been living here in Tasavalta? Did he have any trouble recognizing them? It was too bad his father was away.

"Kristin." As he called her by her name, he wondered if it was the last time he would ever be able to do so. "Stop it. Have you nothing real to say to me? Why didn't you *tell* me?"

There was a pause, in which Kristin drew a deep breath, like a woman who wondered if it might be her last.

"Yes," she said then. "I must say something very real to you, Mark. For the sister of a Princess Regnant to have married a—commoner, and a foreigner as well—that would have been very hard. Very nearly impossible. But I would have done it. I wanted to marry you. I wanted it so much I was afraid to tell you who I was. And I was going to marry you, wherever that path led. I hope you will believe that."

"Kristin, Princess . . ."

"Wait! Let me finish, please." She needed another pause to get herself together. "But my sister Rimac is dead. She died childless and unmarried, and I am ruler now. For a Princess Regnant to marry a commoner, let alone a foreign soldier, *is* impossible. Impossible, except—again I hope you will believe me—I would have done it anyway. It would have meant resigning the throne, probably leaving the country; I would have done that for you. But . . ."

"But."

"But you must have heard them! There isn't anyone else to rule! You heard Rostov. If I hadn't come back to take the throne, there would have been a civil war over the succession. Even with attackers threatening us from outside. I know my people. We probably seem to you a happy, peaceful country, but you don't know . . ."

Again Mark was silent.

"I . . . Mark, our land and people . . . we owe you more than we can ever repay. We can give you almost anything. Except the one thing that you want. And that I want . . . oh, darling."

This time the embrace lasted longer. But as before, the Princess broke it off.

Mark was conscious that he still had a duty to perform, and drew himself up. "I am the bearer of certain messages, that Sir Andrew, whom I serve, has charged me to deliver to the ruler of the Lands of Tasavalta."

Kristin, as never before conscious of duty, drew herself up, too, and heard the messages. They were more or less routine, diplomatic preliminaries looking to the establishment of more regular contacts. Sir Andrew had long resisted adopting the diplomatic pretense that he was still actually governing the lands and people that had been stolen from him; but he had recently been persuaded of the value of taking such a pose, even if the facts were otherwise.

Mark concluded the memorized messages. "And

now, I am ordered to place myself at Your Majesty's disposal." Again, in the fog of his exhaustion, the feeling came over him that none of this really had anything to do with him; he had stumbled into the middle of a play, there were certain lines that he was required to read, and soon it would all be over.

Kristin said, "I am glad to hear it. You will need a few days in which to rest, and recover from . . ." She had to let that trail away. With a toss of her head she made a new start. "You will be assigned— modest quarters here in the palace." *Quarters far from my own rooms.* So Mark understood the phrase. "Then—you heard what I told Karel. I mean to send you on a special mission. This should not pose any conflict with your orders from Sir Andrew, if they are to place yourself at my disposal. I hope that you will accept the assignment willingly."

He could feel only numbness now. "I am at Your Majesty's disposal, as I said before."

"Good." Kristin heaved an unroyal sigh: part of an ordeal had been passed. "The mission you are to perform for Tasavalta is a result of some magical business of Karel's. In divination . . . you will be given more details later. But according to him, the indications are so urgent that he dared not wait even until tomorrow to confront me with the results.

"You are to go and find the Emperor, and seek an alliance with him for Tasavalta—and an alliance with him for Sir Andrew too, if you feel you are empowered by Sir Andrew to do that. I leave that to your judgement."

"The Emperor. An alliance with him?" Even in Mark's present state of embittered numbness, he had to react somehow to the strangeness of that proposal. An *alliance*, as if the Emperor were a nation, or had an army? Of course the indications were, Mark thought, that the Emperor was, or at least could be when he chose, a wizard of immense power.

Curious in spite of everything, he asked, "Me, negotiate for you in such a matter? I'm not even one of your subjects. Or a diplomat. Why me?"

"Karel says it should be done that way. Though I don't think that he himself knows why. But I've learned over the years that my uncle usually gives his monarch good advice."

"Karel wants to make sure I'm out of the way."

"There is that. But sending you back to Sir Andrew would do that just as well. No. There's something about the Emperor—and about you. I don't know what."

The Emperor, thought Mark. *The man that Draffut, after fifty thousand years of knowing human beings, trusted at first meeting. The man who had said that he, Mark, should be given Sightblinder.*

The man in whose name a simple incantation had twice, in Mark's experience, repelled demons. . . .

The sorcerer Karel—it was, Mark supposed, foolish to think he had not been listening—was back in the room now, as if on cue.

After all that had already happened today, Mark had no real capacity left for surprise, so he felt no more than dull curiosity when he observed that the magician was carrying a sheathed Sword.

Karel in his soft, rich voice said to him: "It is Coinspinner, and it has come to us in a mysterious way. And you are going to take it with you to help you find the Emperor."

Mark's dinner that evening was eaten not in the palace, but in the vastly humbler home of his sister Marian. It had turned out that she was now living in the town, really a small city, not far below.

Mark had by now had a little time in which to savor the great news that his father Jord, who he had thought for ten years was dead, was alive after all. And not only was Jord still alive but well and active at last report, off now on some secret mission for the Tasavaltan intelligence service. Neither Mala nor Marian appeared to know where Jord had been sent or when he might be back, and Mark, with some experience in these matters himself, did not press to find out. For now it was enough to know that he at least had a good chance of someday seeing his living father once again.

At dinner—a good dinner, evoking marvelous memories—Mark heard from his mother and sister how his surviving family had come to Tasavalta years ago, after more years spent in homeless wandering, following the destruction of their old village.

In the nine years or so since then, much had happened to them all, and they had much to talk about. Marian was married now, her husband off somewhere with Rostov's army. Her two small children gaped through dinner at this newly discovered uncle, and warmed up to him gradually.

It was almost midnight, and Mark was having to struggle at every moment to stay awake, before he said goodnight. His "modest quarters" in the palace had no attraction, and he was about to go to sleep on cushions on the floor in the room where they had dined and talked.

Marian had already said goodnight, and had taken the children upstairs to bed.

But Mark's mother lingered. There was a suppressed urgency in her manner. "Walk me home. I stay nearby, here in town, while Jord is gone. It's only a little way."

"Of course."

Once they were outside, Mala clung to her son's arm as if she needed his support to walk, though she was not yet forty and all evening had seemed full of energy, rejoicing in their reunion. But now her mood became suddenly tinged with sadness.

"You've just come back to us," she said. "And before we can begin to know you, you must go off again."

"I must, Mother."

"I know, I know." Mark had yet to encounter anyone at all, in either town or castle, who did not know of his relationship with Kristin, and the potential problems that it raised.

Mother and son walked, slowly. He was very tired. He thought that his mother seemed now to be on the brink of telling him something. She kept asking him, "You'll come back to Tasavalta, though?"

"I'll be here a couple of days yet. I'll see you again, and Marian, before I go."

"Yes, of course. Unless the plan for your departure is changed. In these matters of secrecy, plans can change very quickly, I've learned that. But after this mission, you'll come back?"

"To report on my mission, I suppose, yes, I'll have to. And be sent off again. I can't stay here. The Princess's commoner lover, and a foreigner to boot. If my father had been the Grand Duke Basil, or

Prince Something-or-other, things would probably be different."

They were at her door now. It was a modest place, but looked comfortable; probably the government here provided quarters for its secret agents' families.

Mala, her voice quivering as if she were doing something difficult, said: "Mark, come in, there's something I must tell you, while I have the chance. The gods know if I'll ever have the chance again."

It was about an hour later when he emerged from the humble apartment where his parents lived. He stood in the narrow street for a little while, looking up at the stars. They looked the same as always. Beyond tiredness now, Mark remained standing there in the street for what felt to him like a long time. And then he went to his modest quarters in the palace, knowing that he had to get some rest.

Two mornings later, well fed, well dressed, and reasonably rested, armed with the Sword Coinspinner at his side . . . and Woundhealer left safely in Karel's care . . . Mark left the Palace. His departure was quiet, without fanfare official or otherwise. Mounted on a fine riding beast and at the head of a small escort similarly well equipped, he was on his way to seek the Emperor.

Mark looked back only once. He saw a figure that he was sure was Kristin, watching his departure from a distant upper window. But he made no sign that he had seen her.

CHAPTER 10

Over the long decades since his human eyes had
gone in sacrifice, and demonic senses had been
engrafted magically upon his own, the Dark King
had come to be unsure sometimes whether he was
awake or dreaming. He saw the Mindsword the
same way in either case, as a pillar of billowing
flame long as a spear, with his own face glowing
amid the perfect whiteness of the flame. He could
tell that the eyes on his own face of flame were open
and seeing. Whether he was dreaming or awake,
that fiery stare for some reason always reminded
him that he had never seen with his own natural
eyes any of those who were now his closest associates and chief subordinates. The demon showed
him his human wizards and warlocks as strange,
hunched, wizened figures, and his generals as little
more than animated suits of armor; but all of them
appeared with exaggerated caricature-faces, that
amplified all of their subtleties of expression, so
that the Dark King might better try to read them.

Whereas demons, in the demonic vision, appeared with noble, lusty, youthful bodies, usually naked and always intensely human, except in their very perfection, their large size, and in the bird-like wings they often sprouted. The Dark King knew of course that they had no real bodies, or wings either, and he did not believe at all in their faces as they were presented to him, shining with kindliness and honor.

Now that the King was in the field with his army, on the march almost daily, the demons sometimes appeared to him on a smaller scale, fluttering in the air inside his tent like monkbirds. Vilkata dwelt now in a tent much smaller than his grand pavilion, because speed was of importance. And he thought that speed was vital now, because of the reports that had recently come in, first announcing and then confirming that Sir Andrew's troops were at last out of the swamp. The army in orange and black was moving in the direction of Sir Andrew's old lands, as if the Kind Knight for some reason thought the time might be ripe to reclaim them.

This news of course made Vilkata wonder what his erstwhile ally, the Silver Queen, might now be planning. As far as he knew she still controlled those lands.

The report of Sir Andrew's movement had also confirmed Vilkata's recent decision that his own strategy had best be altered. Now, he determined to destroy Sir Andrew first, before turning his attention to his other surviving enemies and rivals. Vilkata had arrived at this decision to change his plans largely out of the feeling that his enemies must now know too much about them as they stood.

First of all, the Dark King was now convinced

that he had entertained a spurious Burslem, some damned spy, at that memorable council meeting at the main camp, the one where the King had first displayed his Mindsword, and which the gods had so gratifyingly attended later. The real wizard Burslem, Vilkata's head of Security and Defensive Intelligence, had at last returned, and had been positively identified, this time, by careful questioning. How the spy had managed to resist the Mindsword's influence, as he or she evidently had, was something else for the King to worry and wonder about. The Sword Sightblinder was so far the only really convincing explanation to be suggested, and the presence of that in one of his enemies' hands was far from reassuring.

Today, as Vilkata moved about his small field tent in his routine of morning preparations, the small demon that served him as sensory aid presented him as usual with a vision of the tent's interior. Certain things, in accordance with his own long-standing orders, were edited out of the scene as he perceived it. For example, the body of last night's concubine, curled now at the foot of the bed in sleep or a good imitation thereof, was most clearly visible by its shapely torso, the breasts and buttocks particularly emphasized. The irrelevances of hands and feet, and especially the face—who would care about trying to read the innermost thoughts of such a woman?—blurred away into a semi-transparent obscurity. In the case of a bed-partner, better a blur than a face, no matter how well-formed and schooled in smiling. Even such smiles could sometimes be disquieting.

And the Dark King had recently ordered that, when the next battle came, the dead should be edited away too, out of his perception. He had observed frequently, on other battlefields and in other areas where much killing was required, that the dead were a notable distraction. Obstacles when removed ought to disappear, resources once used up were only waste materials. The dead tended to stink, and were in general esthetically unpleasing. He had finally decided to order them filtered out. Someone else could count them up when necessary.

He had decided, too, that many of the wounded, most of them in fact, should also be expunged from his vision. Those remaining should be only the ones still able to play an active part in the day's events, enough to present some possible danger to the Dark King's person, or his cause. This might not always be easy for a busy demon to judge; in doubtful cases the filtering familiar was to let the wounded person remain visible, even if esthetically offensive.

This morning, when Vilkata left his small tent and mounted his war-steed, amid the usual thunderous applause of his troops and officers, his army appeared before him in his demon-sight as neat ranks of polished weapons, the human form attached to each blade or bow not much more than a mere uniformed outline.

A look at the best maps he had available had persuaded him that it ought to be possible to intercept Sir Andrew's force if he moved swiftly, staring at first daylight. The morning's march was hard and long. Scouts, some of them human beings mounted or afoot, some of them winged beasts, kept coming in with reports of what appeared to be the rear guard of Sir Andrew's force not far ahead. They estimated that the enemy army was even a little smaller than earlier intelligence estimates had made it out to be.

But Vilkata, still prudent despite the overwhelming advantage that he thought he held, ordered his infantry forward as against a foe possibly almost their equal in numbers. He also ordered a swift cavalry movement, a reconnaissance in force, to move around Sir Andrew's army, to try to engage the enemy front and if possible prevent successful flight. Meanwhile he maneuvered the main body of his own troops into battle array. Stationing himself just behind the front of this force, near the center, he awaited more reports, and remained ready to draw the Mindsword for what he calculated would be maximum effect upon foe and friend alike.

The first skirmishes broke out ahead. The Dark King drew his weapon of great magic and advanced, mounted, holding overhead what he himself perceived as a spear of fiery glory. He saw the enemy rearguard, in a view tailored by his familiar to his wishes, as mobile though inanimate man-sized obstacles. Still he could see their shapes and their numbers perfectly well, and even note the fact that many of them wore orange and black.

Vilkata saw also, and felt with joy, the terror that he inspired in those men and women ahead when they first saw him, and how swiftly that terror was altered by his Sword's magic into a mad devotion.

He saw with delight how Sir Andrew's soldiers, who at first glance would have formed a rank and fought him, at sight of the Mindsword fell down and worshipped him instead. And how, when he presently roared orders at them, they rose and turned, and went running like berserkers against their former comrades, who must now be just out of sight and trying to get away.

One of the last to bend to the Mindsword's power was a woman, a proud sorceress by the look of her, no longer young and evidently of some considerable rank. One counterspell after another this arrogant female hurled back at the Dark King and his Sword; but they had all failed her, as he knew they must, and as she too must have known; and she too turned at last, snarling with mad joy, like the others, at being able to serve the future ruler of all the Earth.

Denis the Quick had been offered the chance to remain in the swamp, along with a handful of wounded and others who could not travel quickly, when Sir Andrew led his army out. Reports had come in indicating that it would not be wise for Denis to attempt to make his way home alone to Tashigang, and Sir Andrew could afford no escort for him. The situation around the city had deteriorated rapidly since Denis's departure. Strong patrols of the Dark King's forces were in the very suburbs now, challenging the few troops that the Silver Queen had in the region. The wealthy owners of suburban villas had fled, into the city or far away from it. This news offered hope of a kind to Sir Andrew and his people, as it was evidence that the situation between King and Queen was now moving rapidly toward open conflict.

But Denis had declined to stay in the swamp. There was no telling how long he'd be stuck there if he did so, or when a better chance of getting out would come, if ever. He preferred to be out in the great world, to know what great events were happening. He was willing to take his chances on getting back eventually to the city he loved, and to the two women there whose images still stirred his dreams.

On the afternoon of the third day since the army had left the swamp, Denis was walking with some members of Sir Andrew's staff. Sir Andrew himself was on hand at the moment; the Knight had been riding up and down the column of his army, trying to preserve its organization—years of guerrilla tactics in a swamp were not the best practice for a long overland march—and had stopped to talk with Denis about conditions among the people in Tashigang.

They talked of the White Temple, and its hospitals, in some of which Denis had worked during his apprenticeship as Ardneh's acolyte. They began a discussion on how to put Woundhealer to the best possible use; this was of course purely theoretical, as Denis had been unable to deliver it as charged. Sir Andrew still did not appear to blame him, however. Doomgiver was with the column, being carried by an officer of the advance guard, who, as it had seemed to Sir Andrew, had the greater likelihood of encountering the enemy today.

Their conversation was interrupted by the arrival of a small flying scout, with a message from the rear guard.

The true bird, intelligent enough to manage elementary speech, cackled at them: "Black and gold, black and gold. Many many."

"Then Ardneh be with my Dame," Sir Andrew muttered, reining in his mount, and looking behind him fiercely. Dame Yoldi was in the rear. "And with us all."

He cried out then for swift messengers to go ahead, to summon back with all speed the trusted friends who were carrying Doomgiver in the van. Then the Knight tried the movement of his helmet's visor, and with more shouted orders set about turning what few units of his army were in direct range of his voice, and heading them back to the relief of the rear guard. These did not amount to much more than a handful of his own bodyguard and friends.

And Denis heard, even as he saw, Shieldbreaker come out of its sheath now. He heard the legendary pounding sound, not fast or loud as yet but dull and brutal. The matchless magic of the Sword of Force beat out from it into the surrounding air, not with the tone of a drum whose voice might stir the blood, but rather with the sound of some relentless hammer, nailing up an executioner's scaffold.

Now the Knight himself and his close bodyguard, all mounted, set out for the rear of their army, or what had been its rear, at a pace that Denis on foot could not hope to match.

But, as he would be otherwise left virtually alone, he tried to keep up. He might have run in the other direction instead, but he thought the rest of the army would soon be pouring back from there, and he would have to face round again and join them, or appear as a deserter.

Denis was about a hundred meters behind Sir Andrew and his mounted companions, and losing more ground rapidly, when to his surprise he saw at a little distance to his right what looked like the deserted remnants of a carnival, set down for some reason right out here in the middle of nowhere. The booths and counters, the apparatus for the games of skill and chance, were all broken and standing idle. No one was in sight at the deserted amusement place, as Denis halted nearby, panting. The people belonging to the show—and who could blame them?—appeared to have run off even before the tramp of marching armies had drawn near.

Sir Andrew and his bodyguard had not yet got out of Denis's sight, when a cry went up from the same direction and only a short distance ahead of them. Denis, turning his head away from abandoned tents and wagons, saw what had to be Sir Andrew's rear guard, running toward Sir Andrew and his immediate companions, who had just halted on a little knoll. It appeared to be a desperate retreat, though as far as Denis could see the rearguard was not yet panicked totally. They had not thrown their weapons away as yet . . . and then he saw that what he had first taken for a retreat was in fact a charge. The rearguard, running from downhill, and already swinging their weapons like madmen, collided full tilt with Sir Andrew and his little group who had been riding to their rescue. The cry and noise of battle went up at once, and the would-be rescuers, taken by surprise, were many of them already down in their own blood.

"A trick! An enchantment!" Despairing cries went up from those riding with Sir Andrew.

It was no trick as simple as switched uniforms. Denis, dazedly continuing to move nearer, was now close enough to recognize Dame Yoldi's face among those who charged uphill, swinging their weapons, and shrieking mad battlecries. She was headed directly toward the little knoll where Sir Andrew and the surviving handful of his bodyguard and officers were now surrounded and under heavy attack.

Sir Andrew might have tried to turn his mount, break free of his assailants who were on foot, and get away. But he could not or would not try to flee. Instead he kept shouting to his traitorous assailants, calling them by name, trying to command them. He stood his ground, and his bodyguard would not make an effort to break away if he did not.

The hammering sound of Shieldbreaker went up and up, louder and faster now, syncopated into an irregular rhythm. Already it had drawn around its master an arc of gleaming steel and fresh blood. Sir Andrew's mount stumbled and went down, hacked and stabbed by half a dozen weapons, but no attacking point or blade could come far enough within the arc of the Sword of Force to reach his skin.

The Knight, tumbled from the saddle of his dying mount, rolled over on the ground, never losing his two-handed grip on the great Sword. Even when Sir Andrew lay on his back it never faltered in its action. And when he stood upright again, it was as if the Sword itself had pulled him up to fight. Shieldbreaker seemed to drag him after it, spinning his heavy body with its violence, right to left and back again, pulling him forward to the attack when one of his attackers would have faltered and pulled away.

Still, those who an hour ago had been his loyal friends came on against him by the score, shrieking their new hatred, calling on their new god, the Dark King, to strengthen them. Shieldbreaker fought them all. It smashed their weapons and their bones impartially, carved up their armor and their flesh alike.

Denis, hypnotized by what he saw, no longer fully in control of his own actions, crept a little closer still. He had a long knife at his own belt but he did not draw it. It was as if the thought never occured to him that he might possibly make any difference in the fight that he was watching.

Sir Andrew's bodyguard, greatly outnumbered by berserk fanatics, were all down now, their dead or dying bodies being hacked to pieces by their mad attackers. But Shieldbreaker protected the man who held it. It continued to make its sound, yet faster now and louder. It worked on, its voice still dull despite its blinding speed, its dazzling arc. It worked efficiently, indifferent as to whom or what it struck, indifferent to whatever screams or words went up from those it disarmed or cut apart, indifferent equally to whatever weapons might be plied against it. Denis saw axeheads, knives, swordblades, shafts of spears and arrows, flying everywhere, whole and in a hail of fragments. Human limbs and armor danced bloodily within the hail, and surely that bouncing, rolling object had once been a head.

The mouth of the Kind Knight opened and he screamed, surely a louder and more terrible roar than any coming from the folk he struck. Denis, creeping closer still as if he were unable to help himself, saw that Sir Andrew was now covered with blood from head to foot. It was impossible to tell if any of it might be his own. But if he were wounded, still the mad vigor of his movements, energized by magic, continued unabated.

The Knight roared again, in greater agony than

before. Denis saw that Dame Yoldi, possessed, a creature of evil hatred, her face hideously transformed, was closing in on Sir Andrew. Her hands were outspread like claws, as if to rend, and she cried out desperate spells of magic. Even Denis the unmagical could feel the backwash of their deadly, immaterial power.

To the Sword of Force the tools of magic were no more than any other weapons. They were dissolved and broken against that gleaming curve almost invisible with speed, that brutal thudding in the air. Dame Yoldi's hatred propelled her closer, closer, to the man she would destroy, and closer still, until the edge of the bright arc of force touched her, hands first, body an eyeblink later, and wiped her away.

Denis saw no more for the next few seconds. When he looked up again, there was a pause. Sir Andrew stood alone now, knee-deep in a small mound of corpses, all in his own colors of orange and black. The Sword in his hands still thudded dully; for those of his former friends who still survived as maddened enemies were not through with him yet. A small knot of them, the wounded, those who had been slow to charge, the calculating, were gathering at a little distance, scheming some strategy, hatred forced into patient planning.

Denis hurried to Sir Andrew's side. The young man thought, as he approached, that Sir Andrew was trying to hurl Shieldbreaker from him; the Sword was quieter now in the Knight's hands, its sound reduced to a muted tapping. But if he was trying to be rid of it, it would not let him go. Both of his hands still gripped it, fingers interlocked around the hilt, white-knuckled where the knuckles could be seen through blood.

Sir Andrew turned a hideous face to Denis. The Knight's voice was a ghastly whisper, almost inaudible. "Go, catch up with the advance guard. Find the man who is carrying Doomgiver, and order him in my name, and for the love of Ardneh, to return here as fast as he can."

Denis had hardly got out of sight in one direction before Sir Andrew, looking the opposite way, was able to see the main body of Vilkata's troops in the distance, a black-gold wave advancing toward him. A trumpet sounded from that line. On hearing it, such remnants of Sir Andrew's corrupted troops as were still on the field abandoned their hopeless attack, turning in obedient retreat to join the forces of their new master.

There, in the distance, that man, whitehaired and mounted under a gold-black banner, must be Vilkata himself. In those distant hands a weapon that Sir Andrew knew must be the Mindsword flamed, the sun awakening in it all the fires of glory. To Sir Andrew's eyes, it was not much more than a glass mirror; Shieldbreaker in his own hands protected him from that weapon too. It negated all weapons except itself.

And it was quite enough, he thought; it had quite destroyed him already.

Again a horn sounded, somewhere over there in the army of the Dark King. Next, to the Knight's numbed surprise, Vilkata's hosts that had only just appeared began a measured withdrawal, going back over the rise of land whence they had come. Sir Andrew tried to think that over, his mind working in a newly confused way. He supposed that to Vilkata's calculation the withdrawal was only sense: why order an army to chew itself to tatters, to no purpose, upon Shieldbreaker's unbreakable defense?

Sir Andrew might have pursued that army, he might have run screaming at that central banner bearing the black skull until everyone beneath it had been turned to chopped meat at his hands. But they would not wait for him. Vilkata was mounted and would get away. And anyway he, Sir Andrew, was too weak to run, to pursue and catch up with anyone.

Now that the immediate threat to Sir Andrew himself was over, the strength of magic that had been given him through the Sword was draining rapidly away. The dread sound of Shieldbreaker's hammer thumped more softly, tapping slower, tapping itself down into silence.

He saw himself as if from outside, an old man standing alone on a hill, knee-deep in corpses of those he once had loved. His arms ached, as if they had been pounded by quarterstaffs, from the drill that Shieldbreaker had dragged them through. Careless of the blood, he put the Sword into its sheath.

It was all Sir Andrew could do now to remain on his feet.

It was almost more than he could do, to go and look at what was left of Yoldi.

After that, trying to see his way through tears, he made his legs carry him away. He was not sure where he was going, nor even of where he ought to go. He got no farther than the next small hillock of the field, coming again within sight of the flimsy ruins of the carnival, when the great pain struck him inside his chest. It felt like a spearthrust to the heart.

He collapsed on his back. A fighter's instincts made him draw the great Sword again before he fell. But he faced no weapons now, and the Sword of Force was lifeless.

As Sir Andrew lay in the grass the sky above him looked so peaceful that it surprised him. He considered his pain. It feels, he thought, as if my heart were bursting. As perhaps it is.

He took a look back, quickly and critically, at what he could see at this moment of his own long life. He found the prospect of death, at this moment, not unwelcome.

The pain came again, worse than before.

"Yoldi . . ."

But she did not answer. She was not going to answer him ever again.

When it seemed that the pain was going to let him live yet a little longer, Sir Andrew flung Shieldbreaker away from him, using two hands and all of his remaining strength. He had tried to throw the great Sword away before, tried again and again when he saw Yoldi running at him and realized what must have happened to her, and what was going to happen. But the Sword's magic would not leave him then. This time, now that it was too late, it left his hands as obediently as any stick thrown for a dog. The blade whined faintly, mournfully, turning through the air.

The Knight did not want to die alone. If only there could be a friend nearby—someone.

He closed his eyes, and wondered if he would ever open them on this world's skies again. Would it be

Ardneh that he saw when he opened his eyes again, as some folk thought? Or nothingness?

He opened them and saw that he was still in the same world, under the same sky. Something compelled him to make the effort to turn his head. A single figure, that of a man in gray, was walking toward him from the direction of the carnival, the abandoned showplace that Sir Andrew had been perfectly sure was quite deserted. A man, not armed or armored, but . . . wearing a mask?

The gray-clad figure came close, and knelt down beside him like a concerned comrade.

Sir Andrew asked: "Who're you?"

The man raised a hand promptly and pulled off his mask.

"Oh." Sir Andrew's voice was almost disappointed in its reassurance. "You," he said, relieved and calm. "Yes . . . I know who you are."

Denis, returning mounted and at full speed, leading a small flying wedge of armed and armored folk who were desperate to relieve their beloved lord, found the battlefield deserted by the living. Sir Andrew lay dead, at a little distance from the other dead. His body, though covered with others' gore, was unmarked by any serious wound. The expression on the Kind Knight's face was peaceful.

Presently Denis and the others began to look for Shieldbreaker. They looked everywhere among the dead, and then in widening circles outward. But the Sword of Force was gone.

CHAPTER 11

The field cot was wide enough for two—for two, at least, who were on terms of intimate friendship—but tonight, as for many nights past, only one person had slept in it.

Or tried to sleep.

The Silver Queen's field tent was not large, not for a shelter that had to serve sometimes as royal conference room as well as dwelling. According to certain stories she had heard, it would not have made a room in the great pavilion that usually accompanied the Dark King when he traveled with his army.

She felt great scorn for many of the Dark King's ways. But there were other things about him that enforced respect, and—to herself, alone at night, she could admit it—tended to induce fear as well.

The Queen of Yambu was sitting in near-midnight darkness on the edge of her lonely field cot, wearing the light drawers and shirt she usually slept in when in the field with her troops. She could hear rain dripping desultorily upon the tent, and an occasional word or movement of one of the sentries not far outside.

Her gaze was fixed on a dim, inanimate shape, resting only an arm's length away beside the cot. In midnight darkness it was all but impossible to see the thing that she was looking at, but that did not really matter, for she knew the object as well as her own hand. It rested there on a trestle as it always did, beside her when she slept—or tried to sleep. It was a Swordcase of carven wood, its huge wooden hilt formed by chiseled dragons with their long necks recurved, as if they meant to sink their fangs into each other. Just where the case had originated, or when, the queen of Yambu was not sure, but she thought it beautiful; and after the best specialist magicians in her pay had pronounced it innocent of any harm for her, she had used it to encase her treasure, which she kept near her almost always— her visit to Sir Andrew in the swamp had been one notable exception—as her last dark hope for victory.

A thousand times she had opened the wooden case, but she had never yet drawn Soulcutter from its sheath inside. Never yet had she seen the bare steel of that Blade in what she was sure must be its splendor. She was afraid to do so. But without it in her possession she would not have dared to take her army into the field now, risking combat with the Mindsword and its mighty owner the Dark King.

Some hours ago, near sunset, a winged half-intelligent messenger had brought her word of Vilkata's latest triumph. He had apparently crushed what might have been Sir Andrew's entire army. Then, instead of coming to attack her as she kept expecting he would do, Vilkata had turned his own vast forces in a move in the direction of Tashigang.

Maybe the Dark King's scouts had lost track of where her forces were. But for whatever reason, her own certainty that she would be the first one attacked by Vilkata was proven wrong, and that gave cowardice a chance to whisper in her ear that it might not be too late for her to patch up an alliance with the King. Of course cowardice, as usual, was an idiot. Her intelligence told her that her only real hope lay in attacking the Dark King now, while she might still hope for some real help. Sir Andrew was already gone. When Tashigang too had fallen, then it would certainly be too late.

When the news of Vilkata's most recent triumph had come in, Yambu had first conferred briefly with her commanders, then dismissed them, telling them to let the troops get some rest tonight. But she herself had not been able to sleep since. Nor, though her own necessary course of action was becoming plainer and plainer, had she been able to muster the will to be decisive, to give the orders to break camp and march.

Who, or what, could stand against the Mindsword? Evidently only something that was just as terrible.

And Sir Andrew had been wearing Shieldbreaker, ready at his side. With her own eyes, on her visit to the swamp, she had seen the small white hammer on the black hilt. Vilkata with his Mindsword had evidently won, somehow, even against that weapon. Did Vilkata now have possession of both those Blades? But even if he did, each terrible augmentation of his power only made it all the more essential to march against him without delay.

The Silver Queen stood up and moved forward one short pace in midnight blackness, trusting that the tent floor was there as usual, and no assassin's knife. She put out her hand and touched the wooden case, then opened it.

She stroked with one finger the black hilt of her own Sword. This Sword alone among the Twelve bore no white symbol on its hilt. No sense of power came to her when she touched it. There was no sense of anything, beyond the dull material hilt itself. Of all the Twelve, this one alone had nothing to say to the world about itself.

She glanced back at her solitary cot, barely visible in the dulled sky-glow that fell in through the tent's screened window. She visualized Amintor's scarred shoulders as they sometimes appeared there, bulking above the plain rumpled blanket. Amintor was wise, sometimes. Or clever at least. She doubted now that she herself knew what wisdom was, doubted she would recognize wisdom if it came flying at her in the night like some winged attacking reptile.

Quite possibly she had never been able to recognize it, and only of late was she aware of this.

The one adviser whose word she would really have valued now had been gone from her side for years, and he was not coming back. She was never going to see him again, except, possibly, one day across some battlefield. But perhaps when they met in battle he would be wearing a mask again (she had never understood why he did that so often) and he would go unrecognized.

And now, at this point in what had become a

familiar cycle of thought, it was time for her to think about Ariane. Ariane her daughter, her only child, and of course his daughter too.

The Silver Queen's intelligence sources had confirmed for her the stories, now four years old, that Ariane was four years dead, had perished with some band of robbers in an attempt to plunder the main hoard of the Blue Temple. Well, the girl was better off that way, most likely, than in Red Temple slavery.

Had that plot, to put Ariane on the throne of Yambu, been a real one? Or had the real plot been to force her, the Silver Queen, to get rid of her daughter, her one potentially trustworthy ally? Even when convinced of the danger, Queen Yambu had been unable to give the orders for her daughter's death. And besides, the auguries had threatened the most horrible consequences for her royal self if she should do so. In the end, as certain of the auguries appeared to advise, she had sold Ariane into Red Temple slavery.

Her own daughter, her only child. She, Queen Yambu, had been lost in her own hate and fear. . . .

Would Amintor, she wondered, if he had been with her then, have had the courage to advise her firmly against destroying her own daughter? Not, she thought, once he knew that she was determined on it.

. . . and now, of course, in this pointless cycle of thought, remembrance, and self-recrimination, it was time for her to recall those days of her love affair with the Emperor, before her triumphant ascension to the throne. Only rarely since that triumph had she felt as fully alive as she did then, in that time of continuous, desperate effort and danger. Then her life had been in peril constantly. She had been in flight day after day, never sleeping twice in the same place, alert always to escape the usurpers' search parties that were frantically scouring the country for her.

That was when she had met him, when the love affair had started, and when it had run its course. She had been an ignorant girl then, only guessing at the Emperor's real power; then, as now, he had had no army of his own to send into the field. But he had saved her more than once, fighting like a demon at her side, inspiring her with predictions of victory, outguessing the enemy on which direction their search parties would take next.

There had been hints, she supposed, in those early days of love, as to what he expected as his ultimate reward. More than hints, if she had been willing to see and hear them. Still she had begun, naive girl as she then was, to think him selfless and unselfish. And then—landless, armyless, brazen, bold-faced opportunist after all!—he had proposed marriage to her. On the very day of her stunning victory, when enough of the powerful folk of Yambu had rallied to her cause to turn the tide. The very day she had been able to ascend the throne, and to order the chief plotters and their families put to a horrible death.

The man who called himself the Emperor must have read her instant refusal in her face. For when she had turned back from giving some urgent order, to deliver her answer to him plainly, he was already gone. Perhaps he had put on one of his damned masks again; anyway he had vanished in that day's great confusion of unfamiliar figures, new bodyguard and new courtiers and foreign dignitaries already on hand to congratulate the winner.

She had refused to order a search, or even to allow one. Let him go. She was well rid of him. From that day forward she would be Queen, and her marriage, when she got around to thinking of marriage, would have to be something planned as carefully and coldly as an army's march.

There had been, naturally enough, other lovers, from that day almost twenty years ago till this. Amintor was, she supposed, the most durable of the bunch. *Lovers* was not really the right word for them though; useful bodies, sometimes entertaining or even useful minds.

But the Emperor—yes, he had been her lover. That fact in some ways seemed to loom larger as it became more distant down the lengthening avenue of years.

But, she thought now (as she usually did when the thought-cycle had reached this point), how could any woman, let alone a Queen, have been expected to live with, to seriously plan a life and a career, with a man like that . . . ?

The Silver Queen's thoughts and feelings, as usual, became jumbled at this point. It was all done with now. It had all been over and done with, a long time ago. The Emperor might have made her immortal, or at least virtually ageless, like himself. Well, as a strong Queen she could hire or persuade other powerful magicians to do the same for her, as they did for themselves, when it began to seem important.

Only after she had refused the Emperor's offer of marriage, and after she had banned that impossible pretender, that joker and seducer, from her thoughts (the banning had been quite successful for a time)—it was only then, of course, that she had realized that she was pregnant.

Her first thought had been to rid herself of the child before it was born. But her second thought—already she was beginning to pick up more hints of the Emperor's latent power—was that the child might possibly represent an asset later. As usual in her new life as Queen, far-sighted caution had prevailed. She had endured the pregnancy and birth.

There was no doubt of who the father was, despite the baby's fair skin and reddish hair, unlike those of either parent. The Emperor had been her only lover at the time. Besides, the Queen could find redheads recorded on both sides of her own ancestry. As for the Emperor's family . . . who knew? Not any of the wizards she had been able to consult.

One thing certain about him; he had been, still was, a consummate magician. The Silver Queen appreciated that more fully now. At the time, as a girl, she had only begun to recognize the fact.

And even now—actually more often now than in those early years of her reign—the idea kept coming tantalizingly back: what if she actually had married him?

That would have been impossible, of course. Quite socially, politically impossible for a Queen to marry one that the world knew as a demented clown. No matter that the wise and well-educated at least suspected there was more to the Emperor than that. But what if she *had* done it, used her new royal power to make it work? There would of course have had to have been a strong concurrent effort to revive her husband's title in its ancient sense, one of well-nigh supreme power, of puissance beyond that of mere Kings and Queens.

Would she have been acclaimed as a genius of statecraft for marrying him and trying to do that? Only, of course, if it had worked. More likely she would have become a laughingstock.

In any case it was nonsense to think about it now. She had been only a girl then, unwise in the ways of ruling, and how could she ever have made such an attempt succeed?

But *he* might have been able to make it work. What if she had let him rule beside her, had let him try . . .

Maybe, she thought, it was the memory of the Emperor's fierce masculinity that was really bothering her tonight. On top of everything else. There had been something stronger about him in that way than any other man she had ever invited to her cot, though physically he was not particularly big.

Enough. There in the dark privacy of her tent, not giving herself time to think about it, she clasped her right hand firmly on Soulcutter's hilt and drew it halfway from its sheath. Still there was no glow, and still no power flowed from it. Rather the reverse. It was as she had feared and expected it would be, but worse; worse than she had thought or feared. Still she could bear it if she must.

Queen Yambu slammed this most terrible of all Swords back into its sheath, and sighed with relief as the midnight around her appeared to brighten instantly. Then she closed the ornate case around Soulcutter, and got up and went to the tent door to cry orders to break camp and march.

CHAPTER 12

Of course the Dark King knew better, when he stopped to think about it. But through the visualization provided him by the demon he had been able to see Shieldbreaker in Sir Andrew's distant hands only as a kind of war-hammer rather than a Sword, a picture matching the sound that reached Vilkata's ears from that distant combat. Soulcutter Vilkata had not yet seen at all, but he knew that it was there now, somewhere behind him, in the hands of the Silver Queen. He knew it by his magically assisted perception of an emptiness, a presence there to which he was truly blind. Any Sword that he did not own could frighten him, and he owned only one out of the Twelve. And now he found himself between two enemies armed with two Swords that seemed to him particularly powerful.

Between the Mindsword in the Dark King's hands behind them and the Dark King's cavalry in front of them, Sir Andrew's little army had certainly been destroyed. That much had been accomplished. Under ordinary conditions a victory of such magnitude would have been enough to make the King feel truly optimistic. But conditions were not ordinary, if they ever were. There were the two Swords Shieldbreaker and Soulcutter, and himself between them.

When the report came in that the Silver Queen was advancing on his rear, Vilkata sent a flying messenger to recall most of his advanced cavalry, and set about turning his entire army to confront her. It was a decision made with some reluctance, because he longed to go instead to search personally on the battlefield for Shieldbreaker. A flying scout had reported seeing from a distance that Sir Andrew hurled the Sword away from him, when the fight at last was over. And what subordinate did the Dark King dare to trust with succeeding in that search?—but at the same time he dared not fail to meet the Silver Queen's advance with the Mindsword in his own hands. He could not be in two places at once.

Anyway Vilkata did not really believe the report about Sir Andrew throwing Shieldbreaker away. Whether the Sword of Force would be dropped and abandoned by any living person on any battlefield was, in his mind, very doubtful to say the least. In the end he ordered certain patrols to the place where Sir Andrew was last seen, to search for the Sword, or to make what other valuable discoveries they could, while he himself turned back to meet the advancing columns of Yambu.

As it turned out, Yambu's main army was not nearly as close as had been reported. The flying, half-intelligent scouts often had trouble estimating horizontal distances; but the King could not take chances. He had not much more than got his army into motion in that direction, when additional disquieting reports came in. These told of gods and goddesses seen in the vicinity of Tashigang, doing extravagant things in the Dark King's name, and proclaiming him their lord and master, the new ruler of the world. That in itself would have been well enough, but the reports also told of the deities offering him human sacrifice, and holocausts of grain and cattle. Besides the waste of valuable resources, it made Vilkata uneasy to realize that the divinities who had pledged loyalty to him were not really under his control. Should he send word to them of his displeasure? But he did not even know where they were right now. Or where they were going to be next, or what they might be intending to do.

The trouble is, he thought, they worship me but I am not a god. Having arrived at that thought, he felt as if he had made some great, vaguely alarming discovery.

Mark and his escort had not been many days out from Tasavalta when they were forced into a skirmish with a strong patrol of the Dark King's troops. This fight had cost them some casualties. But Coinspinner in Mark's hands, altering the odds of chance in his favor at every turn, saw him and most of his small force through the fighting safely. He had experienced the workings of the Sword of Chance before, and he trusted it—to a degree; it was really the least trustworthy of the Twelve—and felt almost familiar with it. The soldiers of his escort had done neither until now.

When the skirmish was over, the enemy survivors driven into flight, Mark and his troops rested briefly and moved on. He was confident, and the soldiers, who earlier had only grimly obeyed orders, now picked up that attitude from him. Since what he truly wanted now was to locate the Emperor, then to the Emperor Coinspinner's luck would lead him, in one way or another.

As they rode Mark paused periodically to sweep the horizon with the naked tip of the Sword of Chance. When he aimed it in a certain direction, and in that direction only, a quivering seized the blade, and Mark could feel a faint surge of power pass into his hand through the hilt. In that direction was the Emperor. Or, at least, that was the way to go to ultimately reach him.

For several days Mark and his surviving Tasavaltan escort journeyed in safety. Then they began to observe the unmistakable signs of armies near. And then at last there was the noise of a battle close ahead.

From a distance Mark watched an enemy force of overwhelming strength, what he thought had to be the main body of the Dark King's troops, first advance in one direction, then reverse themselves— though not as in defeat, he thought—and trudge in mass formation the other way. The actual fighting had been somewhere beyond them, where he could not see it.

When the enemy had moved out of the way, and almost out of sight, Coinspinner still pointed him toward the place where the battle had been.

When Mark with his small escort reached the battlefield, they found it almost devoid of living things, except for a few scavengers, gathering on wing and afoot. There were a hundred human dead or more, concentrated mostly in one place. Among the fallen Mark could not see a single one in Vilkata's colors. The only livery visible was Sir Andrew's orange and black.

On the field one human figure was still standing. Slightly built, it was garbed in a robe that had once been white, and looked like one of Ardneh's servants who had been through some arduous journey and perhaps a battle or two as well. When Mark first saw it, this figure was bending over one of the dead men who lay a little apart from the others. Then, even as Mark watched, the figure in white began to labor awkwardly at digging—a grave, Mark supposed—using the blade of a long knife.

As Mark and his troops, in the colors of Tasavalta, rode nearer, the figure in white took note of them and stopped what it was doing to await their approach. But it did not try to run.

When Mark got closer, he recognized the isolated dead man as Sir Andrew. In war it was no great surprise, particularly on a field of slaughter like this one, to find a comrade and a leader dead. But still the discovery was no less a shock.

Mark jumped down from his mount and put his hand on the gore-spattered head of the Kind Knight, and remarked his peaceful face. "Ardneh greet you," he muttered, and for a moment at least could feel real hope that it might be so.

Then Mark stood up. Taking Denis for a genuine Ardneh-pilgrim who had probably just wandered onto the scene, Mark asked, "But where are his own people, all slaughtered?" He looked round him at the few score dead. "This can't be his entire army!"

Denis answered. "Many were slaughtered, I fear.

The Dark King's cavalry attacked also, ahead, beyond those hills. The officers remaining are trying to rally whatever troops are left. Sir Andrew's close friends wanted to bury him—what I am trying to do—but they decided Sir Andrew would have wanted them to see to the living first. As I am sure he would."

"You knew him, then?"

The youth in ragged white nodded assent. "I had been with him for some days. I think I came to know him, in a way. I am called Denis the Quick, of Tashigang." And Denis's quick eyes flicked around Mark's escort. "I did not know that there were Tasavaltan troops nearby."

"There are not many. My name is Mark."

Nor had Denis failed to notice the large black hilt at Mark's side. "There was a man of that name who had—and still has, for all I know—much to do with the Twelve Swords. Or so all the stories say. But I didn't know that he was Tasavaltan."

"I am not Tasavaltan, really . . . and yes, I have had much to do with them. Much more than I could wish." Mark sighed.

But even as he spoke, Mark was tiredly, dutifully drawing Coinspinner again. While Denis and the Tasavaltan soldiers watched in alert silence, he swept it once more round the horizon. "That way," Mark muttered, as he resheathed the Blade. "And nearby, now, I think. The feeling in the hilt is strong."

The Sword has pointed in the direction of the abandoned carnival, which was just visible over the nearest gentle rise of ground.

Mark began to walk in the direction of the carnival, leading his mount. His escort followed silently,

THE THIRD BOOK OF SWORDS 221

professionally alert for trouble. Denis hesitated for a moment, then abandoned his gravedigging temporarily and came with them too. The ruined show was only about a hundred meters distant.

Standing on the edge of the area of dilapidated tents and flimsy shelters, Mark looked about him with a frown. "This is very much like . . ."

"What?"

"Nothing." But then Mark hesitated. His voice when he replied again was strained. "Like one carnival in particular that I remember seeing once . . . long ago."

It was of course impossible for him to be certain, but he had a feeling that it was really the same one. Something about the tents, or maybe the names of the performers—though he could not remember any of them consciously—on the few worn, faded signs that were visible.

Yes. Nine years ago, or thereabouts, this very carnival—he thought—had been encamped far from here, in front of what had then been Sir Andrew's castle. That had been the night of Mark's second encounter with a Sword, the night on which someone had thrust Sightblinder into his hands. . . .

One of the mounted Tasavaltan troopers sounded a low whistle, a signal meaning that an enemy had been sighted nearby. Mark forgot the past and sprang alertly into his saddle.

There was barely time to grab for weapons before a patrol of the Dark King's cavalry was upon them. Vilkata's troops abandoned stealth when they saw that they were seen, to come shouting and charging between the tents and flimsy shacks.

Mark, with Coinspinner raised, met one mounted

attacker, a grizzled veteran who fell back wide-eyed when he saw his opponent brandishing a Sword; the magnificent blade made the god-forged weapons unmistakable even when the black hilt with its identifying symbol was hidden in a fist. Other fighting swirled around them. Mark's riding beast was slightly wounded. He had to struggle to control it, as it carried him some little distance where he found himself almost alone. The Sword of Good Luck could create certain difficulties for a leader, even when it perhaps simultaneously saved his life. He waved a signal to such of his Tasavaltan people as he could see, then rode to lead them in a counter-attack around a wooden structure a little larger than the rest of the carnival's components.

In a moment he discovered that his troops had evidently missed or misread his hand signal, and he was for the moment completely alone. Swearing by the anatomies of several gods and goddesses, he was wheeling his mount again, to get back to his troops, when his eye fell on the faded legend over the flimsy building's doorway.

It read:

THE HOUSE OF MIRTH

And just outside the House of Mirth, a man was sitting, waiting for Mark. The man, garbed in dull colors, sat there so quietly on a little bench that Mark had ridden past him once without even noticing his presence. Mark was sure at once that the man was waiting for him, because he was looking at Mark as if he had been expecting him and no one else.

The man on the bench was compactly built, of

indeterminate age, and wrapped in a gray cloak of quiet but now somewhat dusty elegance. His face, Mark thought, was quite calm and also quite ordinary, and he sat there almost meekly, unarmed but with a long empty scabbard at his belt.

Coinspinner pointed straight at the man. Then the Sword seemed to leap and twist in Mark's hand, and he could not retain his hold upon it. The man on the bench had done nothing at all that Mark could see, but the Sword of Chance was no longer in Mark's grip, and the scabbard at the Emperor's side was no longer empty.

Even apart from Coinspinner's evidence, Mark had not the least doubt of who he was facing. He had heard descriptions. He had heard enough to make him wonder if, in spite of himself, he might be awed when this moment came. But in fact the first emotion that Mark felt was anger, and his first words expressed it. They came in a voice that trembled a little with his resentment, and it was not even the taking of the Sword that made him angry.

"You are my father. So my mother has told me."

The Emperor gave no sign of feeling any anger in response to Mark's. He only looked Mark up and down and smiled a little, as if he were basically pleased with what he saw. Then he said: "She told you truly, Mark. You are my son."

"Return my Sword. I need it, and my troops need me."

"Presently. They are managing without you at the moment."

Mark started to get down from his riding beast, meaning to confront the other even more closely. But at the last moment he decided to hold on to whatever advantage remaining mounted might afford him—even though he suspected that would be none at all.

He accused the seated man again. "It was a long time afterward, my mother said, before she realized who you really were. Not until after I was born. You were masked, when you took her. For a while she thought you were Duke Fraktin, that bastard. Playing tricks, like a . . . why did you do that to her? And to my father?"

Mark heard his own voice quiver on the last word. Somehow the accusation had ended more weakly than it had begun.

The Emperor answered him steadily. "I did it, I took her as you say, because I wanted to bring you into being."

"I . . ." It was difficult to find the right words, properly angry and forceful, to answer that.

The man on the bench added: "You are one of my many children, Mark. The Imperial blood flows in your veins."

Again Mark's injured riding beast began to give him trouble, turning restively this way and that. He worked to control it, and told himself that if only he had his Sword he would have turned his back on this man and ridden away, gone back to join the fight. But his Sword was gone. And now as soon as the animal looked directly at the Emperor it quieted. It stood still, facing the man on the bench and trembling faintly.

And is it going to be the same with me? Will I be pacified so easily? Mark wondered. Already his intended fury at this man was weakening.

Mark said; "I have been thinking about that, too. The Imperial blood. If I have it, what does that mean?"

The Emperor stood up slowly. There was still nothing physically impressive or even distinctive about him. He was neither remarkably tall nor short, and, to Mark's dull senses at least, he radiated no aura of magic. As he walked the few paces to stand beside Mark's trembling mount, he drew Coinspinner and casually handed it up to Mark, hilt first. "You will need this, as you say," he remarked, as if in an aside.

And then, as Mark almost dazedly accepted the Sword, the Emperor answered his question. "It means, for one thing, that you have the ordering of demons. More precisely, the ability to order them away, to cast them out. What words, what particular incantation you employ to do so matters little."

Mark slid Coinspinner back into the sheath at his own side. Now he was free to turn and ride away. But he did not. "The demons, yes . . . tell me. There was a girl named Ariane, who was with me once in the Blue Temple dungeon. Who saved me from a demon there. Was she . . . ?"

"Another of my children. Yes. Did she not once think that she recognized you as a brother?"

"She did. Yes." Now even weak anger was ebbing swiftly, could not be called anger any longer. Now it had departed. Leaving . . . what?

Again the Emperor was smiling at him faintly, proudly. "You are a fit husband, Mark, for any Queen on Earth—or any Princess either. I think you are too good for most of them—but then I may be prejudiced. Fathers tend to be." The man in gray stood holding on to Mark's stirrup now, and squinting up at him. "There's something else, isn't there? What else are you trying to ask me?"

Mark blurted out a jumble of words, more or less

connected with the memorized version of Princess Kristin's formal request for an alliance.

"Yes, that's what she sent you after me to do, isn't it? Well, I have a reputation as a prankster, but I can be serious. Tell the Princess, when you see her, that she has an alliance with me as long as she wants it."

There had been another alliance that Mark had meant to ask for. But it was too late now. "Sir Andrew has just been killed."

"I know that."

The calmness in the Emperor's voice seemed inhuman. Suddenly Mark's anger was not dead after all. "He died not half a kilometer from here. If you would be our ally, why aren't you fighting harder on our side? Doing more?"

His father—it was suddenly possible now to think of this man also in those terms—was not surprised by the reproach, or perturbed either. He let go the stirrup, and stroked the riding beast's injured neck. Mark thought he saw, though afterward he was not sure, one of the small wounds there wiped away as if it had been no more than a dead leaf fallen on the skin. Mark's newly acceptable father said, "When you are as old as I am, my son, and able to understand as much, then you can intelligently criticize the way I am behaving now."

The Emperor stretched himself, a weary movement, then moved back a step and looked around. "I think this present skirmish at least is yours. One day you and I will have a long time to talk. But not just now. Now that you have completed your mission for the Princess, I would advise you to get your remaining people to Tashigang, and quickly inside the walls. And warn the people in the city, if they do not already realize it, that an attack is imminent."

"I will." Mark heard himself accepting orders from this man, the same man he had sought for days, meaning to confront in accusation. But this change was not like that brought about by the Mindsword's hideous warping pressure. This inward change, this decision, was his own, for all that it surprised him.

His revitalized mount was already carrying him away. His father waved after him and called: "And you can give them this encouraging news as well— Rostov is bringing the Tasavaltan army to their aid!"

CHAPTER 13

The little column of refugees was composed for the most part of cumbersome carts and loadbeasts, and for several days it had been moving with a nightmarish slowness over the appalling roads. Now and again it left the roads, where a bridge had been destroyed or the only roads ran in the wrong directions, to go trundling off across someone's neglected fields. In this manner the train of carts and wagons had made its way toward Tashigang. The people in the train, all of them villagers or peasants who had been poor even before the war started, were fearful of the Dark King's cavalry, and with good reason. Behind them the land was death and ruin, under a leaden sky hazed at the horizon with the smoke of burning villages. The wooden-wheeled carts groaned with their increasing burden of people who could walk no more, and of the poor belongings that the people were still stubbornly trying to keep. The loadbeasts, in need of food and most of all of rest, uttered their own sounds of protest.

Riding in the second wagon were four people, a man named Birch and his wife Micheline, along with their two small children. The man was driving at the moment, urging on their one loadbeast that pulled the wagon. In general he kept up a running stream of encouraging comments, directed at the animal and at his family indiscriminately. He was not getting too much in the way of answers. His wife had said very little for several days now, and the children were too tired to speak.

Just now the train of wagons was coming to a place where the poor road dipped between hills that had once been wooded, to ford a small, muddy stream. Most of the trees on the hills looked as if they might have been individually hacked at by a hundred axes, then pulled apart by a thousand arms, of people needing firewood or wood for other uses; quite likely someone's army had camped near here not long ago.

The little train of half a dozen wagons and carts now stopped at the ford. All of the travelers wanted to let their animals drink, and the people who were not carrying fresher water with them in their vehicles drank from the stream too. Birch and his family did not get out of their cart. At this point they were not so much thirsty as simply dazed and exhausted.

While the company of refugees was halted thus, a patrol of the Dark King's cavalry did indeed come into sight. Those who were sitting in their wagons or standing beside them held their breath, watching fatalistically. But the patrol was some distance off, and showed little interest in their poor company.

They were greatly relieved. But hardly had the cavalry ridden out of the way when one of the women stood up in her wagon screaming, and pointed in a different direction.

Over one of the nearby hills, studded with its broken trees like stubble on a tough chin, the head and shoulders of a god had just appeared. There was more nearby smoke in the air in that direction, from some farm building on the other side of the hill burning perhaps, or it might have been a haystack or a woodpile smoldering; and the effect of seeing the god's figure through this haziness was somehow to suggest a truly gigantic figure kilometers away, moving about, at the distance of an ordinary horizon.

Birch, the man in the second cart, froze in his position on the driver's seat. His wife, Micheline, who was sitting beside him had clamped a painful grip upon his arm, but he could not have moved in any case. Behind them, peering out from where they had been tucked away amid furniture in the large two-wheeled cart, their two small children were frozen too.

Birch could tell at first glance that the mountainous-looking god coming over the hill was Mars. He could make the identification at once by the great spear and helm and shield of the approaching being's equippage, even though the man had never before seen any deity and had not expected to see one now.

Mars was almost directly ahead of the people in their wagons, advancing toward them from almost the same direction that the train was headed. And the Wargod had certainly taken notice of them already; Birch thought for a moment that those distant eyes were looking directly into his own. Now Mars, marching forward out of the smoke, appeared as no more than three times taller than a man. Now he was lowering his armored helm as if in preparation for battle; and still he tramped thunderously nearer, a moving mountain of a being, kicking stumps and boulders out of his way.

He was descending the near side of the nearest hill now, taller than the treetops of the ruined grove as he moved among them. Before Birch could think of any way he might possibly react, Mars had reached the muddy little ford.

Once there, he raised his arms. Looking preoccupied, as if his divine thoughts were elsewhere, and without preamble or warning, he spitted the man who had been driving the first wagon neatly on his spear, which was as long as a tall tree itself, and only a little thinner. That man's wife and children came spilling around him from their cart, and rolling on the ground as if they could feel the same spear in their own guts.

Mars moved quickly, and came so close that he was hard to see, like a mountain when you were standing on it. Birch felt his own wagon go over next. If that great spear had thrust for him too, it had somehow missed. All Birch could feel was a fall that left him half stunned, and then a growing pain in his leg and hip, and a numbness that threatened to grow into a greater pain still, and the awareness that he could not move. Near him Micheline and the children lay huddled and jumbled in the midst of their spilled belongings. Except for Birch himself they all appeared to be unhurt, but Micheline was gasping and the children whimpering softly in new terror. Still connected to the wagon by the leather straps of the harness, their only loadbeast lay twitching, its whole body crumpled into an impossible position. It had been slaughtered, butchered by a mere gesture from the passing God of War.

Mars' windstorm of a voice roared forth, above the cowering humans' heads: "What's all this talk I hear, these last few years, about twelve special Swords? I've never seen them and I don't want to. What's so great about them, really? Can anyone here answer me that? My war-spear here does the job as neatly as it ever did."

If the god was really talking to the humans he had just trampled, and whether he expected any of his surviving victims to actually enter into a dialogue, Birch never knew. The voice that did rumble an answer back at Mars was deeper and louder by far than any human tones could be. It came rolling down at them from the hillside on the other side of the ford, and it said: "Your spear has failed you before, Wargod. It will again be insufficient."

Birch did not recognize that voice. But Mars did, for Birch saw him turn, with an expression suddenly and almost madly joyful, to face its owner. The God of War cried out: "It is the dog! The great son of a bitch that they call the Lord of Beasts. At last! I have been looking for you for a long time."

Birch was still lying on his back, aware that Micheline and the children were still at his side, and evidently still unhurt; but beyond that he could not think for the moment about himself or his family, nor speak, though his dry lips formed words. Even his own pain and injury were momentarily forgotten. He could only watch. He had never seen a single god in his whole life before, and now here were two at one time.

Lord Draffut came walking downhill, toward the ford and the few crouching, surviving humans, and the poor wreckage that was all that was left of the train of carts. Draffut's towering man-shaped form splashed knee-deep through the small river, now partially dammed by the jumble of wrecked vehicles, murdered loadbeasts and human bodies, all intermingled with the poor useless things that the humans had been trying to carry with them to safety inside the walls of Tashigang. The bloodied water splashed up around those knees of glowing fur, and Birch saw marveling that the elements of water and mud were touched with temporary life wherever the body of Draffut came in contact with them.

"Down on four legs, beast!" the Wargod roared, brandishing his spear at the other god who was as tall as he.

Lord Draffut had nothing more to say to Mars just now. The Beastlord only bared his fangs as he crossed the stream and halted, slightly crouching, almost within reach of the God of War.

The first thrust of the great spear came, too swift and powerful for watching Birch to see it plainly, or for Draffut to ward it in just the way he sought to do. It pierced Draffut's right forearm, but only lightly, in and out near the surface, so that he was still able to catch the spear's shaft in both his hands. A moment later he had wrenched the weapon out of the grasp of Mars completely, and reversed it in his own grip.

Mars had another spear, already magically in hand. The two weapons clashed. Then Draffut thrust again, with such violence that the shield of Mars was transfixed by the blow, and knocked out of the Wargod's grasp, to go rolling away with the spear like some great cartwheel on the end of a broken axle.

Mars cried out, a bellow of rage and fear, thought Birch, not of injury. Even to witness the fear of a god was terrible. In the next moment Mars demonstrated the ability to produce still more spears at will, and had now armed himself with one in each hand.

Draffut lunged at him and closed with him, and locked his massive arms around his great opponent, clamping the arms of Mars against the cuirass protecting the Wargod's body. At the same time Draffut sank his enormous fangs into god-flesh at the base of the thick armored neck. At the touch of the Lord of Beasts, even the magical armor of Mars melted and flowed with life, treacherously exposing the divine flesh that it was meant to guard.

The giants stamped and swayed, the earth quivering beneath their feet; even though his upper arms were pinioned, Mars tried stabbing at his attacker with the spears he held in both his hands. Birch, beyond marveling now, saw how one spearhead was converted by Draffut's life-powers to the giant head of a living serpent, and how the serpent's head struck back at the arm and wrist of the god who held it. Mars shrieked in deafening pain and rage.

Micheline, seeing the fight in her own terms, as an opportunity for human action, demanded of her husband whether he was hurt, whether he could move. Birch, taking his eyes off the contending giants only for a moment, told her that yes, he was hurt, and no, he could not move, and that she should take the children and get on away from here, and come back later when it was safe.

She protested briefly; but when she saw that he really could not move, she did as he had said. The fighting gods were much too busy to notice their departure, or that of any of the other people who could still move.

The spearhead in the right hand of Mars had not been changed by Draffut's touch; it stubbornly refused to flow with life. "You will not melt this weapon down!" Mars cried, and with its bright point and edge he tore open a wound along the shaggy ribs of the Lord of Beasts. And meanwhile Mars had managed to cast the treacherous biting serpent from him.

Now the God of Healing could no longer entirely heal himself. He bled red sparkling blood, from his side and from his wounded arm as well.

Yet he closed with Mars and disarmed him again of his remaining spear. He seized Mars in a wrestler's grip, and lifted him and threw him down on rocks, so that the earth shook with the shock of impact, and the water in the nearby stream leapt up in little spouts.

But as soon as he was free of Draffut's grip, Mars bounced up, a spear once more in each hand, just as before. He was bleeding too, with blood as red as Draffut's, but thicker, and so hot it steamed, rushing out from the place where Draffut's fangs had torn his neck.

Mars said: "You cannot kill a true god, dog-being. We are immortal."

Draffut was approaching him again, closing in slowly and methodically, looking for the best chance to attack. "Hermes died. If I cannot kill you . . . it is not because you are a god. It will be because. . ."

And now again—Birch did not understand, or hope to understand, everything that he was seeing and hearing—it seemed that Mars was capable of fear. "Why?" the Wargod asked.

Draffut answered: "Because there is too much of humanity in you. Human beings are not the gods' creation. You are theirs. You and all your peers who meet in the Ludus Mountains."

This brought on a bluster of roaring and insults from Mars, to which Draffut did not bother to reply. Meanwhile the two giants continued their steady, stealthy circling and stalking of each other.

But, finally, it was as if Draffut's calm statement about humanity had struck deeper than any planned insult. It must have struck so deep as to provoke even the God of War to that ultimate reaction, thought.

Mars rumbled at the other, "What did you mean by that foolishness? That we are their creation?"

"I mean to tell you what I saw, on that day when I stood among you, on the cold mountaintop, with the Sword of Stealth in my hand . . . Sightblinder let me see into the inward nature of the gods, you and the others there. And since then I have known . . . if I could not kill you the last time we fought, and I cannot kill you now, it is because there is in you too much of humanity."

"Bah. That I cannot believe." Mars waved his spears.

Stalking his enemy, bleeding, Draffut said it again. "You did not create them."

"Hah. *That* I can believe. What sort of god would be bothered to do that?"

"They created you."

Mars snorted with divine contempt. "How could such vermin ever create anything?"

"Through their dreams. Their dreams are very powerful."

The two titans closed with each other again, and fought, and again both of them were wounded. And again they both were weakened.

The only human observer left to watch them now was the man named Birch. He would certainly have crept away by now, too, with his wife and children, if he had been able to move. But he could not move. And by now he was no longer even thinking particularly of his own fate. He watched the fight until he fainted, and when he recovered his senses he watched again, for the fight was still in progress. When his thirst became overpowering, he made a great effort and managed to turn and twist himself enough to get a drink from the muddied, bloodied water of the small stream. Then he lay back and kept his mind off his own pain and injury by watching the fight some more.

The sun set on the struggle. It went on, with pauses—Birch supposed that even gods in this kind of agony must rest—through the night. The dark was filled with titanic thrashings and groanings, and splashing in the river where it gurgled gorily and patiently over and around the new dam that had been made out of human disaster.

At least, Birch told himself in his more lucid moments, he was not going to have to worry about predatory animals coming and trying to make a meal of him as he lay wounded. What ordinary beast would dare approach this scene?

When dawn came, Birch found himself still alive, somewhat to his own surprise. In the new daylight he beheld the ground, over the entire area around the ford, littered with broken spearshafts and spearheads, and with monstrous dead or lethargic serpents that had once been spears, all relics of the fight that still went on.

Or did it? This latest interval of silence seemed to be lasting for a longer time than usual—

There was a great, startling, earth-quivering crash, somewhere nearby, just out of Birch's sight, behind some overturned and smashed-up wagons that screened a large part of his field of vision. The ground shook with the renewed fight, which once more seemed to terminate in a final splash. In a moment the watching human was able to see and feel the waves indicating that the two combatants, still locked together, had plunged into the partially dammed pool of the river.

Now for a time Birch could no longer hear them fighting, except for occasional splashes that gradually decreased in violence. But now he could hear the two gods breathing. Ought gods to have to breathe? Birch wondered groggily. Maybe they only did it when they chose, like eating and drinking. Maybe they only did it when they needed extra strength.

Time passed in near silence. Then as the newly risen sun crept higher in the sky, a shadow fell across Birch where he lay. The man opened his eyes, to behold the figure of yet another god. Thank Ardneh, this one had not yet noticed the surviving human either.

Birch knew at once, by the leather-like smith's apron worn by the newcomer, and by the twisted leg, that this was Vulcan. The lame god was wearing at his side two great, blackhilted Swords, looking like mere daggers against the gray bulk of his body. He squatted on his haunches, looking down into the pool where the two fighters had gone out of Birch's field of vision. Now there was a renewed stirring in the pool, at last. A muttering, a splash. A great grin spread across the face of the Smith as he stood up and leisurely approached the combat a little more closely. Before he sat down again, on a rock, he kicked a broken cart out of his way. This incidentally cleared the field of view for the injured man, of whose existence none of the three giants had yet taken the least notice.

"Hail, oh mighty Wargod!" The salutation came from Vulcan in tones of gigantic mockery. "The world awaits your conquering presence. Have you not dallied here long enough? What are you doing down there, exactly—bathing your pet dog in the mud?"

Birch could see now how red the mud and water were around them both. Of the two combatants, Draffut could no longer fight, could hardly move. The God of War was little better off than his bedraggled foe. But now, slowly, terribly, with great gasping efforts, Mars dragged himself free of his opponent's biting, crushing grip, and stood erect, ankle-deep in mud.

When the Wargod tried to speak his voice was half-inaudible, failing altogether on some words. It seemed that he could barely lift the arm that he stretched out to Vulcan. "A spear—a weapon—I have no more spears. Lend me your Sword, Smith.

One of them, I see that you have two. This business must be finished."

Vulcan sighed, producing a sound like that of wind rushing through a smoldering forge. He remained where he was, still some twenty meters or so distant from the other two. "Give you a weapon, hey? Well, I suppose I must, since you appear to be the victor in this shabby business after all. How tiresome."

Mars, though tottering on his feet, managed to draw himself a little more fully erect.

"How mannered you suddenly grow, Blacksmith. How fond you suddenly are of trying to appear clever. Why should that be? But never mind. Put steel here in my hand, and I'll finish this dirty job."

"I grant you," said Vulcan, "there is a need that certain things be finished." And the Smith stood up from where he had been sitting, and his ornaments of dragons' scales tinkled as he chose and drew one of his Swords.

" 'For thy heart'," he quoted softly, clasping and hiding the black hilt delicately in his great, gray, hardened blaksmith's hand. He held the Sword up straight, looking at it almost lovingly. " 'For thy heart, who hast wronged me.' "

"Wait," said Mars, staring at him with a suddenly new expression. "What Sword is—?"

His answer did not come in words. Vulcan was moving into a strange revolving dance, his whole body turning ponderously, great sandaled feet stamping rock and mud along the wagon trail, flattening earth that was already trodden and beaten and bloody from the fight, squashing the already dying serpents that had once been spears. The

Sword in the Smith's extended arm was glowing now, and it was howling like the bull-roarer of some primitive magician.

Mars, half-dead or not, was suddenly galvanized. He sprang into motion, fleeing, running away. Running as only a god can run, Mars went ducking and twisting his way through the remnants of the hillside grove. He dodged among great splintered treetrunks, and splintering further those trees that got in his way.

Birch saw Vulcan throw the Sword, or rather let it go. After the Smith released it, the power that propelled it came only from within itself. The speed of Mars' flight was great, but the Sword was only a white streak through the air. Virtually instantaneously it followed the curving track of the Wargod's flight.

At the last moment, Mars turned to face doom bravely, and somehow he was able to summon yet one more spear into his hand. But even his magic spear of war availed him nothing against the Sword of Vengeance. The white streak ended abruptly, with the sound of a sharp impact.

Even with Farslayer embedded in his heart, Mars raised his spear, and took one stumbling step toward the god who had destroyed him. But then he could only cry a curse, and fall. He was dead before he struck the earth, and he demolished one more live tree in his falling. That last tree deflected the Wargod's toppling body, so that he turned before his landing shook the earth, and ended sprawling on his back. Only the black hilt and a handsbreadth of Farslayer's bright blade protruded from the armored breastplate on his chest.

CHAPTER 14

At the largest land gate in the walls of Tashigang, which was the Hermes Gate giving onto the great highway called the High Road, one thin stream of worried citizens was trying to get out of the city when Mark and Denis arrived, while another group, this one of country refugees, worked and pleaded to get in. There was obviously no general agreement on the safest place to be during the war that everyone thought was coming. The Watch on duty at the Hermes Gate were implacably forbidding the removal of foodstuffs, or anything that could be construed as military or medical supplies, while at the same time denying entrance to many of the outsiders. To gain entrance to the city it was necessary to show pressing business—other than that of one's own survival, which did not necessarily concern the Watch—or to bring in some substantial material contribution to the city's ability to withstand a siege. Denis, on identifying himself as an agent of the House of Courtenay, was admitted with no further argument. And Mark, along with his escort, was passed as a representative of Tasavalta, as his and his soldiers' blue-green clothing testified.

Mark thought that some of the Watch on duty at the gate recognized Coinspinner at his side—it was not mentioned, but he suspected that the fact of the Sword's presence was quickly communicated to the Lord Mayor. Mark informed the officer who spoke to him that he too could be reached at the House of Courtenay, and alerted the guardians of the gate to expect the survivors of Sir Andrew's army. That group, two or three hundred strong, was traveling a few hours behind Mark and Denis; it would, they agreed, make a welcome addition to the city's garrison, that Denis said was chronically undermanned.

It was the first time Mark had ever entered a city as large as this one—he had heard some say that there were none larger—and he saw much to wonder at as Denis conducted him and his handful of Tasavaltan troopers through the broad avenues and streets. This was also, of course, the first time that Mark had seen the House of Courtenay, and he was duly impressed by the wealth and luxury in which his old friends Barbara and Ben were living. But he was given little time today in which to be impressed by that. The household, like the rest of the great city around it, was in a state of turmoil and tension. Soon after entering Mark got the impression that none of its members knew as yet whether they were preparing for war and siege, or for evacuation. Packing of certain valuables as if for possible evacuation was being undertaken, by a force of what Mark estimated as at least a dozen servants and other workers, while simultaneously

another group barricaded all but a few of the doors
and windows as if in expectation that the House
must undergo a siege.

Almost immediately on entering the building's
ground floor, coming into the clamorous confusion
of what must be a workshop, Denis immediately
became engaged in conversation with a man he
introduced to Mark as the steward of the household, named Tarim.

Denis was already aghast at some of the things
Tarim was telling him.

"Evacuation? Tashigang? Don't tell me they're
seriously considering such a thing."

"We have heard something of the Mindsword's
power," said Tarim worriedly. He turned his aging,
troubled eyes toward Mark. "Perhaps you gentle-
men who travel out in the great world have heard
something of it too."

Denis was impatient. "I think we've some idea
about it, yes. But we're not helpless, there are other
weapons, other Swords. We've even brought one
with us . . . and if they evacuate this city, half a mil-
lion people or however many there are, where will
they all go?"

Tarim shrugged fatalistically. "Flee to the upper
hills, I suppose, or the Great Swamp. I didn't say
that it made sense to evacuate."

Someone else had just entered the ground floor
room. Turning, Mark saw the man who all his life
he had thought of as his father. Who was his father,
he told himself, in every sense that truly mattered.

And so Mark called him at first sight. For the time
being, the Emperor was forgotten.

Mark had been only twelve the last time he saw
Jord, then lying apparently dead in their village

street. But there was no mistaking Jord, for the older man had changed very little. Except for being dressed now in finer garments than Mark had ever seen him wear before. And except for . . .

The really exceptional transformation was so enormous, and at the same time appeared so right and ordinary, that Mark at first glance came near accepting it as natural, and not a change at all. Then, after their first embrace, he wonderingly held his father at arms' length.

Jord now had two arms.

Mark's father said to him, "What the Swords took from me, they have given back. I'm told that Woundhealer was used to heal me as I lay here injured and unconscious. It did a better job even than those who used it had hoped."

"The Sword of Mercy has touched me too," Mark whispered. And then for a little time he could only stand there marveling at his father's new right arm. Jord explained to Mark how the arm had begun as a mere fleshy swelling, then a bud, and then in a matter of a few months had passed through the normal stages of human growth, being first a limb of baby size, then one to fit a child. It was as large and strong as the left arm now, but the skin of the new limb was still pink and almost unweathered even on the hand, not scarred or worn by age like that on Jord's left fist, visible below the sleeve of his fine new shirt.

Suddenly Mark said, "I've just come from seeing Mother, and Marian. When they hear you have a new arm . . ."

The two of them, father and son, had many things to talk about. Some things that were perhaps of even greater importance than a new arm—and

Mark still had one problem to think about that he was never going to mention to this man. But they were allowed little time just now for talk. Ben and Barbara were arriving from somewhere in the upper interior of the house to give Mark a joyful welcome.

Barbara jumped at him, so that he had to catch and swing her. She threw wiry arms around his neck and kissed him powerfully, so that he held her, as he had Jord, at arms' length for a moment, wondering if in her case too there had taken place some change so great as to be invisible at first glance. But then he had to drop her, for Ben, less demonstrative as a rule, came to almost crush Mark in a great hug.

They were followed by a plump nursemaid, introduced to Mark as Kuan-yin who was carrying their small child Beth. The toddler was obviously already a great friend of Jord's, for she went to him at once and asked him how his new arm was.

Kuan-yin, released from immediate duty, at once went a little apart with Denis. Mark could see that the two of them, standing face to face amid the confusion of workers packing and barricading, had their own private greetings to exchange.

"We'd like to get a welcoming party for you started right away," Ben was saying to Mark, "but we can't. It'll have to wait at least until tomorrow. The Lord Mayor has called a council of leading citizens, and Barbara and I are invited. Substantial people now, you know. Master and Lady Courtenay. And the Mayor knows we have some kind of a hoard of weapons, to help defend . . . what's that at your side?"

Ben grabbed the sheath, and looked at the Sword's hilt. "Thank Ardneh, Coinspinner! We've got to go to that meeting, and you've got to come too, and bring this tool along, to see that they don't decide on some damned foolishness like surrendering. You'll be welcome, bringing word from outside as you do. And also as a representative of Tasavalta. And bringing another Sword . . . that'll stiffen up their spines. Townsaver is in town already."

Mark grinned at him. "Doomgiver is on the way."

"Thank all the gods!" Holding Mark by the arm, Ben lowered his voice for a moment. "We can't surrender, and we certainly can't evacuate. Imagine trying to take a three-year-old on that . . . you and I know what it would be like. But if the rest of the city goes, we'll have to try."

The Lord Mayor's palace, like every other part of the city that Mark had seen so far, was a scene of energetic, confused, and doubtfully productive activity. Here as elsewhere the inhabitants appeared to be striving to make ready for some all-out effort, whose nature they had not yet been able to decide upon.

Mark, Ben, and Barbara were admitted readily enough at the main doorway of the Palace. This was a building somewhat similar to the House of Courtenay, though even larger and more sumptuous, and with reception rooms and offices on the ground floor instead of workshop space. Soon they were conducted up a broad curving stair of marble, past workmen descending with newly crated works of art.

On the way, Mark's friends were trying to bring

him up to date on the situation that they were about to encounter.

"We're likely," Ben warned, "to run into our old friend Hyrcanus at this meeting."

Mark almost missed his footing on the stair. "Hyrcanus? Is he still Chief Priest at the Blue Temple? But he—"

"He still is," Barbara assured him. "And the Blue Temple is an important faction here in Tashigang."

"I suppose they must be. But I never thought about it until now," Mark murmured. "Hyrcanus. I remember hearing somewhere that he was certain to be deposed. I thought he was gone by now, it's four years since we robbed him. Plundered his deepest rathole, as nobody else has ever done before or since."

"Thank all the gods for that rathole," Barbara murmured. "And send us another like it. A handful of its contents has done well for Ben and me. I hear that the Temple are now considering moving their main hoard of treasure into Tashigang. We just wanted to warn you, Hyrcanus will probably be here, and he won't be happy to see us."

"He thinks I'm dead," Mark murmured. But it was too late now to try to preserve that happy state of affairs.

They had now reached the door of the conference room, a large, well-appointed chamber on an upper floor, and were ushered in without delay. Even after being warned it was a shock for Mark to behold Hyrcanus with his own eyes; it was the first time that he had ever actually seen the man, but there was no doubt in Mark's mind who he was. The Blue Temple's Chairman and High Priest, having survived the efforts that must certainly have been made to depose him after the sacrilegious robbery of the Temple's main hoard four years ago, was still in charge, and had indeed come here today for the Lord Mayor's conference.

Hyrcanus, the High Priest, small, bald, and rubicund, his face as usual jovial, looked up as the three of them entered. His cheerful smile did not exactly disappear, but froze. He must have recognized Ben, at least, by description, at first sight.

The Chairman studied Mark too, and could hardly fail to identify him also, especially as their escort announced his name along with the others in a loud voice. The others who were gathered round the table, a dozen or so men and women, mostly the solid citizens of Tashigang, rose to return greetings and extend a welcome to the new arrivals. Their faces were cheered, Mark thought, at the sight of the Tasavaltan green and blue that he still wore. And their expressions altered still more, with new hope and calculation, at the sight of the black hilt at his side. Mark let his left hand rest upon it, loosely, casually; he did not want Hyrcanus, at least, to be able to read which white symbol marked that hilt.

Mark supposed the fact that he was appearing in Tasavaltan colors might at least give the cheery-looking old bastard pause, and perhaps cause him to at least delay the next assassination attempt.

The Lord Mayor, named Okada, was a clerkish-looking man on whom the robes of his high office looked faintly preposterous. Yet he presided firmly. The arrival of Mark, Ben, and Barbara had interrupted Hyrcanus in the midst of a speech, which he now resumed, at the Mayor's suggestion.

It was soon apparent as Hyrcanus spoke that the

Blue Temple Chairman's thoughts were not now on revenge and punishment of past transgressors, but, as usual, were concentrated on how best he could contrive to save the bulk of the Blue Temple's treasure. A siege of the city, a storming of the walls, were to be avoided at all costs—at least at all costs to others outside the Blue Temple. Mark, listening, assumed that Hyrcanus had already made some arrangement, or thought he had, with the Dark King, by which the Blue Temple holdings in Tashigang would be secure, in exchange for co-operation with the conqueror.

Mark could recognize one other face at the council table, though no reminiscences were exchanged in this case either. Baron Amintor was here as the personal representative of the Silver Queen. He recognized Mark also, and gazed at him in a newly friendly way, while Mark looked stonily at this old enemy of Sir Andrew. The Baron, Mark was sure, recognized Ben and Barbara as well.

Hyrcanus continued the speech he had begun, urging that one of two courses be adopted: either outright surrender to the Dark King, or else the declaration of Tashigang as an open city. That last, Mark thought, must amount, in practical terms, to the same thing as surrender.

The speech of the High Priest did not evoke any particular enthusiasm among the citizens of Tashigang who made up the majority of his listeners. But neither were they vocal in immediate objection; rather the burghers seemed to be waiting to hear more. Now and again their eyes strayed toward the black hilt at Mark's side.

Hyrcanus might have gone on and on indefinitely, but Mayor Okada at length firmly reclaimed the floor. Who, he asked, wanted to speak next?

Baron Amintor had been impatiently waiting for his chance. Now he arose, and as representative of the Silver Queen, argued eloquently that the city must be defended to the last fighter. Though he was careful, Mark observed, not to put it in exactly those terms. Rather the Baron was strongly reassuring about the walls, the city's history and tradition of successful resistance to outside attack, and about the commitment of the Silver Queen to their defense.

Hyrcanus interrupted him at one point to object. "What about the Mindsword, though? What are any walls against that?"

Amintor took the objection in stride, and assured the others that Yambu was not without her own supremely powerful weapon. "In her wisdom and reluctance to do harm, she has not employed it as yet. But, faced with the Mindsword . . . I am sure she will do whatever she must do to assure the safety of Tashigang."

One of the burghers rose. "When you mention this weapon that the Queen has, you are speaking of the Sword called Soulcutter, or sometimes the Tyrant's Blade, are you not?"

"I am." If Amintor was offended by the plain use of that second name, he did not show it.

"I know little about it." The questioner looked around the table. "Nor, I suppose, do many of us here. What can it do to protect Tashigang?"

Amintor glanced only for a moment at Hyrcanus. "I would prefer not to go into tactical details regarding any of the Swords just now," the Baron answered smoothly. He almost winked at Mark, who carried Coinspinner, as if they had been old comrades instead of enemies. "Later, under conditions of greater security, if you like. I will say now only that the Queen is wise and compassionate"—for some reason, no one in the room laughed—"and that she will not use such a weapon as Soulcutter carelessly. But neither will she allow this city that she so loves to be taken by its enemies."

Mark had to admit to himself that he had little or no idea what Soulcutter might do. It was the one Sword of the Twelve that he had never seen, let alone had in his possession. Almost all he knew of it was contained in the verse that everyone had heard:

> *The Tyrant's Blade no blood hath spilled*
> *But doth the spirit carve*
> *Soulcutter hath no body killed*
> *But many left to starve.*

Glancing at Ben and Barbara, he read an equal lack of knowledge in their faces.

The Lord Mayor now looked at Mark expectantly. It was time that the meeting heard from the emissary from Tasavalta.

Mark stood up from his chair and leaned his hands on the table in front of him. With faith in what the Emperor had told him, he was able to announce that the Tasavaltan army was on the march, under the direct command of General Rostov, coming to the city's relief. Rostov's was an impressive name, one fit to go with the reputation of the walls of Tashigang itself, and once again most of the faces around the table appeared somewhat cheered. That the Tasavaltan army also was small by comparison with the Dark King's host was not mentioned at the moment, though everybody knew it. Even should the Silver Queen arrive with her army at the same time, Vilkata would still have the advantage of numbers.

"Does anyone else have anything to say?" the Lord Mayor asked. "Anyone else, who has not spoken yet?"

Ben spoke briefly, and Barbara after him. They added nothing really new to the discussion, but reminded everyone again of the city's tradition and promised to help arm the defense from their store of weapons. Before she spoke, Barbara faced Mark momentarily, and her lips formed the one word: *Doomgiver?*

Mark shook his head very slightly. He wanted to keep that news in reserve, to stiffen the council's resolve if they should be swayed toward surrender after all. Right now he judged that was unlikely.

Shortly after Barbara spoke, the Mayor called for a show of hands. "How many are ready to fight for our city?"

Only one hand was not raised. Hyrcanus sent black looks at Ben, and Mark, and Amintor.

Before the Chairman of the Blue Temple could make a final statement and a dramatic exit, an aide to the Mayor entered to announce the arrival of a flying courier with a message for the Lord Mayor. The courier and message container were both marked with the black and silver insignia of Queen Yambu herself.

The beast-courier—Mark recognized it as one of a hybrid species prevented, in the interests of secrecy, from ever acquiring speech—was brought into the room. The message capsule of light metal was opened and the paper inside unfolded.

Okada read through the single sheet alone, in anxious silence; then he raised his head.

"It is indeed from her most puissant Majesty, the Silver Queen herself, and, as the marking on the capsule indicated, addressed personally to me. I will not read the entire message aloud just now; it contains certain matters I do not need to proclaim in council." There followed a look at Hyrcanus, to say wordlessly that important military secrets were not going to be announced in front of him, not in view of the attitude he had just taken. The Mayor continued: "But, there are other parts that I think we all should hear at once."

The Silver Queen's words that the Mayor read were very firm, and could be called inspiring in terms of fear if not otherwise: there was to be no talk of surrendering the city, under penalty of incurring her severe displeasure.

Her message also confirmed that she was already on the march with her army, coming to the relief of this her greatest city—as she put it, indeed the greatest and proudest city in the world. And that she intended to achieve victory by whatever means were necessary.

Hyrcanus walked out. He did it unhurriedly, almost courteously, with considerable dignity, Mark had to admit. The High Priest did not waste time on threats, now that it would have been obviously useless and even dangerous to do so; a behavior somehow, at this stage, thought Mark, more ominous than any threats would be.

The Lord Mayor, looking thoughtfully after the High Priest, was evidently of the same opinion.

Okada immediately called in an officer of the Watch from just outside the conference room, and calmly gave the order to arrest the High Priest before he could get out of the Palace; once out, he would easily be able to give some signal to his troops. The Blue Temple Guards in the city, Ben had said, were one of the largest trained fighting forces within the walls.

Now it became at least possible for the council to discuss the city's means of defense in more detail, without the virtual certainty that a potential enemy was listening and taking part in the debate.

Amintor immediately put forward a plan to neutralize the Blue Temple troops by meeting any attempt on their part to rescue Hyrcanus with a countermove against the local Temple and its vaults, whipping up a street mob for the purpose if no regular forces could be spared. Barbara whispered to Mark that Denis would probably be a good man to see to the organization of such an effort.

In succeeding discussion, it quickly became plain that the key to the regular defense of the city's walls against attack from outside would be the Watch, a small but well-trained body of regular troops loyal to the Lord Mayor. They were only a few hundred strong against Vilkata's thousands, but their numbers could be augmented by calling up the city's militia. Ben whispered to Mark that the quality of the militia was, regrettably, not so high as it might be. But certainly the city's long tradition of defending itself ought to help.

Then there were the fragments of Sir Andrew's army to be considered, the survivors who had followed Denis and Mark to Tashigang, along with the ten or a dozen at most of Mark's surviving Tasavaltan escort. Mark could assure the Lord Mayor that Sir Andrew's people were all good, experienced fighters, though at present somewhat demoralized by the sad death of their noble leader. Given the chance, they would be eager to exact revenge.

Mark revealed now that the Sword he wore at his side was Coinspinner, and he proposed that they consult the Sword of Chance at once to try to determine the best means of obtaining a successful defense of the city. All were agreeable; and all, particularly those who had never seen a Sword before, were impressed by the sight when Mark drew his.

"It points . . . that way. What's there?"

They soon determined that something outside the room was being indicated. They had to leave the council room, and then go up on the roof of the Palace to make sure.

The Sword of Chance was pointing at someone or something outside the city walls, in fact at the very center of Vilkata's advancing army. The Dark King's force had just now come barely into sight, through distant summer haze. It was still, Mark thought, well out of Mindsword range.

And Coinspinner pointed as if to Vilkata himself. Mark looked at Ben, and got back a look of awe and calculation mingled.

CHAPTER 15

The delegation from the palace, two women and one man, arrived at Mala's door very quietly and unexpectedly. It was the afternoon after she heard of Mark's departure from Tasavalta on a mission for the Princess. Her first thought on seeing the strangers at her door was that something terrible had happened to her son or her husband, or to both; but before she could even form the question, one of the women was assuring her that as far as was known, both were well. The three of them had come to conduct Mala to the palace, because the Princess herself wanted to see her.

The Palace was not far above the town, and less than an hour later Mala was there, walking in an elaborate flower garden, open within high walls. The garden had tall flowering trees in it, and strange animals to gape at, hybrid creatures such as the highborn liked to amuse themselves with, climbing and flying amid high branches.

Mala was left alone in the garden, but only for a

few moments. Then a certain fat man appeared, well dressed and with an aura of magic about him. He introduced himself as Karel, which name meant nothing to Mala; and he, though obviously a person of some importance, appeared quite content that it should be so. He walked along the garden path with Mala, and asked her about her family, and tried to put her at her ease. That he succeeded as well as he did was a tribute to his skill.

And then he asked her, in his rich, soft voice: "Do you know the Sword of Mercy? Or Sword of Love, as it is sometimes called?"

"I know of it, sir, of course; you must know who my husband is. But if you mean have I ever seen it, no."

"Then have you any idea where it is, at this moment? Hey?" Karel's gaze at her was suddenly much more intense, though he was still trying to appear kind.

"When my son was here, there was a story going about that he—and the Princess—had brought it with them to Tasavalta. But he himself said nothing to me of that, and I did not ask him. I knew better than to be curious about state secrets. Nor could I guess where it is now."

Karel continued to gaze at her with a steady intensity. "He did bring it, and it was here yesterday after he left. That's no state secret." The magician suddenly ceased to stare at her. Shaking his head, he looked away. "And now it's gone, and I don't know where it is either. And whether that ought to be a secret or not . . ." He sighed, letting the words trail off.

Mala felt vaguely frightened. "I don't know either, sir."

"No, of course you don't. I believe you, dear lady, now that I have looked at you closely . . . and there is one other matter that I want to ask you about."

Her frightened look said that she could hardly stop him.

He sighed again. "Here, sit down." And he led her to a nearby marble bench, and sat on it beside her, puffing with relief when his weight came off his feet. "No harm will come to you or Mark for a truthful answer, whatever it may be. I think I know already, but I must be sure . . . who is Mark's real father?"

Under the circumstances the story of more than twenty years ago came out. Mala had thought at the time that the man might be Duke Fraktin. Later she had been convinced that it was not. And later still, slowly and gradually, the truth had dawned.

"But sir, I beg you, my husband . . . Jord . . . he mustn't know. He's never guessed. Mark is his only living son. He . . ."

"Hmmm," said Karel. And then he said: "Jord has served us well. We will do all we can for him. The Princess is waiting to see you. I told her that I wished to speak to you first."

The magician heaved himself up ponderously from the bench, and guided Mala through an ornamental gate, and into another, smaller garden, where there were benches that looked like crystal instead of marble, and paths of what looked like gravel but was too soft for stone; and here the Princess was standing waiting for her.

She looks like a nice girl, was one idea that stood out clearly in the confusion of Mala's thoughts.

Kristin had been hopelessly curious as to what

the mother of the man she loved was like; this was largely because she was still curious as to what Mark himself was like, having had little time in which to get to know him. It was all very well to order herself, with royal commands, to forget about him. To insist that Mark was her lover no longer, that if she ever saw him again it would only be in passing, in some remote and official contact; but somehow all these royal commands meant nothing, when the chance arose to talk to Mark's mother in line of duty, in this matter of the Swords.

When the minimum necessary formalities had been got through, the two women were left sitting alone on one of the crystal benches, and Karel had gracefully retired; not, Kristin was sure, that he was not listening. She knew Karel of old, and the fat wizard had more on his mind just now than Swords, or a missing Sword, important though those matters were.

Mala was saying to her: "I had hoped that one day I would get the chance to talk to you, Highness. But I did not want to seem to be a scheming mother, trying to get advantage for her son."

"You are not that, I am sure . . . unless you are scheming for Mark's safety only. Any mother would do that."

Kristin had questions to ask, about Mala, Jord, their family; when she asked about Mark's father, she thought that his mother looked at her strangely; but then how else would the woman look, being brought here suddenly like this, to talk to royalty?

And the questions kept coming back to Mark himself.

More time had passed than Kristin had realized,

but sill not very much time, when there was an interruption, a twittering from an observant small beast high in a branch above them.

Kristin swore, softly and wearily. "There is now a general who insists on seeing me, if I have learned to interpret these jabbering signals correctly. I have so much to do, and all at once." She seized Mala by the hands. "I want to talk to you again, and soon."

A minute later, Mala was gone, and Kristin was receiving General Rostov.

The General began by reporting, in his gravelly voice, that the man Jord had a good reputation in the Intelligence branch. There was no actual Tasavaltan dossier on the son as yet—rather, one had just been started—but he seemed to have a good reputation with Sir Andrew's people. And a long and strange and intimate connection with the Swords, as Jord did too, of course.

"Nothing to connect either of them, though, Highness, with the disappearance of Woundhealer."

"No, I should think not, General . . . now what are your military plans?"

Rostov drew himself up. "It's like this, Highness. The best place to defend your house is not in your front yard, but down the road as far as you can manage it. *If* you can manage it that way."

"If that is a final . . . what is it, Karel?"

The wizard had reappeared at the ornamental gate. "A matter of state, Highness. You had better hear it before completing any other plans, military or otherwise."

"One moment," said the Princess, and faced back to Rostov. "I believe you, General. And I have decided to go with you. If you are saying that the army must march to Tashigang, because that is where the fate of our people is being decided, then that is the place for me to be also."

Choking in an effort to keep from swearing, General Rostov disputed this idea as firmly as he was able.

"Both of you," said Karel, "had better hear me first. What I have to say is connected with the woman who was just here."

CHAPTER 16

They were kilometers in length, and tall as palaces. They wound uphill and down, in a great tail-swallowing circle, in curves like the back of the legendary Great Worm Yilgarn. They were the walls of Tashigang, and at long last they stood before him.

The taking of the city, even the planning of its capture, were turning out to present considerably greater problems than the Dark King had earlier envisioned. He had once pictured himself simply riding up to the main gate on the Hermes Road, and brandishing the Mindsword in the faces of the garrison, who had been conveniently assembled for him on the battlements. Then, after a delay no longer than the time required for his new slaves in the city to open up the gate, he would enter in triumph, to see to the disposal of his new treasure and the elimination of some of his old enemies.

That last part of the vision had been the first part to turn unreal and unconvincing, which it did almost as soon as Vilkata began to think about it. The Mindsword would seem to rob revenge almost entirely of its satisfaction. If one's old enemies had now become one's loyal slaves, about as faithful as human beings could be, then what was the point of destroying or damaging them?

In any case, Vilkata could see now that Tashigang was not going to fall into his hands as neatly as all that. On the last night of his march toward the city, the night before he first faced the ancient serpentine walls directly, the Dark King had received a warning from his demonic counselors. They had determined, they said, that the Sword Doomgiver had just been carried inside the city's walls, where it was now in the possession of some of the most fanatical defenders. Therefore he, the Dark King, stood in danger of having his most powerful magic—aye, even the power of the Mindsword— turned against him when he tried to use it in an attack.

After receiving this grim caution, Vilkata sat in blind silence for a time, dispensing with the demon's vision the better to concentrate on his own thoughts. Meanwhile those of his human counselors who were attending him waited in their own tremulous silence around him, fearing his wrath, as they imagined that he still listened to the demonic voices that only he could hear.

The Dark King tried to imagine the direst warnings of his inhuman magical counselors coming true. It would mean the devotion of all his own troops would turn to hatred. And also, perhaps, it would mean all of the evil that he had ever worked on anyone now within the walls of Tashigang coming back on himself, suddenly, to strike him down.

And he was warned, too, that the Sword Townsaver might also be within the city. The Sword of
Fury in itself ought not to blunt the Mindsword's
power. But what Townsaver might do, to any
portion of an attacking army that came within a
bladelength of its wielder, was enough in itself to
give a field commander pause.

The Dark King shuddered, the fear that was
never far below the surface of his thoughts suddenly coming near the surface. As he shuddered, the
humans watching him thought that he was still listening to the demons' speech.

And then, there was the matter of Farslayer, too.
Until he had that particular weapon safely in his
hands, he had to be concerned about it. Any monarch, any man, who dealt consistently in such great
affairs as King Vilkata did, was bound to make enemies and would have to be concerned. There were
always plenty of short-sighted, vengeful little folk
about . . . and neither the Dark King's wizards nor
his immaterial demons could give him any idea of
who possessed the Sword of Vengeance now.

If only he had been able to pick up Shieldbreaker
from the field of battle! But no, another distraction,
another threat, had intervened to prevent that. And
now no one could tell him where that trump of
weapons was located either.

Coinspinner was another potential problem. It,
too, was now thought by the Dark King's magical
advisers to be present inside the walls of Tashigang.
And he was sure that the Sword of Chance would
bring those damned impertinent rascals good luck,
good fortune of some kind, even in the face of the
Mindsword's influence. Vilkata kept trying to

imagine what kind of good luck that would be.
Whatever it was, it would not be good for him.

But despite all of the obstacles and objections, he
could be royally stubborn, and he was going forward. None of his fears were great enough to prevent that. In the end he decided to keep his own
supernal weapons under wraps for the time being,
and to try what he might to induce the city to surrender under threats.

The afternoon he arrived before the walls, he had
his great pavilion erected within easy sight of
them—though not, of corse, within missile range.
At the same time Vilkata ordered a complete envel-
opment of the city, and entrenchment by his troops,
as if for a lengthy siege, all along their encircling
lines.

Even his great host was thinly spread by such a
maneuver, which necessitated occupying a line
several kilometers long; but Vilkata intended to
concentrate most of his troops in a few places later,
if and when it actually became necessary to assault
the walls. Meanwhile he wanted to give an impression not only of overwhelming force but of
unhurried determination. And still he was not
satisfied that things were going well; he kept urging
both his scouts and his wizards to provide him with
more information.

At dusk on the second day of the siege, the Dark
King's vaguely growing sense of some impending
doom was suddenly relieved. The last flying messenger to arrive during daylight hours brought in a
report saying that the troublesome Beastlord
Draffut was finally dead, and the god Mars—who
was also troublesome, because he had managed to
remain free of the Mindsword's control—was dead

with him. And that Vulcan, triumphant over both of them, was headed toward the city of Tashigang, waving the Sword Shieldbreaker and crying his own eternal loyalty to the Dark King.

When the half-intelligent courier was asked to predict the time of the god's arrival, it gave answers interpreted to mean that the progress of the Smith across the countryside was slow and erratic, because he was stopping frequently to offer sacrifice to his god Vilkata, and also because he walked a zig-zag course; but Vulcan continually cried out that he was coming on to Tashigang, where his other Swords were gathering, and where he meant to do honor in person to the King.

His other Swords? Vilkata pondered to himself. Of course the Smith had forged them all, and perhaps that was all that he meant by the use of such an expression. In any case, there was nothing Vilkata could do about the Smith, or any other god, until they came within the Mindsword's range. And the Dark King did not want to appear to be worried by what sounded, on the surface, like very good news indeed. Therefore he gave permission for a celebration of Vulcan's triumph to begin, and sent out trumpeters and criers to make certain that the death of Draffut and the advance of the victorious Vulcan were made known within the walls of Tashigang as well.

Vilkata even took part in the revel himself, at least as far as its middle stages. He retired comparatively early, thinking that in any case he was giving himself time to sleep and recover before Vulcan could possibly arrive. He wearied himself with women, and came near besotting himself with wine, and then tumbled into his private bed to sleep.

His awakening was hours earlier than he had expected, and it came not at the gentle call of his valet, or some officer of his bodyguard. The sound that tore Vilkata out of dreams of victory was the ripping of his pavilion's fabric, not far from his head, by some enemy weapon's edge.

No matter how mad the odds seemed against success, when merely human calculation was applied, Coinspinner had insisted that the defenders of the city organize a sally against Vilkata's camp; a military maneuver involving the sending of what could be at most a few hundred troops, to fight against the Dark King's many thousands. At least this was the only interpretation that could finally be placed on the way that the Sword of Chance, whenever it was consulted, pointed insistently into the heart of the enemy camp.

Mark, Ben, and Barbara, along with the other members of the Lord Mayor's council, discussed the possibility of sending one or two agents or spies, armed with Coinspinner, out into the camp, to try to achieve whatever the Sword was telling them to do there. But Mark had experience of the Dark King's security systems, and without Sightblinder to help he could imagine no way of accomplishing that.

On the other hand, the more carefully the idea of a surprise sally was considered, the less completely mad it seemed. It could, of course, be launched by night, and it certainly ought to take the enemy by surprise. The Mayor drew out secret maps. It was noted that one of the secret tunnels leading out of the city—like most places so elaborately fortified, Tashigang was equipped with several—emerged from a concealed opening under the bank of the Corgo, behind the enemy front line and only about a hundred meters from where Vilkáta's pavilion had been set up.

A plan was hastily worked out. Both Ben and Mark would accompany the attacking force, Mark with Coinspinner in his hands. Ben, after speaking strongly against surrender of the city, could not very well avoid the effort now; nor did he want his old friend to go without him. The handful of Tasavaltan troops who had escorted Mark to Tashigang now volunteered, to a man, to go with him again. He was somewhat surprised and gratified by this; either his leadership or his Sword had inspired more confidence than he knew.

The bulk of the raiding force, which was two hundred strong in all, was made up from the survivors of Sir Andrew's slaughtered army. They proved to be as eager for revenge as Mark had expected them to be.

The deployment of the force into the secret, stone-walled tunnel took place in the late hours of the night. The city end of the tunnel was concealed in the basement of an outbuilding of the Mayor's palace.

Waiting in the cramped, dark, and dripping tunnel for some final magical preparations to be made, Mark had some time to talk with his old friend Ben. He told Ben something of his meeting with the Emperor.

When Mark first mentioned the name of Ariane, Ben shook his head, not wanting to hear more; but when he heard that the Emperor had claimed the red-haired girl as his daughter, the huge man turned hopeless eyes to Mark. "But what does it mean? What does that matter now? She's dead."

"I don't know what it means. I know you loved her. I wanted you to hear what he told me."

Ben nodded, slowly. "It's strange . . . that he said that."

"What do you mean?"

"When we were leaving the treasure-dungeon— right after she was killed—I looked up onto that headland, the Emperor's land they said it was, right across the fjord. I thought for a moment I saw—red hair. It doesn't mean anything, I don't suppose."

And now, suddenly, there was no more time for talk.

The Mayor's most expert sorceress was squeezing her way through the narrow tunnel, marking with a sign each man and woman of the raiding party, as she passed them. When he hand touched his own eyes briefly, Mark found that now he could see a dim, ghostly halo behind the head of everyone else in the attacking force. When fighting started in the darkness, they ought to be able to identify each other. At least until the enemy magicians solved the spell, and were able to turn it to their own advantage. Most likely they were more skillful than this woman of the Mayor's. But it was necessary to take what seemed desperate chances. That was what Coinspinner was for.

The party moved out. The tunnel extended for more than a kilometer, and its lower sections were knee-deep in water. An occasional loud splash or oath, the shuffle of feet, the chink of weapons, were for some time the only sounds.

The outer end of the tunnel, in which an advance party had been waiting for some time, was quietly opened. Two by two, moving now as quickly and silently as possible, the raiders launched themselves out of the tunnel into shallow water, and up and out into the open night.

Mark, with Coinspinner in his hands, was the second or third fighter to emerge. Now there could be no mistake about it. The Sword of Chance was directing him, ordering the whole attack, straight to Vilkata's pavilion. The huge tent stood plain in the light of several watchfires near it, its black-gold fabric wrinkling in a chiaroscuro wrought by the night breeze.

The first few of the Dark King's soldiers to blunder innocently into the way of the advancing column were cut down in savage silence. For those few endless-seeming moments, the advantage of surprise held. Then the alarm went up, in a dozen voices at once. The thin column of raiders broke into a charge; still, half or more of their total number had not yet come out of the tunnel.

Now resistance began, weapon against weapon, fierce and growing stronger. But it was still too disorganized to stop the charge. Mark, near the front of the attack, used Coinspinner as a physical weapon. Troops were gathering to oppose the raiders; the alarm was spreading. But now for a moment the pavilion was within reach, the Sword of Chance could touch its fabric. Fine cloth parted with a shriek before its edge.

Men who had been inside burst out with weapons in their hands to bar the way. Already a counterattack was taking form, against both sides of the column and its front. The formation shattered, with

its front forced back by opposing swords and
shields; the fight became a great melee, a free-for-
all.

A different and even deadlier resistance was gathering too. Above the watchfires, over the huge tent
itself, the air roiled now with more than rising heat.
The demonic guardians of the Dark King and of his
chief magicians were readying themselves to
pounce upon intruders.

The Lord Mayor's best sorceress, stumbling near
Mark's side in the darkness, stopped suddenly and
seized Mark by the arm. He could feel the woman's
whole body quivering.

"Do what you can," she demanded of him. "And
quickly! Else we are all lost. I had hoped they would
not be this strong . . ."

Mark himself with his experience had been
grimly certain that they would. Still the Sword had
brought him here. And he had another power of his
own, already tested once.

His faith in it was tested now. Suddenly the
Emperor was only one more man, and far away,
while the ravening airborne presences that lowered
themselves now toward Mark were the most over-
whelmingly real things in all the universe.

Mark had rehearsed no incantations beforehand.
If he meant to trust the Emperor, he would trust
him in that as well, that no special words were
needed. The words that came to him now were
those of Ariane, uttered in the Blue Temple cave
four years ago:

"In the Emperor's name, forsake this game, and
let us pass!"

Vilkata, awakened by the sounds of the attack,

had just rolled groggily out of bed. The demon that served as his eyes, recalled abruptly to duty, had just begun to send sight-images to the Dark King's brain. Then in a moment the demon was catapulted into a blank distance, and those images were blanked away again.

For a moment the Dark King did not grasp the full import of his full and sudden blindness. Certainly some emergency had arisen, and his first thought was for the Mindsword. He groped for it, but his hands found only a tangled fall of cloth; part of his pavilion was collapsing around him. And the weapon was not where he thought it ought to be. Could he possibly, in last night's drunkenness, have failed to keep the Sword with him, beside his bed as always? He could remember, at some time in the party, using it in sport, trying to drive one of his women mad with devotion to him. But after that. . .

Surrounded by the sounds of fighting, groans, oaths, and the clash of arms, he groped frantically about him on the floor, amid soft pillows and spilled wine. Between the confusion of his awakening and his sudden blindness he was disoriented. No, he had brought the Mindsword with him to his bedchamber, he remembered and was sure. But now he could not find it. Where was it?

The clamor of the fighting continued very near him. The fabric and the supports of the tent must have been assaulted; the bodies of people running and fighting had jostled into it, and more great sheets of loosened cloth were falling, crumpling. They settled and collapsed right on the groping blind man.

The Sword had to be right here, he knew that it

was here. But still he could not lay his hands on it. Frantically, sightlessly, he burrowed into the heaps of soft, fine fabric that were coming down and piling up like snow. But his searching fingers were baffled by the cloth, as the eyes of a normally sighted man would be in fog.

And Vilkata was aware by now that not only his vision-demon but all the other demons as well were gone, a great part of his defense dissolved. It was unbelievable, but true. Somehow they had all been hurled away. In the middle distance he could hear the voice of Burslem, screaming incantations, trying to call other, non-demonic, forces of magic into play. What success the magician might be having, Vilkata could not tell. His ears assured him that the physical fight still raged nearby, but the enemy weapons had not yet found his skin. Perhaps, under this baffling cloth, he was invisible as well as blind.

And still, in his confusion, he could not find the Sword. He'd grope his way back to his bed, and start over again from there. If only he knew which way to crawl to find his bed.

Mark was wielding Coinspinner constantly now, as a physical weapon in his own defense. The demons had been satisfactorily expelled, at least for the time being, but minute by minute the Dark King's other defenses were becoming better organized. Confusion still dominated, and because of that fact the bulk of the attacking force still survived. Mark thought that, to the enemy, his attacking force must have seemed to number in the thousands; it would seem inconceivable to the Dark King that any force much smaller than that would dare to attack him in this fashion.

In the outer darkness around the periphery of the struggle, the Dark King's people must often have been fighting one another. Closer to the pavilion, in the light of the watchfires, they prospered better, and began to assert some of the real advantage of their numbers. Mark was wounded lightly in his left arm, when even superb luck ran thin, by a blow that doubtless would have killed him outright but for his possession of the Sword of Chance.

He had lost sight of Ben, and of the sorceress. His Tasavaltan guard were fighting near him. Coinspinner still pointed at the half-collapsed pavilion, but Mark no longer saw how he could get there. The whole invading party was being forced back now, farther away from it.

Only Doomgiver, in the hands of one of Sir Andrew's officers, saved the attacking party from complete annihilation at this point. It repelled blows, missiles, and magic spells, making its holder a center of invulnerable strength, turning each weapon used against him back upon its user. Alone it worked considerable destruction in the ranks of the Dark King's guardians. And, along with the Sword of Chance that Mark still had in his grasp, it allowed a tenacious survival for the attackers even after their hopes of being able to seize the Mindsword had dwindled almost to the vanishing point.

"Back!" Whether Mark was the one who actually voiced the word or not, it was in his throat. "We must retreat. We can't let our two Swords be captured here."

So what had been a forced withdrawal became a calculated one. Now Coinspinner, faithful as always to its users' wishes, also pointed the way back. Mark fought, and moved, and fought again, hampered by his wounded arm, swinging the Sword of Chance as best he could. His Tasavaltan bodyguard was trying to keep close around him, and more than once they saved his life.

"By all the gods, what's that?"

It was not all the gods, but only some of them. No more than three or four, perhaps. They were out near the horizon, kilometers from the walls of Tashigang and the field of human combat. Several large sparks, like burning brands, could be seen out there in the distance, moving back and forth over the earth erratically. Those sparks must be whole burning treetrunks at the least.

Momentarily a near-hush spread across the battlefield, as most of the people on it became aware of that sight in the distance; and in that moment of half-silence, the singing voices of the distant gods were audible. What words they sang were hard to catch, discordant as those far voices were, and whipped about by wind; but enough could be heard to be sure that they sang praise to Vilkata.

And the earth below the moving firebrands, and the sky above them, were no longer fully dark; the greater fire of dawn was on its way.

It was enough, it was more than enough, to turn the retreat into a mere scramble for survival. Even if the gods did not come soon to the Dark King's aid, daylight would; daylight would end the confusion in Vilkata's camp, let his people see how few they really fought against. Whether the scramble for escape was ordered or not, it was already under way.

Many of the city's defenders were able to get back into the tunnel before the tunnel was discovered by Vilkata's people, and a concerted effort made by them to block its entrance. Ben was just a bit too late to be able to use the tunnel, and Mark was later still.

By chance, perhaps, the two things on which the Dark King's hopes depended came back to him almost simultaneously, even as they had been taken: the Mindsword, and his demonic powers of sight. As the first shouts were going up from some of his people near his tent proclaiming victory over the raiders, his hand fell at last on the black hilt. The Sword was still lying where he had left it, undisturbed and unseen, while fighting raged around it. And at the same time the demon, able now to return to duty, brought back Vilkata's sight. His first view was of the Sword in front of him, the column of fire that was his usual vision of the blade now muffled and enfolded within the leather sheath.

The Sword once more in his hand, the Dark King ordered his vision expanded. He got a good look at the partial ruin and still widespread confusion that prevailed around him in his camp. His chief human subordinates were just discovering that he was missing. They were unsure whether he was still alive, and many of them, Vilkata was convinced, were hoping that he was not.

That would change drastically, as soon as he showed them the Blade again. He got to his feet. Now that he could see, it was easy to disentangle himself from fallen fabric. If he had believed in thanking gods, he would have thanked them now.

The Dark King's sense of triumphant survival, of being indestructible, was short lived. Haggard in the early daylight, knowing that he must look weakened and distraught, afraid of trying to seek sleep again, afraid as well of appearing tired or uncertain in front of his subordinates, Vilkata used his private powers of magic to chastise his returning demons. Where they had been, they could not or would not say.

It was different when he demanded to know from them what power had been able to drive them so completely and easily away. Then they responded sullenly that it was the name of the Emperor that had been used against them.

"The Emperor! Are you joking?" But even as he said the words, Vilkata realized that they were not. In his own long study of magic and the world, he had from time to time encountered hints of genuine Imperial power; hints and suggestions and too, of a connection between the present Emperor and the being called Ardneh, the Dead God of two thousand years ago, still worshipped by the ignorant masses. Those hints and suggestions Vilkata had long chosen to ignore.

The Dark King punished his demons, and constrained them as best he could to serve him faithfully from now on. Then he went, exhausted as he was, to confer again with his human wizards, who after the night just passed were quite exhausted too.

The magicians pulled long faces when their lord mentioned the Emperor's name to them. But they had to admit that there might be some truth to the claim of driving demons away by such a means.

Vilkata demanded, "Then why cannot we use it too?"

"We are none of us the Emperor's children, Sire."

"His children? I should hope not. Are you mad?" The term "Emperor's child" was commonly used in a proverbial way, to describe the poor, the orphaned, the unfortunate.

Before the subject could be pursued any farther, there arrived a distraction. It was welcomed heartily, at least at first, by the magicians; and it came in the form of the morning's first flying messenger, bearing news that the Master of the Beasts thought too important to be delayed. It told Vilkata that the Silver Queen's host had now actually been sighted, marching against his rear. This time, Vilkata was assured, the report was genuine.

The observed strength of the army of the Silver Queen was not enough in itself to give the Dark King much real concern. But there was the dread Sword that he knew she carried; and, perhaps equally disquieting, the thought that her timely presence here might well mean that his enemies had worked out some effective plan of co-operation against him.

This last suspicion was strengthened when the Tasavaltan army was also reported to be now on the march, and also approaching Tashigang. Rostov would make a formidable opponent. But it would be a day or two yet, according to report, before his army would be on the scene.

And there was Vulcan—Vulcan was now almost at hand. It struck Vilkata more forcefully now than ever before, that the gods were often stupid, or at least behaved as if they were, which in practice of course came to the same thing.

Holding the Mindsword drawn and ready in his

hand, the Dark King rode out to confront this deity who said that he had come to do him honor.

Riding a little ahead of a little group of trembling human aides, his vision provided by a demon now equally tremulous with fear, Vilkata flashed the Mindsword over his head. At the same time he cried out in a loud voice, demanding the Smith's obedience.

Vulcan's first answer was a knowing grin, shattering in its implications. Then the god laughed at the human he had once been forced to worship.

With a wicked gleam in his huge eyes, Vulcan brandished the smoldering tree-trunk that once had been a torch, and announced that he meant to have revenge for that earlier humiliation.

"Did your scouts and spies, little man, take seriously what I shouted to them about my coming here to do you honor? Good! For as soon as I have time, I mean to do you honor in an unprecedented way. Ah, yes.

"I am a god, little man. Remember? And *Shieldbreaker* is now in my hand! Can you understand what that means? I, who forged it, know. It means I am immune to all other weapons, including your Mindsword. There is no power on earth that can oppose me now."

The Dark King, as usual at his bravest when things seemed most desperate, glared right back at the god, and nursed a silent hope that Doomgiver in some human hand might still bring this proud being down. Or Farslayer . . . then he saw another sheath at Vulcan's belt, another black hilt, and he knew a sinking moment of despair.

Vulcan, taking his time, had yet a little more to say. He was going to have his revenge on Vilkata, but not just yet. "First of all, little man, there are more Swords that I must gather. Just to be sure . . . therefore I claim this city and all its contents for my own. And all its people. They will wish that Mars still lived, when my rule begins among them.''

And the god turned his back on the King, and marched off to claim his city. However many companions the Smith had had when he came over the horizon, he was now down to just one, a four-armed male god that Vilkata was unable to identify offhand. Not, he supposed, that it much mattered.

As long as Vilkata was actually in Vulcan's presence, he had been able to confront the Smith bravely enough. But when the confrontation was over, the man was left physically shaking. Still, in a way he was almost glad that Vulcan was now openly his enemy. Always, in the past, it had taken a supreme challenge of some kind to rouse Vilkata to his greatest efforts and achievements. When he knew a crisis was approaching, fear gnawed at him maddeningly, and sometimes came near to disabling him. But when the crisis arrived, then he was at his best.

As was the case now. Rejoining the main body of his army, he called his staff together and issued orders firmly. In a new, bold voice, the Dark King commanded them to abandon the siege that they had scarcely yet begun. Once more he set his whole vast host in motion, turning it to meet the Silver Queen and Soulcutter.

Vulcan's turn would come, and soon. There were still certain weapons to which even a god armed with the Sword of Force would not be immune, the tools of boldness and intelligence. Meanwhile, for the time being, Vilkata would abandon the city of Tashigang to the gods.

CHAPTER 17

In the hour before dawn, at a time when two hundred of the loyal defenders of Tashigang were fighting outside the walls, there was treachery in the Lord Mayor's palace. Money changed hands, and weapons flashed, in a corridor on an upper floor, where one room had been made into a cell for holding an important prisoner. Chairman and High Priest Hyrcanus of the Blue Temple was freed, in steps of bribery and violence.

The move to rescue Hyrcanus was planned and executed by his immediate subordinates in the Blue Temple, as part of a general insurrection, in accordance with the High Priest's own previous orders. The intention was to seize control of the city, and welcome in the Dark King and his army.

Attempts by the Blue Temple Guard to seize the walls and gates from inside were unsuccessful. The concurrent try to assassinate the Lord Mayor failed also, nor were the Blue Temple raiders able to capture the palace—not all of the Watch there were easily subverted or taken by surprise. And Hyrcanus was wounded in his escape, so that he had to be half carried, gasping and ashen-faced, back to the Blue Temple's local headquarters on a street not far away.

Once there, propped up on a couch while a surgeon worked on him, the Chairman demanded to be brought up to date on how the situation stood, inside the city and out. When his aides had informed him as best they could, one of his first orders was to dispatch a company of thirty Blue Temple Guardsmen against the House of Courtenay. Their orders were to take or destroy the building, and seize whatever Swords and other useful items they could discover—along with any available gold and other valuables, of course. They were also to take the important inhabitants of the house prisoner if possible, or kill them as second choice; and in general to crush that place as a possible center of resistance.

Then Hyrcanus began to lay his plans to attack the walls and gates once more.

When the first Blue Temple raid struck the palace, in the hour before dawn, Baron Amintor was waiting in a ground floor room for a good chance to see the Mayor privately. When the Baron saw the Guard in its capes of blue and gold come swirling in to the attack, he immediately decided that he could best serve his Queen's interests and his own by remaining alive and active in the city, whatever the outcome of this particular skirmish might prove to be. The fate of the palace and the Mayor still hung in the balance when Amintor prudently retired, and set out through the streets to carry warning to the

House of Courtenay. He of course remembered that
that was where the young man named Denis lived,
who was supposed to be able to set a counterattack
of looters in motion against the Blue Temple.

When the Baron reached his destination—not
without a minor adventure or two along the
way—he found the House already on the alert, its
doors and windows sealed. It took him some time
and effort, arguing and cajoling, to get himself
admitted to speak with someone in authority.

Once inside, he found himself face to face with
the tiny woman who had been introduced to him at
the palace as the Lady Sophie. Now, surrounded by
her own determined-looking retainers, she received
his warning with evident suspicion, which he in
turn accepted philosophically.

"I can only suggest, Madam, that you wait and
see if I am right. Wait not in idleness, of course;
order your affairs as if the Blue Temple were indeed
leading a revolt. I will await the result with confidence."

"You will await the result in a room by yourself.
Jord, Tamir, disarm him and lock him in that
closet."

The Baron's capacity for philosophical accept-
ance became somewhat strained; but at the
moment he had no real choice.

The attack by the Blue Temple against the house
began presently, just as the Baron had predicted,
with fire and sword and axe against the walls and
doors and windows. But the attackers met fierce
resistance from the start. Brickbats and scalding
water were dumped on them from the flat roof, and
the first window that they managed to break open

immediately sprouted weapons, like teeth in a warbeast's mouth.

Denis was not there to aid in the defense. Barbara had taken the Baron's warning seriously enough to dispatch the young man with orders to put into operation whatever looting counterattack he could. The street connections made in his early life ought to serve him well in the attempt.

And even a feint, or the suggestion of an attack, might serve as well as the real thing. In a city this big, the Blue Temple vaults must hold vast treasure; and Denis had already begun to spread among the city's street people the rumor that the Blue Temple's main hoard, an agglomeration of wealth well beyond the capacity of most people to comprehend, had already been moved into Tashigang for safekeeping. It was unlikely that even a large mob could succeed in looting the Temple here, but even the threat ought to make the misers squirm and roar, and pull in their claws to defend that which they valued more than their own lives and limbs.

As the direct attack on her own house began, Barbara's first act was to see to it that her daughter, with Kuan-yin as caretaker and Jord as personal bodyguard, was put into the safest and strongest room available.

Then Barbara ran upstairs to get Townsaver. If this warning and attack were only part of an elaborate hoax to discover where it was hidden, the Baron was safely locked up now, and would never see. A few days ago the Lord Mayor, perhaps trusting the security of this house as much or more than that of his own palace, had asked Master and Lady Courtenay to keep it here.

She was still climbing stairs when a great crash

from below told her that a door had somehow already been broken in. Smoke and the cries and clash of battle rose from below, as Barbara knelt to bring the great Sword out of its hiding place under her bedroom floor.

Fighting nearby, threatening innocent noncombatants in their home, had wakened the Sword of Fury already. The weighty steel arose with magical ease and lightness in her grip, the Sword already making its preliminary faint millsaw whine. For a moment as she held it, there crossed Barbara's mind the thought of Mark's hands, a small boy's hands then, the first time he had held this Sword, his grip no stronger then perhaps than hers was now upon this very hilt ... she was already hurrying back toward the stairs.

From below there sounded a new crash, a shout of triumph in the invaders' voices.

Their joy would be short lived. In Barbara's hands, Townsaver screamed exultantly, and pulled her running down the stairs.

CHAPTER 18

Ben, caught in Vilkata's camp when the retreat turned into a desperate scramble for survival, bulled his way into the fighting at the mouth of the no-longer-secret tunnel. But it was quickly obvious that the tunnel was now hopelessly blocked as a means of escape. Having no other real choice, he promptly committed himself to the river instead. Many other bodies, alive and dead, were afloat in the Corgo already. All of them, swimming or bobbing, would eventually reach one or another of the great water-gates that pierced the city's walls only a few hundred meters downstream.

Ben splashed and waded and swam his way well out into the current, trying to avoid the hail of missiles, slung stones and arrows, now being launched by enemy troops along the bank. The steadily growing lightness of the eastern sky brightened the water as well. The enemy certainly had the tunnel now. Not that it was going to do them any good as an invasion route; it had been designed for complete and easy blockage at the point where it approached the walls, and also at the inner end, almost below the palace.

The bottom fell off steeply under Ben as he moved out from the shore. And now he had to slip out of his partial armor, and drop his heavier weapons, strong swimmer though he was, if he was going to keep from drowning.

He swam downstream, missiles still pattering like heavy hail upon the water's surface round him. He went under water for a while, still swimming, and came up for air and swam again. The high walls rose up before him swiftly; the river ran fast here, and swept him down upon them. The gray-brown of their hardened granite was brightening in the new daylight. Now Ben could see that this portion of the walls, along with the upstream water-gates, was being manned in force by the Watch in gray-green uniforms. More of the Watch were down at water level, just inside the gate ahead of him, admitting one at a time through a turnstile arrangement the returning survivors of the sally. There was already enough daylight to let them do this with security.

Ben swam a few more strokes, and then could pull himself up, first on rock and then on steel bars, magically protected against rust. Around him a steady trickle of other survivors were doing the same thing; a bedraggled crew, he thought, but not entirely defeated. He did not see Mark anywhere, but that did not necessarily mean anything.

Once he had been let in through the turnstile, Ben's way led upward, into and behind the wall, along a flight of narrow steps. His last glance at the scene outside the city showed him that Vulcan and some other god, a many-armed being Ben did not recognize, were approaching, now no more than a few hundred meters away.

Others soldiers were stopping on the stairs to watch. Ben, for his part, had had more than enough of confrontations and fighting for a time; he was anxious to get home and see what was happening there.

Among the Watch officers who were seeing to the admission of returning fighters, confusion reigned. It was the situation more often than not in any military, Ben had observed. Someone was announcing that the survivors were to stand by for debriefing and then reassignment on the walls. But someone else, not an officer, passed on a rumor that the Blue Temple was in revolt, and the House of Courtenay under attack within the city. Ben on hearing this ducked out and hurried through the streets toward his home. In the confusion no one appeared to notice his departure.

The streets of Tashigang were largely empty, what stores and shops he passed were all of them closed and shuttered. Once he observed, a few streets away, a running group that looked like some detached fragment of a mob. Ben stayed out of their way, whatever they were about.

Tired and generally battered, though essentially unhurt, he stumbled at last into the familiar street. There was his house, at least it was still standing, and his heart leaped up in preliminary joy; this was followed in a moment by new anxiety, when he saw how the building was scorched and still smoking above ground level, and how the windows and doors to the street were battered. Now he could see part of what looked like a bucket brigade of his faithful workers, stretching between the house and the nearby river.

Ben ran panting through the broken front door, into the main room of the ground floor, and stopped. Carnage was everywhere. Amid broken furniture and weapons were piled hewed and mangled bodies, the great majority of them wrapped in cloaks that had once been blue and gold.

Barbara, elated, looking unhurt, came bounding from somewhere to greet him.

"Townsaver," she explained, succinctly, indicating the condition and contents of the room. "They started a fire, and broke in ... but then some of them were glad to get away."

Then, in sudden new worry, she was looking behind her husband, at the empty street. "Where's Mark?"

"I don't know. We were separated. He may be all right." And from the way the question had been asked, Ben understood that she would have preferred him to be the one still unaccounted for.

Vulcan, standing waist-deep in the swift Corgo, was unhurriedly rending open one of the huge water-gates of steel and iron bars. He might of course have climbed the city wall, or flown over it somehow, but this mode of entry struck him as more appropriate. He had made the city his now, and he was going to enter his city through a door.

Shiva, his recently acquired companion, was squatting nearby on the riverbank and watching. The rivets and other members of the gate were breaking one at a time, parting with loud pops as Vulcan bent his strength upon them, the fragments flying now and then like crossbow bolts.

Vulcan was speaking, but, as often, his words were addressed mainly to himself. "If I were capable of mistakes, that would have been one ... letting my twelve Blades go so meekly, after I had them forged. Giving them away to Hermes like that, to be dealt out to the human vermin for the Game ... a mistake, yes. But now I'll make no more."

Now Shiva pitched into the river the smoldering treetrunk that he had still been carrying. The huge spar of wood went into the water with a steamy splash.

As if in reply, there was a swirling in the water, and the nebulous figure of Hades appeared just above its surface. On the high city wall there were a few human screams. The few human watchers who had remained in the immediate area were quickly gone, getting themselves out of sight of that god's face, of which it was said that no man or woman might look on it, and live thereafter.

Hades said, in his formless voice, that he had come to bring a warning to his old comrade Vulcan. It was that anyone who used Farslayer could never triumph thereby in the end.

Vulcan glared at him. "To a true god, there is no end. Was that a warning, troglodyte, or a threat? If you choose to deal in threats, Farslayer is here at my side again, and as you say, I do not hesitate to use it."

The almost shapeless words of Hades' answer came back to him: *Death and darkness are no more than portions of my domain, Fire-worker; such threats do not concern me.*

And again there was a stirring of the river and the earth, and Hades was gone.

Vulcan cast aside the remnants of the gate he had now torn down, and waded through the stone arch it had protected, and went on into the city. From the inside, Tashigang looked about as he had expected; he had heard that this was the largest city that the human vermin had ever built. He noted with indifference that the four-armed god Shiva was still following him.

There was a running human figure nearby, caped in blue and gold, and Vulcan bent down and shot out a hand and scooped the creature up, inflicting minimal damage; he wanted some information from it.

"You, tell me—where is the place you call the House of Courtenay? I hear that they are hiding some of my Swords in there."

He got his directions in a piping voice; the man pointed with the arm that had not been broken by Vulcan's grab.

The Smith let the creature fall, and limped away briskly through the streets. But now Apollo's head loomed over a nearby rooftop.

"Beware, Smith. We must meet and think and try to talk about all this. I am calling a council—"

"Beware yourself. We've met and talked enough, for ages, and got nowhere. And think? Who among us can do that? Maybe you. Who else wants to? I don't. I just want what is mine."

He marched on, moving quickly in his uneven gait. A street or two later, there was another interruption. Atop an indented curve of the great city wall, which was here only about as high as Vulcan's head, a human in green and gray was brandishing some unknown Sword, as if daring the gods to attack him. It must be a Sword in which the man had confidence.

Vulcan detoured to confront this man. Shiva, interested, was staying right with him.

The tiny teeth of the man on the wall were chattering. But he got out the words he was trying to say: "This is Doomgiver! Stay back!"

"Doomgiver, hey?" That particular Sword had been, in the back of Vulcan's thoughts, a lingering concern. Wishing to take no chances, he aimed a hard swing with the Sword of Force. Its thudding sound built in a moment to explosive volume. There was a dazzling flash, a thunderclap of sound, as the two Blades came in contact, opposing each other directly.

Vulcan stood there, blinking at ruin and destruction. A chunk of stone as big as his fist had been blasted out of the wall before his eyes. Of the human being who had been standing on the wall, holding the opposing Sword, there was almost nothing left. Although Shieldbreaker appeared the same as ever, there appeared to be no trace of Doomgiver.

"Doomgiver, gone? Just like that? No, there must be some pieces here; I'll find them, and carry them back to my forge, and make it new!"

But that proved to be impossible. Though Vulcan diminished himself to half his previous height, the better to search for tiny scattered objects, he could not turn up even the smallest fragment of the shattered blade. He found only the black hilt, bearing the simple white circle, a line returning on itself. The Sword of Justice was no more.

He told himself that he might still try to recast it, some day, beginning the job from the beginning again; but he was not sure now that he remembered how he had accomplished it the first time. And anyway, what need had he of a Sword of Justice now? Just twenty years ago, things had been simpler; all the gods knew what they were doing then, and what they were supposed to do; and no human being had yet thought of challenging their rule.

Vulcan was angry, as he went limping on toward the House of Courtenay.

Over rooftops he saw the heads of Apollo, Zeus, and Diana, come to chide and challenge him again.

Diana demanded: "Why did you strike down Mars?"

He snarled at them all: "Because he insulted me, and bothered me! Who needed Mars, anyway? What was he good for? And as for the Great Dog, I'm not even sure he's dead. I wasted no time on him, one way or the other."

As soon as Vulcan swelled himself back to his usual height, and waved Shieldbreaker at them, the protestors fell back out of his way, as he had known they would.

"By my forge, I think that this must be the house."

The four-story building, standing close by one of the branches of the river, had already been attacked by someone else, and was still smoking. On the flat roof of the house, amid vines and flowers and garden paths, a human stood. The little creature was strong and bulky for a mere man, and held another Sword in hand.

Shiva pounced forward, meaning to take that weapon for his own. He ignored Vulcan's rumbled warning.

The Sword in the man's hand screamed with its

own power. By the shrill note Vulcan recognized it, at once and with satisfaction. Townsaver!

The god of the four arms screamed too, in pain, not triumph, and pulled back a badly mangled hand. The injured god ran reeling, devastating small buildings as he crashed into them. His screams continued without pause, as his bounding, bouncing flight took him away to the city walls again, and over the walls and out of sight.

"Hah, the fool!" Vulcan grumbled to himself in satisfaction. "Now I'll take that Sword too. Or else see it destroyed, like the other."

He stepped close to the man on the roof, and slashed quickly with the Sword of Force, right to left and back again. With the motion of his arm his right fist struck a corner of the building, close to the part of the roof where the man was standing. As the two Swords came in contact, and the Sword of Fury disappeared in another explosive flash, the building opened up under the impact of Vulcan's fist, and the man who had been holding Townsaver dropped down inside the walls, disappearing in a cloud of dust and a small landslide of debris.

"That must have been Townsaver, by its voice . . . but, by the Spear of Mars, it's gone now too! Damnation to all human vermin who destroy my property! But there may be other Swords in this nest. He who told me said more than one."

Vulcan considered the battered structure, its roof terrace gaping at the corner where his fist had struck, its lower floors blackened on the outside and still smoldering where someone had earlier tried an assault by fire. It would be easy enough to pull the house down, but it would be awkward to sift the whole pile of wreckage for his Swords afterward. No.

After taking thought for a few more moments, the Smith shrank himself once more, this time to little more than human size. Now he ought to be able to enter most of their rooms and passages. The shrinkage of course left his strength undiminished, and had the extra advantage of making it easier for him to grip Shieldbreaker's merely man-sized hilt.

He kept the Sword of Force in hand and ready, just in case the building when entered might contain surprises.

There was no need to kick the front door in; someone had already taken care of that. Inside, he encountered first a pile of ugly human dead; nothing that he wanted there. He could tell now that there were some live ones also present in the building, but so far they were all trying to hide from him. It didn't matter what they did. He'd seek out what he wanted.

This was some kind of human workshop here. It was well stocked with weapons, but none of divine manufacture.

The Smith shouted: "You might as well bring them out to me! I forged them, all of them, and they are mine!"

Next he kicked open a wall, behind which, his senses told him, there was some kind of a hidden door—but all he uncovered, all that had been hidden here for safety, were a plump human girl and the small child she was trying to shelter.

"Hah! This is their treasure?" The ways and thoughts of humankind were sometimes small beneath all Vulcan's comprehension.

Now a light weight of some kind fell from somewhere to land on Vulcan's neck, and it took him a moment to realize that it was in fact a living human body. A man had just jumped deliberately upon him, from above and behind. A lone man, whose weaponless arms, looked around Vulcan's mighty neck, were straining in an evident effort to strangle him.

The god laughed at this puny assault; laughed at it, when he got around to noticing it for what it was. At first it did not even distract him fully from his search. The Swords, the Swords . . . there ought to be at least one more of them around here somewhere . . . .

He would have them all, or he would destroy them all, to perfect and insure his ultimate power over the other gods and goddesses. So, they thought the Game had been abandoned, did they? Well, it was over now, or very nearly over. But not abandoned. No. He, the Smith, the cripple, was winning it, he had almost won. . . . and, just to be sure of course, he needed the Swords to perfect his power over men and women too. He wanted at some time to be able to put Shieldbreaker down and rest; but he thought that time would not come while even one of the other eleven remained in other hands than his, or unaccounted for.

He had turned away from the girl and the baby, ignoring them even as he forgot the rag of living human flesh that was a large, strong man still hanging on his neck. He would brush that away the next time that he thought of it.

Now Vulcan's progress was blocked by a strong, closed door, and he grabbed with his free hand at a projecting corner of the doorframe, intending to tear the whole framework loose.

But he met startling resistance. Here was mere wood and stone, and of no heroic dimensions, refusing to yield to him.

Still, such was the Smith's impatience that his first concern was still getting through the door, and not wondering why he could not. Instinctively he used Shieldbreaker on the door, which now gave way quite satisfactorily.

Irritated by the delay, and more so by the fact that the room uncovered this time was empty, Vulcan became more fully aware of another irritation, the man who was still hanging on his back. The god, reaching back with his free hand to peel the annoyance off, achieved a belated recognition.

"What's this, human? Grown back your right arm, have you, since last we met? Well, we can fix that. . . ."

But for some reason the puny human body would not peel free. Applying the best grip that he could one-handed, without setting Shieldbreaker down, Vulcan again had the curious sensation of being almost powerless. The link of those two human arms that held him would not part.

It was almost as if the chronic lameness in his leg was growing worse, spreading to other parts of his body. The Smith did not care in the least for the sensation of being without strength. It was becoming really alarming. Not only a stone wall, a wooden door, but even flesh was able to resist him now.

While all the time, in his right hand which felt stronger than ever, the limitless power of Shieldbreaker tapped out its readiness to be used.

". . . we can fix that like *this* . . ."

And Vulcan, reaching behind himself somewhat

awkwardly with the Sword, moved it to cut loose the clinging human flesh. Awkward, yes. His hands that had worked with divine skill to forge this weapon and its peers felt clumsy now when he tried to use it behind his back.

"Aaahrr!" All he had accomplished was to wound himself slightly in the neck.

He aimed his next blind cut more cautiously—*there*.

That time, Vulcan assured himself, the Sword had, it must have, passed right through the body of the clinging man. The trouble was that the man still clung on as tight as ever, giving no indication of being killed. The muscles of those human arms even tightened a little more. Their force should have been inconsequential in terms of what was needed to choke a god, but Vulcan imagined that his own breathing had become a shade more difficult, enough to be annoying, anyway.

Why was he, a god, worrying about breathing? But suddenly it seemed to matter.

The human's mortal breath, gasping with exertion but still full of life, sawed in Vulcan's ear. "I was there with you when you forged this weapon, God of Fire. My blood is in it, and part of my life. I know it—"

Standing in the middle of a large room, beside a fireless forge, Vulcan braced himself and strained with his left hand again. But still he could not break the other's grip.

"—know it as well as you do, Firegod. Better, maybe. I can feel the truth of Shieldbreaker, now that it has touched me again. You cannot hurt me with it, as long as I have no weapon of my own."

By now Vulcan's search for other Swords had

been forgotten. This foolish business of letting a
human being attack him had gone too far, he had to
end it. He had to rid himself of this clinging *thing*,
and do it swiftly.

But even as he strove to do so, another human,
approaching unnoticed by the god in his distraction, leaped upon him. This one was a tiny female
with dark hair. Vulcan moved just as she jumped at
him, so that she almost missed. But still she had
him by one ankle now, and she was trying—who
would have believed such a thing?—to tip him over.

Vulcan used the Sword on her. Or tried to use it
rather. He saw with his own eyes how the blade of
Shieldbreaker passed through her body, or gave the
illusion of dong so, again and again, without leaving the least trace of damage after it.

With his Sword perversely useless now, against
this fragile flesh that grappled with him, the Smith
let out a great roar, of mental pain and choking
rage. He would have thrown the Sword away now,
but it refused to separate from his hand. His fingers
would not release their grip upon the hilt.

All right then, he'd use it, in the only way it
would still work. He laid about him with the
Sword, knocking down furniture and walls, sending
bricks and timber and plaster flying. Dragging his
two human tormentors helplessly with him, he
chewed a passage through the ground floor of their
house. He'd bring it all down on their heads, these
useless human vermin.

A new idea came to him, and he tried to increase
his stature, to swell himself once more to true god-
size. Appallingly, he found that he could not. All the
powers that had once been his were shrinking,
concentrating, being driven minute by minute into

the one focus of his perfect Sword, the blade of Shieldbreaker itself and his right arm and hand that held it.

Now, other humans, emboldened by the survival of the first two, were coming to join in the attack. Human hands fastened on Vulcan's left arm, more human hands on his other leg. Someone's hand snatched Farslayer from its sheath at his belt; not that he'd really dreamed of wasting it on any of these puny . . .

More people were coming at him, a grappling swarm of them. Now they were strong and numerous enough to drag him against his will. They were forcing him a step at a time out of the house, going through some of the very openings he'd just created. He lashed out wildly with the Sword, and more wood and dust and tile came crashing down, on Vulcan's head and all around him, not bothering him much but laying one or two of his assailants low. Through the chokehold on his neck he gurgled minor triumph.

Still more and more of the vermin came pouring out of their holes, now daring to attack him. Jord cried a warning to one of these, but too late. The man had leaped at Vulcan, swinging an axe at the Smith's head. Shieldbreaker tapped once and brushed the weapon away, along with the arms of the man who had been holding it.

Another man tried to grab Vulcan by the Sword-arm. Still too much power there, too much by far, perhaps more power than ever. The man was flung off like mud from a wheel, to break his body on the wall.

But still the other people held on. Half a dozen of them were gripping the god now, each of the vermin seeming to gain determination from the others, each of them sapping some minute portion of his strength.

Vulcan roared out threats, though he knew that it was now too late for threatening. Words and yells did him no good. He fell, and rolled upon the floor, brushing off some of his assailants, crushing others, damaging them all, savaging those who persisted in clinging on. Yet persist they did, and still more came, out of the wreckage of their house. As soon as he rid himself of one, one or two more jumped on him, coming at him endlessly out of the rooms and ruins.

A crossbow bolt came streaking at him, launched by some concealed and unwise hand. Shieldbreaker tapped once again, unhurriedly, and shattered the missile in midair. Fragments of the bolt drew blood from the people who were wrestling with the god.

Jord, in a weakening voice, cried warning once again: "No weapons! No weapons, and we can win!"

Concentrated now in the one Sword was all of Vulcan's power, and all his hope. He knew that he must win with it, or die. Once more, then, behind his back, carefully and hard—there, that must have cut the pestiferous human leader clean in two!

But it had not. Or if it had, the man had been able to survive such treatment handily. The human's legs and feet still behaved as if they were connected to his brain, and he rode the god as if Vulcan were no more than a riding beast.

And Vulcan could feel a new pain in his back, and more of his own blood; once more he'd done himself some damage with the Sword.

Still he fought on, straining to stab, slice up,

destroy, the desperately wrestling human horde. They clung to him and submitted to being battered when he rolled on the ground again. When he was back on his feet, they dragged him about, and would not be shaken off. He slipped and fell, in a patch of his own blood.

And now they picked him up.

Now in their score of hands they bore him, raving, thrashing, screaming, outside the building, and he could no longer try to bring it down upon them. The arc of the Sword of Force flashed at them, passed through their bodies as through phantoms, leaving them unharmed.

The original grip on Vulcan's neck was really choking now. Every muscle of his body was growing weaker and weaker—except those in his right arm. That limb felt more and more powerful, but all that it could do was wield the Sword, and in combat against unarmed flesh the Sword was useless. Meanwhile, Vulcan's blood drained from his self-inflicted wounds.

He relaxed suddenly, playing dead.

In a moment, stunned and battered themselves, the people had all let go of him.

He leaped up, raging, wise enough now to use his first free effort to throw the Sword away from him. But in the presence of his enemies it would not let him go.

A moment later, a huge man, who had just come stumbling out of the half-ruined house, had hurled himself alone at Vulcan, and brought the god down with a tackle.

And then they were all on him again.

Now another group of people, these in white robes, recognizable to the struggling Smith as servants of the Dead God, Ardneh, were running into the street before the house. These, coming late to the scene, were clamoring in protest. From their words Vulcan could tell that they thought they were witnessing a lynching, a mob attack upon some poor helpless man.

The people who were grappling the Smith down tried to explain. "Completely mad, he thinks he's Vulcan." And a kind of exhausted laugh went round among them.

An aged priestess of Ardneh, looking wise and kind, came to take the useless Sword out of the madman's grasp. It came to her easily out of his cramped grip.

"To keep you from hurting yourself, poor fellow, or anyone else . . . my, what a weapon." The priestess blinked at the Sword. "This must be put away, in safety somewhere."

"I'll take it," said Ben.

The old woman looked into the huge man's eyes, and sighed. "Yes, you take it. There is no one better here, I think. Now we must bind this poor fellow for a while, so he does no more harm. How strong he is!—ah, such a waste. But these cords will hold him; carefully, for we must do it out of love."

CHAPTER 19

In all of his fifty thousand and more years of life, the creature named Draffut, the Lord of Beasts, had never been closer to death than he was now. Yet life, his almost inextinguishable life, remained in him. He clung to it, if for no other reason than because there was an injured human being nearby, who cried out from time to time in his own pain. Draffut, still true to his own nature, felt compelled to find a way to help that man.

But he was unable to do anything to help the man, unable even to move enough to help himself. The very stream that laved his wounds seemed to be slowly drawing his life away instead of assisting him to heal.

It was daylight—whether of the last day of the fight, or some day after that, he was not sure—when he became aware that another presence, intelligent but not human, was approaching him.

The Beastlord opened his eyes slowly. A goddess, recognizable to him as Aphrodite, was standing above him at a little distance, looking down at him where he still lay in the mud at the water's edge.

Aphrodite was standing just where Vulcan had stood, and there was a Sword in her hands too. But Draffut knew at once that this was different than Vulcan's approach, and he felt no fear as she drew near him, and raised the Sword.

It struck at him, and he cried out with a pang of new life, as sharp as pain. "Woundhealer," he said, suddenly strong enough to talk again. "And you are Aphrodite."

"And you are the Healer," she said. "Therefore I think it right that you should have this Sword. Humans quarrel and fight over this one, even as they do with all the others. So I took it back from them. And I am weary of trying to decide what to do with it next—so much love allows but little time for pleasure."

With a motion marked by a slight endearing awkwardness, she dropped the Sword of Mercy on the surface of the mud beside him.

Draffut, able to move again, put out his huge hand, weakly and slowly, and touched the blade. "I thank you, goddess, for your gift of life."

"There are many who have life because of me . . . ah, already I feel better too, to be rid of it. But that Sword suits you, I think. You are not much like me."

"Except in one way. We are both of us creations of humanity. But I only in part. And out of their science, not their dreams. I will still exist, if—when—humanity changes its collective mind about me."

The goddess tossed her perfect hair—and was it pure gold, or raven black? "You say that about us, but I don't believe it. If humanity created us, the gods and goddesses, then who could possibly have created them? But never mind, I am tired of all this philosophy and argument. There seems to be no end to it of late. I think the world is changing."

"Again. It always does." And now Draffut was dragging himself to his feet. The mud that had caked upon his fur when he was dying was falling off now, crumbling and twisting even as it fell, moving in the glow of the renewed life within him.

Painfully, a stopped, slow giant carrying the Sword of Mercy, he began to make his way across the muddy ground toward the injured man.

Rostov listened long and intently to what his latest and best source of information had to tell him about what was going on inside the walls of Tashigang, and what had happened last night during the outrageous, heroic sally against the Dark King's camp.

One of Rostov's patrols had luckily picked up the young man, who was carrying Coinspinner in his right hand, in the garden of one of the abandoned suburban villas along the Corgo.

"Trust a bad copper to turn up," the General had growled at first sight of him; then he had allowed his steel-bearded face to split in a tight grin. "The Princess will be anxious to see you, Mark. No, I shouldn't call you that, should I? What's the proper term of address for an Emperor's son?"

"For . . . who? The Princess, you say?" the wounded youth had answered weakly. "Where is she?"

"Not far away. Not far." Rostov still grinned. He could begin to see now what the Princess had seen all along in this tough young man. Who, as it now turned out, not only had good stuff in him, but Imperial blood. That was evidently, in the rarefied realm of magic and politics where these things were decided, something of acceptable importance. Rostov was glad—it was time that Tasavalta had some sturdy warrior monarchs on the throne again.

On a field not many kilometers from Tashigang, the armies of Yambu and Vilkata confronted each other, in a dawn dimmed almost to midnight by an impending thunderstorm. The Silver Queen was preparing herself to draw Soulcutter. She knew that she would have to do so before the Dark King brought the Mindsword into range; if not, her army would be lost to her, and she herself perhaps maddened into becoming Vilkata's slave.

She had recently received a strange report: first the god Vulcan had been seen inside the city, bound helplessly by the gentle hands of white-robed priestesses and priests; and then he was gone again. Some said that an angry unarmed mob had seized the Smith, and the wooden frame he had been bound to, and had thrown him in the river, and he had floated out of the city through the lower gates.

Queen Yambu thought: and is the world now to belong to us humans, after all? If we can overthrow the gods, and kill them—possibly. Not that they had ever bothered to rule the world when it was theirs. Perhaps it has been ours all along.

Without really being startled, she became aware that a man was standing in the doorway of her tent, and gazing in at her impertinently. She assumed he was one of her officers, and was about to speak sharply to him for staring at her thus, when she realized that he was not one of her own men at all. The words died on her lips.

His face was in shadow, and not until she shifted her own position did she see the mask. "You," she said.

He came in uninvited, pulled the mask off and helped himself to a seat, grinning at her lightly. He had not changed at all. Outside she could still hear the sentries walking their rounds, unaware that anyone had passed them.

The Emperor said to her: "I still have not had my answer."

It took the Queen a moment to understand what he was talking about. "You once asked me to marry you. Can that be what you mean?"

"It can. Didn't you realize that I was going to insist on an answer, sooner or later?"

"No, I really didn't. Not after . . . what happened to our daughter. Have you forgotten about her? Or is this visit just another of your insane jokes?"

"I have not forgotten her. She has been living with me." When Queen Yambu stared at him, he went on calmly: "Ariane was badly hurt, about four years ago, as you know. But she's much better now. She and I have not talked about you much, but I think that she might want to meet you again some day."

The Silver Queen continued to stare at her former lover. At last she said, "My reports, and I have reason to trust them, said that Ariane was killed, in the treasure-dungeon of the Blue Temple."

The Emperor scowled his distaste for that organization. "Many have died, in that . . . place. But Ariane did not die there. Even though the young men with her at the time were also sure that she was dead. One of those young men is my son, did you know that? I like to take care of my children, whenever I can. She is not dead."

And still Queen Yambu stared at him. She could not shake off her suspicion that this was all one of his jokes, perhaps the prelude to a hideous revenge—she had never been sure, even when they had been lovers, whether he was a vengeful man or not.

At last her royal poise abandoned her for the moment, and she stammered out: "I—I sold her to the Red Temple."

The frown was turned at her now, and briefly she understood what ancient Imperial power must have been, that Kings and Queens had quaked before it.

"I might have killed you for that, if I had known about it when it happened. But years have passed, and you are sorry for that selling now. She has survived, and so have I. And so have you."

In anger she regained her strength. "I have survived without you, you impossible . . . and you say you want to marry me, still? How do I know you mean what you are saying now?"

"How do you know when to trust anyone, my dear? You'll have to make a choice."

She wanted to cry out that she did not know when to trust anyone; that was her whole problem. "You madman, suppose I were to answer you and tell you yes. Could you defeat the Mindsword for me then?"

"I'll do all I can to help you, if you will be my bride. We'll see about the Mindsword when it comes."

"It's here now. Oh, you bastard. Impossible as

always. Leave now. Get out of here, or I'm going to draw Soulcutter." And she put her hand on the unrelieved blackness of that hilt, that rested as always within reach. "And I suppose you'll go on seducing brides, and fathering more bastards, after we are married?"

He said, softly and soberly, "I will be more faithful to you than you can well imagine. I love you; I always have. Why do you think I fought for you, beside you, when you were a girl?"

"I don't believe it, I tell you. I don't believe any of it. Leave now, or I draw Soulcutter."

"It's your Sword, to do with as you will. But I will leave when you decide to draw it."

She started to draw the Sword, and at the same moment called out in a clear voice for her guards. When they came pushing into the tent a moment later, they found their Queen quite alone, and Soulcutter safely in its sheath, though her hand on the hilt was poised as if for action.

The soldiers found themselves staring half-hypnotized at that hand, both of them hoping that they would be out of the tent again before the Sword was drawn; and already in the air around it, around themselves, they thought they could feel the backwash of a wave of emptiness.

Queen Yambu wasted no more time, but gave the orders necessary to get her troops into the state of final readiness for battle. That done, she ordered an advance.

With Vilkata's ranks still no more than barely in sight, she waited in the middle of her own line, mounted on her famous gray warbeast, ready to draw the Sword of—of what? As far as she knew, this one had only one name.

Now the enemy lines were creeping forward. There, in their center, that would be Vilkata himself, waiting for the perfect moment in which to draw the weapon that he was gambling would be supreme.

The hand of Queen Yambu was on her own Sword's hilt. She urged her mount forward, a little. Not yet.

Now.

The Mindsword and Soulcutter were drawn, virtually simultaneously.

Her own first reaction, to the overwhelming psychic impact of her own Sword, was that she wanted to throw it away—but then she did not. Because she could no longer see how throwing it away would make any difference, would matter in the least.

Nor did anything else matter.

Nothing else in the whole universe.

The Mindsword was a distant, irrelevant twinkle, far across the field, beneath the gloom of thunderclouds. While near at hand, around Queen Yambu herself . . .

Those of her own troops who were closest to her had been looking at her when she drew. After that they were indifferent as to where they looked. Around her a wave of lethargy, of supreme indifference, was spreading out, a slow splash in an inkblack pool.

In the distance, but drawing rapidly nearer, a charge was coming. Vilkata's troops, with maddened yells, the fresh inspiration of the Mindsword driving them.

Some of the Queen's soldiers, more and more of

them with each passing second, were actually slumping to the ground now, letting their weapons fall from indifferent hands. It appeared that they would be able to put up no resistance, that the Dark King might now be going to win easily.

But of course that did not matter either.

With berserker cries, the first of the Dark King's newly energized fanatics rushed upon them. The defense put up by the soldiers in black and silver was at best half-hearted, and it was weaker the closer they were stationed to their Queen.

But the attackers, Vilkata's men and women, were now entering the region of Soulcutter's dominance. It was their screams of triumph that faltered first, and then the energy with which they plied their weapons. Next their ranks came to a jostling, stumbling halt.

The Queen of Yambu—not knowing, really, why she bothered—slowly raised her eyes. The Sword she held above her head was so dull that it almost hurt the eyes to look at it.

The Sword of Despair—she had thought of the other name for it now. Not that that mattered, either. Not that or anything else.

Why was she bothering to hold the Sword so high? She let her arms slump with its weight. When her warbeast, puzzled and suffering, wanted to move, she let it go, sliding from its back. She stood almost leaning on the Sword now, its point cutting shallowly into the earth.

Nor did any of that really mean anything, as far as she could tell.

The fighting that had begun, sporadically, was dying out. Soulcutter was winning, all across the field. If neither victory nor survival mattered, to anyone, there would be no battle.

Yambu was aware, though only dimly and indifferently, that so far the Dark King's weapon had been able to shield him, and a small group of his followers around him, from Soulcutter's dark, subtle assault.

That group began to charge toward her now, yelling warcries. But its numbers shrank, and shrank more rapidly the closer it came to Queen Yambu. One by one the people in it turned aside from the charge, to sit or kneel or slump to the ground, giving up the effort in despiar.

King Vilkata's demons were the last to desert him. And even before that had happened, he himself had given up the attack and was in full flight from the field.

Rostov, out having a personal look around, turned his scouting squadron back when they came to the edge of the field. Ahead of him the General could see what looked to him like the worst slaughter he had ever beheld, in a lifetime spent largely amid scenes of butchery. There were two armies on the field, and as nearly as he could tell from this distance, both of them had been virtually wiped out. But the General turned back, and ordered his soldiers back, not because of what he saw but because of what he felt, what they had all felt when trespassing upon the fringes of that grim arena. Another few steps in that direction, thought Rostov, and he would have been ready to throw down his weapons and his medals and abandon life.

He was wondering what orders to give next, when he saw a giant figure appear in the distance.

With swift, powerful, two-legged strides it drew closer, also approaching the field of despair. It was Draffut, called a god by some; although General Rostov had never seen the Lord of Beasts before, who else could this be?

There was someone else; a man-shape, riding familiarly on Draffut's shoulders.

Draffut did not approach Rostov and his scouting detachment, but instead halted at another point on the rim of that terrible battlefield. There the giant stopped, and set down the man who had been riding on his shoulders; and from that point the man alone, a gray-caped figure bearing a bright Sword in hand, walked on alone into the field of doom and silence.

Rostov, puzzled, tried to make out where the man—was he wearing a mask?—was headed. Then the General realized that there was still one other human figure standing on the battlefield—way out there, at its center.

It was the Silver Queen, leaning on the blade that she was too immobilized to cast down. When Rostov and his soldiers saw the Emperor take it from her hands, and sheath it, they could feel how a change for the better came instantly over the nearby world.

The General turned to his troops, shouting: "They're not all dead out there! Some of the Dark King's hellions are starting to wake up already! What're you waiting for, get out there and disarm them while you can!"

EPILOGUE

When the party of the surviving gods in their retreat had climbed above the snow level of the Ludus Mountains, the blind man they carried with them began to curse and rail at them again. He ranted as if they were still under his command; and Vulcan, listening, began to be sorry that he had picked the man up and brought him along.

The Smith still had other company, present intermittently. Gray-bearded Zeus, proud Apollo, Aphrodite, Hades. They and some others came and went. Hades was, as always, never far from his true domain, the Earth. Diana had walked with them for a while, but had dropped out of the group early, saying only that she heard another kind of call.

Vilkata, the man they had brought with them, was shivering and in rags. The golden circlet had fallen from his head days ago, and his power to command demons had gone with it. He kept groaning, whining that he'd lost his Sword. He was raving now, demanding that food and slaves and wine be brought to him.

Why did I bring him with me? Vulcan pondered once again. The Smith himself had regained some of his strength since the servants of Ardneh, perceiving him as no longer violent and dangerous, had loosed his bonds and let him go. But he was still far from what he once had been, and sometimes he feared that he was dying.

Apollo had told them all several times in the course of the retreat that they were all dying now, or would be soon, himself included. The world had changed again, Apollo said.

The man they carried with them at least gave them all some connection to humanity. Though Vulcan still did not want to admit they needed that.

He said now to the man perched on his shoulder, as if talking to some half-intelligent pet: "We might find some food for you somewhere. But there is no wine—none that you can drink—and certainly no human slaves."

"But I have you as my slaves," the man rasped back. Today his proud voice was weakening rapidly. "And you are gods, and goddesses. Therefore all the Earth is mine."

From behind, Apollo asked: "You cannot feel it, little man?"

"Feel what?" He who had been the Dark King turned his blind face back and forth. In a more lucid voice he demanded: "Where are we?" Then, a moment later, again: "Feel what?"

Apollo said: "That the humans whose dreams created us, and gave us power, are now dreaming differently? That our power, and our lives as well,

have been draining from us, ever since we gave you
Swords to use?"

Among the gods there were still some who could
persuade themselves to argue with this viewpoint.
"It's all part of the Game—"

"The Game is over now."

"Over? But who won?"

That one wasn't answered.

"In the mountains, in the upper air, we'll start to
feel strong again."

They trudged on, climbed on. The capability of
swift effortless flight had once been theirs. Vulcan
thought that none of them were starting to feel
stronger. In fact the thin air was beginning to hurt
his lungs.

He would not have it, would not *allow* it to be so.
Bravely he cried out to Apollo: "You still say that
we are their creations? Bah! Then who created
them?"

Apollo did not reply.

Occasional volcanic rumbles now shook the
Earth beneath their feet; here and there subterranean warmth created bare steaming spots of rock
amid the snow.

Their flight, their climb, was becoming slower
and slower. But it went on. Now where was Aphrodite? Vulcan looked around for her. It was not as if
she had departed, in the old, easy way, for somewhere else, he thought; she was simply and truly
gone.

He had not seen Hades for a long time, either.

Vilkata sensed something. "Where are you all
going?" the man shouted, or tried to shout. "I command you not to disappear. Turn round instead,

take me back down to the world of humanity. I'm going to freeze to death up here!"

Vulcan had no wish to put up with the man's noise any longer, or with his weight that seemed to grow and grow; and the god cast the blind, mewing man aside, down a cliff into frozen oblivion, and moved on.

The Smith summoned up his determination, trying now to regain the purpose with which he had begun this climb, long days ago. He mused aloud: "It was near here—near here somewhere—that I built my forge, to make the Swords. I piled up logs, earth-wood, and lit them from the volcanic fires below. If only I could find my forge again—"

Presently he realized that he was now alone, the man having gone down a cliff somewhere, the last of his divine companions having vanished, as if evaporated upon the wind. The last wrangling voice of them had been chilled down to silence.

But not quite the last.

"Then who created THEM?" the Smith bellowed, hurling forth the question like a challenge to the universe, at the top of his aching, newly perishable lungs.

He looked ahead.

There was something, or someone, lying in wait for him, beyond that last convoluted corner of black rock. Some new power, or ancient one, come to claim the world? Or only the wind?

He was afraid to look.

The whole world was cold now. The Smith could feel the awful cold turning against him, feel it as easily and painfully as the weakest human might.

He wanted to look around the corner of the rock, but he could not. He was afraid. Just in front of him, volcanic heat and gas belched up, turning snow and ice into black slush in a moment.

Vulcan lurched forward, seeking warmth. He fell on his hands and knees. Dying, in what seemed to him the first cold morning of the world, he groped for fire.

THE END